Spies on the Silk Road

The Repurposed Spies are off on another mission!

Prepare yourself for an electrifying and thoroughly entertaining adventure through the heart of Central Asia. An unconventional team of spies, recruited for their unique abilities, embark on a business-critical mission under cover of being researchers. Working on behalf of three very different clients, each seeking a different outcome from the same enterprise, they risk danger, kidnap and death to achieve the recovery of assets – commercial and human.

Following the ancient trails of Marco Polo, navigating a perilous geographical route through territories beyond the reach of conventional law enforcement, the team must dismantle a dangerous black market enterprise. In pursuit of a stolen shipping container, loaded with high tech medical equipment worth millions, the five 'covert researchers' tangle repeatedly with the thieves and their equally dangerous customers.

Can they achieve success, and all make it home? Strap in for a bumpy ride!

Spies on the Silk Road

A novel by
Oliver Dowson
Spies on the Silk Road

BKssss

Published by BKssss Publishing
https://bkssss.com
info@bkssss.com

ISBN: 978-1-7392988-5-2
eBook ISBN: 978-1-7392988-6-9

British Library Cataloguing in Publication Data

A catalogue record for this book is available from the British Library

Contents

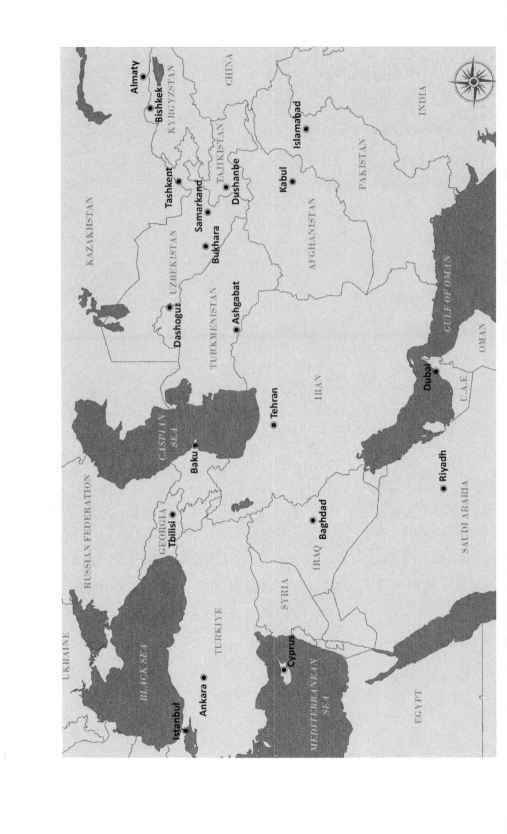

Are they Spies?

Or simply Covert Researchers?

What does the word 'spies' conjure up for you?

For most people, it's those daring individuals who work for state security departments like the CIA, SIS, KGB or Mossad, up against scary individuals in in scary countries. The ones who search for weapon systems, and clandestine operations, or infiltrate political organisations that might threaten their native country. Men and women, some of questionable morality, out to save the world as they or their masters believe it should be. Real life spies like Gary Powers, Kim Philby or Mata Hari, or their literary counterparts James Bond, Matthew Bourne and their ilk. Probably not people we're likely to meet in everyday life – or would want to.

There's another much more common breed. People undertaking industrial and commercial espionage. Gaining trust in a workplace to steal trade secrets from a competitor. Infiltrating government departments to learn about lucrative contract opportunities long before they are published, so their employers can be prepared and steal a march. Penetrating criminal gangs to prevent thefts before they happen and cripple cyberattacks where others have failed. Worming their way into cross-border commercial disputes that prejudice the spies' employer.

There are spies like these all around us in everyday life. Not everyone is who they seem. Most are never found out. Most are relatively ordinary people who work in their own country, doing jobs they understand to a high degree of competence. You may have encountered some of them.

But, just as in every other profession, there is an elite. Teams of skilled individuals who sell their services to a company, delivering one-off projects for an upfront fee, and a substantial bonus on satisfactory completion. Projects that the company simply cannot perform for themselves. Perhaps in other countries, far away, where they have no resources. Perhaps dangerous, where they cannot risk their own personnel. In every such mission, the company cannot afford to be found out, or take the risk of reputational damage if they attempt it themselves and it goes wrong. Contracted the task to the professionals, and the company gets plausible deniability.

Those who perform these missions don't usually like to be called spies. Our team members call themselves 'covert researchers'. But spies are what they really are. Indeed, several of them once worked as spies for government agencies. But not anymore. Meet the Repurposed Spies.

Meet the Repurposed Spies

LAOBAN

'Laoban' means 'boss' in Mandarin, and the boss of the team is what she is. She doesn't admit to being Chinese, though she definitely looks Asian. Probably in her mid-thirties. Known for being pernickety and having a sharp tongue, but a great organiser. Indeed, when she worked for Mr Smith (see below) she was a facilitator or 'project manager'. Because of her reputation for popping up unexpectedly, when and wherever she's needed, with rapid costume changes, Ronald Jones chose to call her 'Chameleon', a pet name that's stuck, but which she detests. She took over what she describes as the legal side of Smith's business after his demise. Laoban is not based anywhere, as far as anyone knows – she just materialises in a new incarnation as and where she feels appropriate.

MARIA

Sometimes called Latviana, especially by Ronald Jones, simply because when they first met she told him she was Latvian. Well, true, she has a Latvian passport, but it's complicated. She's really Belarusian, but doesn't want anyone to know. In her mid-twenties. A facilitator like Laoban in Smith's business, she joined her as a junior partner in the new business. Her role is to run the back office and act as the focal point for communications. She is based in Rotterdam.

RONALD JONES

Now in his late sixties, a man with a colourful history, originally trained as a spy by the British government but psychologically 'repurposed' as a schoolteacher when, in his twenties, his activities went off on a tangent and put the country in danger. A keen linguist, he taught Spanish and Portuguese in a high school in Slough, England for the next thirty years before retiring, and then led a solitary life until recruited by Mr Smith – and then, almost unwittingly, being repurposed back to spying again. After Smith's arrest, realising how much he enjoyed covert research, Ronald first went freelance, but has since joined Laoban's team.

ROBERT

Ronald used to call him 'Pilot' because that's what he is, though, since he often doesn't have a plane to fly, his more important role is as a 'facilitator', making things happen and getting other team members out of trouble. Like Maria, he joined the new company as a junior partner. Impossibly handsome and in his mid-thirties, he is based on a small 'business park' close to an airfield on the fringes of North London. For nearly a year now, despite living in different countries, he and Maria have enjoyed a romantic relationship they've been at pains to keep secret from Laoban (though it's almost certain she knows).

HUMPHREY

A trauma surgeon by profession, though repurposed by the Air Force into espionage, parachuted into remote locations to fix limbs and discover secrets. After an honourable discharge, worked as a surgeon in a London hospital until recruited to the team by Laoban. Now in his early forties. Recently, he and Beatrix became an 'item' and he has joined her as a partner of another sort in her care home business.

BEATRIX

Once an Olympic gymnast, she definitely worked in something governmental and top secret, though she still won't tell even her best friends (or even Humphrey) what she did. The clues are that it was somewhere very cold (speculation is on Antarctica, since she loves everything to do with penguins) and that it proved necessary to maintain and develop her skills in martial arts. Now in her late thirties, she left whatever secret thing it was she was doing to set up care services for wealthy senior citizens. Recruited from there by Laoban, she still keeps the care business operational, now in partnership with Humphrey.

MR SMITH – real name ARBUTHNOT

To outside appearances, a dapper English gentleman, a private consultant. Ten or more years ago, from a base in Mayfair, London, and exploiting a seemingly endless list of personal contacts, he created a global covert research business, specialising in the more illegal (but therefore better remunerated) end of the market. Laoban, Maria, and Robert were the ones who actually worked at the sharp end and made his business possible until things fell apart in several ways during the pandemic. Unpaid and angry, the three conspired his downfall, first getting him arrested in London and then, when he pulled high level strings to get away, in Angola, where he currently languishes in a cell in very insalubrious conditions.

THE OTHER MR SMITH

There really is a Mr Smith who was a partner to Arbuthnot in Smith, Smith & Associates. Not that he knew anything about Arbuthnot's activities; he was simply the rich investor who made them possible. His lack of interest and involvement cost him dear, as when Arbuthnot (masquerading under the name Smith) was arrested, the police simply didn't believe him when he claimed he knew nothing of what was going on, and he befell the same fate as the fake Smith.

EA

The abbreviation for a man only ever acknowledged as 'Executive Assistant', a title he proudly bore when working for Smith (the fake one). Smith's downfall meant he was out of a job, since when he appears to have freelanced for contacts in his former employer's address book, unexpectedly and repeatedly popping up at the more criminal and corrupt end of the market.

1 – Unexpected Sales Literature

Lanzarote, Canary Islands

Startled by the doorbell, Ronald revolved his chair and stood up, in the process tipping most of the haphazard pile of papers balancing on the edge of his desk onto the floor, where they joined their relatives that had suffered the same fate earlier.

"I'm honoured. You've come yourself today," he smiled. "And you're early."

"I'm not here to bring your lunch," Bea replied. "Josefina will come as usual. She might be a little late. Actually, she's preparing you something special."

Ronald salivated. Josefina's meals had become a highlight of his life since returning from Africa and moving to Lanzarote. What retirement should be all about, in his opinion, not that he had any intention of stopping work. Not yet, anyway. Not when he was paid so well simply to analyse possibly dodgy dossiers of documents and to scour foreign news websites for potential lucrative business opportunities that Laoban might find customers interested in muscling in on. A settled life. Though, in truth, he was now beginning to miss the riskier field-based stuff, what he liked to call 'real spying.' The last two years had proved he'd still got it in him; he craved further opportunity.

Beatrix was equally happy in her new environment. If not more so. Her and Humphrey's share of the payout from the African mission had been enough to expand her 'Bea at Home' business to the Canary Islands. The investment had brought with it 'golden visa' resident status. Best of all, Humph had resigned his consultancy at the hospital in London and moved with her, assuming the dual roles of her Medical Director and live-in lover. They'd bought a care home in Lanzarote for a knock-down price from an English couple who, on their retirement a decade earlier, had acquired it as a business opportunity but subsequently proved clueless at running it in any direction except into the ground. Bea had left Janice in charge of the practical end of the home care business back in London and contracted a third-party business manager to look after the finances, safely separating cash assets from temptation and fraudulent opportunity for her employee.

There was a very attractive one-bedroom annex attached to the care home, built by the previous owners in the vain hope that their son and his family would often come and stay. Ronald, his new enthusiasm for travel enhanced by his adventures of the last year, had no desire to return to his old home in Slough, and was thrilled to move in to be close to his new friends. Beatrix and Humphrey were happy to not only get the rent but have a friendly linguist to deal with the Spanish, a language of which they were struggling to master even the basics, and to take on the mountainous and confusing bureaucracy associated with their new business in a foreign land. Laoban was happy because the care home provided a perfect cover story for all three of them, Lanzarote being packed to the gills with well-off Brits. Maria and Robert the Pilot were happy too, as the island had a convenient yet relatively discreet airport, and they could easily fly in for planning meetings the team would hold in *chiringuitos* on the beach, enjoying the winter sun and sipping *sangria* while plotting the next mission.

Ronald was not in the least respect doddery, unlike the six geriatric residents that had come with the home, but was more than happy to be provided with free round-the-clock room service. Since leaving Slough, he'd rather lost the habit of laundry and cleaning. That's what he told Bea, anyway. Bea's unspoken opinion was he was living proof that men were useless when it came to domestic matters. Anyway, she had solemnly promised Laoban that she'd make sure he didn't lapse back into any of his past bad habits that she'd been told about.

Having lunch delivered to his table daily was the icing on his cake. Sometimes literally. Indeed, all the catering was excellent. The service too.

But lunch would come later. Bea was clutching a sheet of paper that she pushed towards him. "Humph wanted you to look over this. He's sent it to you by email as well, but he knows you like things to be printed out."

"It's in Russian."

"You understand Russian, though, don't you?" Bea eyed Ronald hopefully.

"Very little. I have been studying recently, a refresher of sorts, so this will give me something to practise on. What is it? Where did he get it?"

"He thinks it was sent to him by accident, by someone who thinks we're running a private hospital."

"A prospective customer for you?"

"No. Humph says the few headings in English make it appear to be a list of operating theatre equipment. The prices are in Bitcoin. If he converted them right, the first two things on the list are just too cheap, though. Online translation doesn't work, perhaps because it's full of technical words. It might just be junk mail, but he wanted you to check it out. Gut feel, he said."

Well, Ronald thought, it was a practical exercise for his Russian translation if nothing else, and hopefully it would prove more interesting than the minutes of the Brazilian health ministry meetings he had been working on for the last two days. He couldn't understand why Laoban – or her client – wanted those translated. So far, he'd not come across anything that he could imagine might interest a commercial entity. All it proved was that said ministry was at least as incompetent as its counterparts in other countries, and that their weekly meetings were held as a matter of rote, regardless of whether there was anything new to discuss.

It took no time at all for Ronald to realise that his Russian must be very poor indeed, as few words made any sense. Fortunately, just a quarter of an hour later and when he was on the verge of giving up, Josefina arrived with his lunch. "*Filete de rodaballo en salsa de almejas!*" she announced proudly as she carried the tray over the threshold. Ronald was very partial to fish, and turbot with clam sauce sounded delightful and smelt better. Lunch was good every day here, not just because of the quality of the food but especially because Josefina brought hers too, so they lunched together and enjoyed an hour's inconsequential gossip, Ronald's contribution usually being to nod and occasionally utter expressions like "you don't say."

An attractive lady in her late forties, Josefina had been a language teacher like Ronald until escaping from (and subsequently divorcing) her violent husband a year before. She had moved to the island from Sevilla on a whim to get as far away from him as possible, picking Lanzarote only because of an email from a budget airline offering one-way flights for twenty euros. She knew nobody there, and possessed just a few hundred euros she had saved from her housekeeping budget and stashed away over the years in a jar of lentils, correctly calculating that her husband would never look there. Regrettably, the island employment office, her first stop after landing, told her that there were no suitable jobs available, and there would probably be nothing for months since she had arrived at the very end of the peak tourist season. Fortuitously, however, her next stop was the café next door, where she sat at a table adjacent to Ronald, who was immediately alerted to her presence by her perfume. In an earlier life, he had been unconscious – indeed, almost unaware – of toiletries. What changed him was the tutoring he received from Laoban. Or Chameleon, as he called her in those days. Ah, happy memories. Now he regarded himself as something of a connoisseur of scents. He would never be a 'nose', but he knew what he liked, and furthered his education whenever he could without too openly sniffing at passing women and drawing attention to himself. The last thing he wanted was to risk anyone thinking him to be an elderly pervert. This lady's scent was unfamiliar to him, dusky rather than floral, signalling someone who may have depths worth investigating.

Thus attracted, he listened to her telling her story to a waitress and asking her if she knew of any jobs going that she might apply for. As soon as the waitress moved on to another table, Ronald turned his chair, noted that she was as well dressed as she was perfumed, and opened a conversation. In the course of listening to half an hour's nonstop extracts from her life history, he learned that she quite liked elderly people, having spent the last decade caring for her parents back in Seville, and was an enthusiastic amateur cook who had made several unsuccessful applications to appear on the Spanish version of *Masterchef*. ("But I will keep on trying.") Definitely a chatterbox. Firm friends already, Ronald took her back to the care home to meet Bea, who unhesitatingly offered her a job as chef and general factotum with a room in the attic. Job and accommodation sorted, barely four hours after landing. For which she had unceasing gratitude to Ronald.

They had hardly finished their lunch when Bea called again, ostensibly to find out how Ronald was progressing with the translation, but probably really to chivvy Josefina to get back to work. "Come to dinner with us tonight," she said to Ronald as she left. "Laoban will be here." Well, that decided his afternoon. First, he needed to see if there was anything seriously useful in the Russian document. He knew Humphrey would want to use it to show off to Laoban how attentive he was to business opportunities. And he'd have to allow an hour before dinner to bathe, put on clean clothes and pay meticulous attention to his appearance, ensuring there were no hairs showing from his nose or ears and no spots, stains or specks of dandruff on his attire.

Before any of that, though, he needed a Russian dictionary. Without a Russian keyboard, he couldn't use the online version; he needed a printed one. Crossing his fingers that the bookshop in Arrecife would be open and stock one, he ordered a taxi using the app on his phone. Twenty-first century technology conquered at last, he thought to himself. He was getting good at modern life.

The shop was open post lunch and siestas, but the owner of the bookshop was sorry he could not help. There being no other customers in the shop, though, he was eager to chat. "I always try to stock two or three different Russian dictionaries," he told Ronald. "I sold out only this morning. I won't get new stock until next Friday." He clearly saw the doubt on Ronald's face. "Seriously, it's one of my best lines. You've seen how Lanzarote is full of Russians."

"Actually, no," said Ronald. "But I've only been living here for a month. I don't think I've met any Russians."

"Well," replied the bookseller, "it depends where you go. They buy big expensive villas in remote parts of the island and keep themselves to themselves. Like a mafia, they are."

"Really?"

"They bring millions of euros, buy up all the houses and our rotten government gives them those golden visas so they can stay forever," he grumbled.

"I thought you would be happy that they also come into the shop and buy up all your dictionaries," said Ronald.

The owner spat on the floor. "I don't trust them." He bent down and started pulling out books out from under the counter. "I just remembered that I've got this one that one of the Russians ordered but hasn't collected. You can have it. I'll just order him another. Won't do him any harm to wait another week or two."

Buoyed by his purchase and in good spirits, Ronald went to the drug store next door and, from their limited selection, purchased a can of body spray with a picture of a heavily muscled hulk on it. Ronald didn't consider himself macho, he just wanted a perfume strong enough that Laoban would notice his effort.

Returning to his new home, Ronald positioned the dictionary in pride of place on the desk and sat down to apply himself to translation of the strange document. The first four words he looked up couldn't be found, but luckily, the fifth gave him the clue he needed. Pushing the dictionary away, he took a photo of the first paragraph with his phone, opened the online translation app, set it correctly and, hey presto, he was in business.

"It's not Russian," he explained to Humphrey over aperitifs. "Same alphabet, different language. Uzbek. You were right about the medical equipment, though. They're offering operating theatre and x-ray equipment for sale. Brand new, they say. Are you in the market for an MRI scanner and some sort of robot for a hundred and ninety-nine thousand euros?"

"It's all just too cheap. Those things go for north of a million. But why send it to me written in Uzbek? Surely that's only used by people in Uzbekistan?"

"Correct. I'm sure it wasn't meant for you. An elementary mistake in the email address, I suspect." Humphrey looked at Ronald enquiringly. "The email address here is info@hunterhealth.com. But there's a hunterhealth.com.uz as well. Nothing to do with us. A private hospital in Tashkent."

Laoban, who had entered the room while they were talking, chimed in, an uninvited participant to their conversation. "Where did this email come from?" She strode up to the table, snatched the paper from Ronald and perused it closely, as if some other secret message might be hidden there. "Anyway, it's not an email. An attachment?"

Humphrey shook his head. "There was an email, but I had to click on a link and type into a form, name and phone number, stuff like that. I then got sent this as an attachment to a WhatsApp message."

Laoban stared at him. "You idiot! Now they know your name, your number and where you are."

"I'm not that dumb," remonstrated Humphrey. "I used one of the burner phones."

"What email address did you give them?"

"The yahoo one I use for junk mail."

"Hmm. OK. Can I see the original email?"

"Sadly, no. It's disappeared. It's not in deleted items, not in junk, not anywhere. Must have self-destructed. Anyway, do we care? We're not buying any operating theatre equipment, however cheap it is. And Amazon probably doesn't deliver from Uzbekistan to Lanzarote."

"I'm thinking of it from a business perspective," said Laoban, who had moved to the far end of the room, opening and standing cat-like next to the French windows as if she might go outside, but equally, might not. "There could be something in this for us."

At which point, Bea came in carrying a tray. "Dinner is served!" she said brightly. "Laoban, come here and sit down. What are you doing over there, anyway?"

"Escaping the overpowering odour of cheap musk. Mr Jones has overdone it. It's a bit late for him to start exaggerating his sex appeal."

2 – Issuing instructions

Rotterdam, Netherlands

"What do you think, Latviana?" asked Laoban. They were alone together in Maria's apartment in Rotterdam.

"Stop calling me Latviana! We agreed we'd always use Maria. I don't like Latviana any more than you like being called Chameleon. And it stops people getting confused. Me too."

"You're right, sorry. Maria. So, what do you think?"

"Well, first of all, I'm cross that Humphrey didn't ask me to translate it if he thought it was Russian. I could have told him straight away."

"He had Ronald right there, literally on his doorstep, and his first thought was that it wasn't anything of serious interest. Just a mistaken mailshot. Anyway, Humphrey thinks you're Latvian. He doesn't know you are Russian."

"Shhh! I'm not! Belarusian, if you please. But just between you and me and Robert, OK? Officially and for everyone else, yes, I'm Latvian. I have the passport to prove it."

"Though you've never been there and don't speak the language," Laoban said witheringly. Original nationality was something that Maria didn't like to talk about. She'd been gifted a Latvian passport a few years earlier by Mr Smith, about the only good thing he had ever done in her opinion, and she was already worrying how she could renew it when it expired. Still three years to go, though.

Maria studied the translation of the Uzbek document. "I don't know what a lot of these things are, but the x-ray equipment and MRI scanner are pretty obvious. They're asking stupidly low prices for brand new stuff. All of it is physically very big. Conclusions?" She paused and looked up. "It's all stolen. Probably to order, since it's difficult stuff to keep stored away. Presumably stolen in Uzbekistan itself, as the thieves won't want to transport it far. I imagine the low prices are explained by there being very few potential customers, and the few there are would need a big incentive to buy stolen goods."

"Got it in one. Let's find out more."

Maria made no response, but groaned inwardly. She knew that when Laoban said "let's" what she really meant was "you go and do it."

"What are you thinking of, Laoban? You're not planning on setting up a medical centre in Uzbekistan, are you?" Still, she could hardly complain. It was undoubtedly part of her unwritten job description. And she certainly wouldn't trust anyone else in their recently expanded team to do the research. Not as well as she could, anyway.

"Of course not. But I'm thinking that somewhere along the way there could be business for us. Whoever is selling the equipment legitimately must want to know who is stealing it. Or their insurers will. From the other point of view, the thieves must be struggling to find customers if they are desperate enough to send out unsolicited price lists. Find out more, Maria."

Maria was always impressed by how Laoban had seamlessly turned her talents to those of salesmanship. Until only a year ago, they'd been working together as equals, facilitators and euphemistically-titled 'project controllers' for the nefarious Smith, Smith and Associates in Latin America. The final project they had been employed to 'control' exploited the rather haphazard espionage activities of Ronald Jones. Jones, a skilled linguist, who had been a spy in his twenties before being repurposed as a schoolteacher for reasons not known, or, if they were, never revealed. Presumably he had done something terribly wrong or brought the country into disrepute. Or MI6 was just experimenting. Who knew? Anyway, Mr Smith was convinced that Jones could be repurposed back again, and would then be the ideal person to unearth commercial secrets around plans for a new superhighway across Central America. Smith's clients, unknown, but presumably in the construction industry, would thus gain advance intelligence that could lead to pecuniary advantage. Of which Mr Smith would receive a significant share. None of which he intended to part with to reward any of his acolytes.

Unjustly blamed by Smith for the failures of Jones's hapless exploits, Laoban and Maria had been consigned to a lonely house on what was essentially a desert island in the Atlantic to act as prison guards for Jones. There they'd spent over a year sunbathing and seeing out the pandemic, at first disliking each other intensely, but eventually tolerating and then becoming firm friends. Learning from their other associate, Robert, the company pilot and general-purpose Mister Fixit, that Smith had no plans to bring them back or, worse still, to pay them, they hatched a plan to get the truth about Smith and his illegal business into the media and to escape back to England, leaving Jones to die alone. Smith, whose real name they discovered to be Arbuthnot, and his associate Smith (who really was a Smith) had been arrested. Laoban, Maria, and Robert had set up in business for themselves, doing what they had learned – from Smith (the fake one) - to do best.

Laoban was the boss, of course; she was a natural for that role. Initially, they worried that the three of them might end up being nothing more than private investigators following philanderers and drug dealers around the city, but then Laoban had negotiated a hugely valuable contract for a project in Africa that they had carried off surprisingly successfully, if not exactly as originally planned. The most surprising thing of all was that during that mission Ronald Jones had emerged, alive and very much kicking, and was now an enthusiastic member of their team. As a result of that engagement, each of them had enough money to keep them going in comfort for a few years. However, four months on from Africa, they all had itchy feet. They needed a big new project. And if Laoban thought she could turn this piece of dodgy sales literature into rewarding work for them, then that was something worth all the effort Maria could apply to it.

"I suppose I could start by calling the number on the bottom of the list and pretending to be a customer? What country is +976? Uzbekistan, I suppose."

"No, Mongolia." Not a country name Maria would have expected to trip off Laoban's tongue in the way it did. Laoban never admitted her racial or ethnic origins, but Maria, like most, had always assumed her to be Chinese.

Robert had once hazarded Korean. Someone else Japanese. But Mongolian, that was a new one. Might that be her heritage?

"Daydreaming?" asked Laoban sharply. "You need to think through a game plan before you call."

"Obviously," Maria replied with equal acid. "I know how to do my job."

3 – Maria on the hunt for contacts

"Hi, Toshio!"

"Hey, Latviana!"

"Not you too. I'm Maria to everyone now, remember?"

"Oh, sure, sorry. Maria. What's new?"

"If I write a text message in Russian, can you send it to someone in Mongolia, making it look like it comes from an Uzbekistan phone number?"

"I can do better than that. Give me the number so I can check something. I'll get back to you."

Ten minutes later, equipped with a new Telegram account linked to an Uzbek eSIM, setting her Virtual Private Network host to a server in Albania, all of which gave her the feeling she was a technical wizard (even though she was just following Toshio's instructions) she typed in her message to the mystery medical equipment vendor and clicked on 'send'.

Thinking it best to make a very specific enquiry, she'd discussed the 'price list' with Humphrey, who from his career in orthopaedics showed an interest in robotic hip and knee replacement equipment. It was neither the most expensive nor the biggest equipment on offer, but it was a relatively recent development and Humphrey knew of only two manufacturers. Also, being something he actually understood, he thought it might make it easier to determine how the vendor was acquiring it, and where from. "If you do end up buying one, there are quite a few residents here in the care home I can practise on," he chortled. "Nice bit of extra revenue. Bea will love that!"

With no Uzbeks on her contact list, she'd need to communicate in English or Russian. Maria could read and write Dutch, German and Italian too, but didn't completely trust her fluency. She therefore concocted a cover story that she was working for international investors who were planning to open a chain of clinics, one of them in Uzbekistan. She'd say that her boss had been given the price list by a doctor at another hospital who was coming to work for them. She wouldn't tell the vendor any of these things until forced to, of course. It wasn't needed for an initial contact, and she didn't want to get herself tied up in unnecessary detail, but it was enough to answer any immediate questions. The cover story could be fleshed out as they went along.

She made coffee. No reply yet. Assembled a sandwich. Still no reply. Checked time zones. 11am in Rotterdam, so 15:00 in Tashkent, 18:00 in Ulaanbaatar. Maybe, in the unlikely event that the vendor was actually in Mongolia, he'd finished work for the day. If the only article she'd ever read about the country in some travel magazine or other was true, he might be putting his feet up in a yurt or flying a falcon, or doing whatever else Mongolians do in their spare time. Toshio's opinion was that he wasn't there. He speculated the thief had just bought a SIM card or a Skype number, pointing out that if he could make it look like Maria was in Uzbekistan, then a fence selling millions of dollars' worth of dodgy medical equipment could pretend to be anywhere in the world that he or she wanted.

To fill her time usefully while she waited, she searched on the web for more information about the medical equipment. So absorbed was she by the manufacturer's eulogistic insistence that she couldn't live without their amazing world class machinery that she almost missed the 'ping' of the message coming in on her phone. It was in English.

'6 weeks delivery. B5. Reply to confirm interest.'

Five bitcoin. About 200,000 euros. She supposed that was a bargain, but she had no way of comparing it. There weren't any prices on the manufacturer's website. Not that she expected there would be. A bit more searching, this time of local news websites, and she discovered one hospital in America had bought something that sounded similar for $700,000 and one in Germany had bought a 'premium' version for 1.5 million euros. Must be more than one model, then. Maybe the expensive one has leather upholstery.

Just in case the vendor suspected something, she decided to reply in Russian. 'I will discuss with colleagues and will reply tomorrow.'

This time an almost instant reply, again in English. 'Do not delay. I only have one. Ready to go. Lots of interest.'

She sent a message to Laoban. 'Vendor contacted. Next steps tomorrow. Will keep you advised.'

Another instant reply. 'OK. Buy some time.'

So, what next? Maria ate her sandwich and contemplated what she could usefully do. Cuddling up to Rob would of course be the nicest, but that wasn't on the cards, at least not for the next few days while she was in her apartment in Rotterdam and he was in London, supposedly giving free flying lessons to someone who Laoban thought could prove useful to them in the future. Rob wouldn't tell her anything, so she naturally suspected the trainee pilot was young, female, attractive, and available. Not a thought to dwell on if she wanted to achieve anything with her evening.

Back in the early Smith period, when she had occasionally shared his bed, she had taken advantage of his post-coital snoring to photograph the pages of his address book. Recently, she had spent fruitful time interpreting his spidery writing, crossings-out and ink blots to turn the information into a digital contact list. Many of the names had meant nothing to her or to Laoban, so she had looked them up on LinkedIn and X/Twitter and added useful background information like skills and places of work. She had even set up a fake LinkedIn account for a 'Mariuz Loban', adding the face of a rather smart moustachioed man she had found online, and promoting this fictitious individual as the CEO of their company, CASCADA. From this account she had sent messages to all Smith's contacts she could find, discreetly telling them they offered specialist research services they had previously shown interest in from another provider who was sadly (sic) no longer in business.

More than a hundred thus contacted, but only one reply so far. Very worthwhile, though, as it came from a certain Gideon Caesar. He had contracted them for the African mission they had successfully concluded a few months ago, proving himself to be as dishonest as Smith, but nevertheless paying up in the end.

Maybe Smith knew someone who'd be helpful to this project. If it turned out to be a project, of course. Her gut told her she wouldn't be wasting her time, and it wasn't as if she had anything more urgent to do. She opened the file and started paging through the names and biographies.

Surprised that she had been riveted to the screen for three hours and three coffees – who knew that studying a Rolodex spreadsheet could be so addictive? – she had filtered out two people who she thought might be worth contacting.

Ben Fullerton-Price (aptly named, she thought, as he was so full of himself in the bio) was a 'Freelance International Sales Warrior'. His bio said he facilitated the sale of industrial equipment, but his use of the word 'warrior' and his previous employment at Lockheed and BAE Systems suggested what he sold was probably armaments. Indeed, from the way he described himself, gushingly and using every character of the maximum length allowed on a social media platform, he would no doubt sell anything he could dress up as a guided missile. His business address was in Zurich, but his frequent LinkedIn posts were from all over the world, including, recently, several from Azerbaijan. Was that near Uzbekistan? She made a note to check.

Unsurprisingly, he listed both his phone and email on his LinkedIn page. She sent him an email from an account in the name of Dr Johannes Jung. Just a few words. 'Do you represent any medical equipment suppliers?' Should be just enough to pique his interest.

Sonia Azevides was listed as a project coordinator for a syndicate of underwriters at Lloyds of London. Maria knew all about what 'project coordinator' could mean. Variations on a theme of dogsbody. Unlike Fullerton-Price, her bio was minimal. Just about enough to say 'I exist and I work here'. No picture. She was on Instagram, though. No public posts, but an attractive display picture. If that was to be believed, she must be a brunette with impressively wavy hair and aged, at a guess, somewhere between 25 and 35. Why would Smith have contact details for a secretary in an insurance company who must have been in her very early twenties when he filed away her name and number? She put the number into WhatsApp. Not known. She dialled it. Unobtainable. On to Plan B.

Maria possessed three fake Instagram IDs that she used now and again when she needed to research people who were active on social media as well as the occasional business contact. Each of the three was illustrated with pictures of other girls she had plucked from the web. Ones who looked vaguely like her but who weren't. Maria A was the girly girl who posted pictures of lipstick and painted nails and swirly dresses. Maria B was a book nerd, shy, reposting reviews of romance and fantasy novels with titles that she liked. Maria C, the one she was going to use now, was professional Maria, posting clips mostly about women's rights but interspersed with pictures of bottles of white wine and colourful cocktails. She searched for, found, liked and reposted a post about #insurancefraud and another that seemed to be about a women's society at #lloydsoflondon, then went to Sonia's profile. Private, so she couldn't tell how active she was. Just sixty-three posts, but over two hundred followers. Following a thousand. Someone who contributed little but enjoyed looking, then. She clicked on 'follow'.

Needing to clear her mind ready to plan the next task, she went to the convenience store adjacent to her apartment block and on her return ran back up the four flights of stairs to her front door to compensate for the half packet of chocolate biscuits she was about to gorge (she was disciplined enough to put the other half in a tin, knowing that if she ate from the packet, she'd eat the lot). Returning to her desk balancing yet another coffee on the plate of biscuits, she saw Sonia had already followed her back. She scrolled through her posts. Into fashion, then. Maybe Maria A would have been a better fit. But she had liked what Maria C had posted, too. She looked at posts from people that Sonia followed. Nothing serious there. Nothing to suggest that there was a business reason for Smith to have her in his contacts list. So… probably the same reason as he had Maria's details in there.

No harm in testing the water. Maria C composed a short direct message to Sonia. 'Hey there! I wonder if you knew or worked for a Mr Smith in Mayfair a few years ago?' Only seconds passed before the reply. 'That bastard!' That's a yes, then.

Still no answer from Ben, the self-styled sales warrior, though. Maria, rather proud of her afternoon's research, called Laoban to update her. They agreed Maria should contact the vendor again in the morning and ask for detailed information about the equipment offered, and continue to work on befriending Sonia. Until they knew more, Laoban thought the insurance loss angle was the most likely to be productive. "If all this expensive equipment is being stolen, then whoever owns it must be claiming on insurance. The insurers will do what they can to keep big losses secret, and some underwriters somewhere will be nursing significant negative numbers in their accounts." Even though there were other global reinsurance offices, Laoban was convinced that somebody in Lloyds of London would know about it. And that somebody would be interested in stopping the thefts.

Early the next morning, Maria started her day by emailing the vendor. 'We are interested. Advise manufacturer and model number and delivery location.'

A curt reply. 'Meet in Almaty Monday 14th. Ritz Carlton Hotel lobby. 10am.'

Five days from now. I doubted even Laoban could find a customer for our services and get them signed up in that time.

'Impossible. Monday 28th?'

'Monday 21st. Will not be available after that.'

Twelve days to find a customer and get to Almaty. Wherever that was. Kazakhstan? Wasn't the document in Ukrainian? That's if Laoban wanted to proceed, of course.

Well, time to pursue the insurance angle. Maria messaged Sonia. 'I suspect we had similar experiences. Want to meet to chat?'

'Yes, for sure, anytime. Call me.' And she left her phone number.

She knew Laoban would expect her to follow up as soon as she could. So, message Rob to ask how soon he could fly over to Rotterdam and pick her up. It felt like ages before he replied. "Sorry, no can do. Lessons for the next few days and not safe to bring you into Elstree. No passport control here." Maria was angry now. Rob had flown over to see her lots of times. It was only in the last two weeks that he had started making excuses about giving lessons. Exuding grim determination, she checked regular flights. 11:10. Two hours from now. Thank goodness she was based in a city with an efficient small airport that was only ten minutes away. She could make that flight. Stupidly expensive ticket, though. Last-minute rip-off. Not her money, ultimately, though. Legitimate business expense. She stowed her laptop and charger in a rucksack, grabbed the bag she always kept packed ready for emergencies, called an Uber, checked everything was locked and the alarms were on and headed for the airport.

She was even more furious when she had boarded and had to put her phone in flight mode. She'd messaged Rob from the taxi, telling him she was en route to London. At the very least, she'd expected to spend the night together, better still, a dinner invitation. Ninety minutes and nothing. Two blue ticks, so he'd read the message. And decided not to answer.

This was Laoban's fault, she theorised. The three of them were partners in the business, but Rob and Maria had been keeping their personal relationship secret from Laoban. They knew she would disapprove, officially, and say it could prejudice their professional activities. In that, she'd be right, of course. But they had been careful, and Maria thought they could go on keeping it discreet. And Bea and Humph had managed it. They were out in the open. Still, it was complicated, as jealousy crept into the picture too. Back in Sal, where Laoban and Maria had spent more than a year guarding Ronald Jones in his sealed apartment, their only visitor ever was Rob, who dropped in occasionally. He flew executive jets between Europe and South America, and made stopovers when he could, bringing them much-appreciated little luxuries, like Belgian chocolate and expensive biscuits. Both the girls had worked with Rob for Smith for a couple of years before that, and both had become somewhat besotted with him. Rob respected Laoban but wasn't attracted to her at all, so to defuse a difficult situation, he had told them he was gay. It was obvious to Maria that Laoban didn't believe him, and that had contributed to her decision when they set up as a partnership that he should be based in London and Maria in Rotterdam. That hadn't kept them apart, though; when they hadn't been busy with projects, Rob had flown over to Holland often and spent nights with her. They had kept it all super-discreet. Until Africa, where they had let down their guard just a little. So... joining the dots, Maria could easily imagine that Laoban had instructed Rob to stay away and find another girlfriend. If that's what he'd done, that would be difficult. Extremely difficult. They'd still have to work together. And now there would be ice!

4 – Making a new Best Friend Forever

London, England

With dark speculations about Rob occupying her mind, it was just as well that the flight was only forty minutes. She turned on her phone even before the plane braked to a sharp halt at the end of the runway at London City airport. Ping! A reply from Sonia to the message she had sent before she left Rotterdam. Still nothing from Rob. Sonia told her she worked at Lloyds, as Maria already knew, of course, and that she finished at five. Maria suggested meeting at the rooftop bar of a hotel she knew facing the Tower of London. Posh, fashionable, discreet, and a ten-minute walk from Sonia's office. She agreed in a heartbeat. Lonely, Maria concluded.

Maria caught the Docklands Light Railway from the airport to Tower Gateway. She had four hours before meeting Sonia; the air fare had been expensive enough, she calculated eight euros a minute, no point in lashing out more on an expensive London cab ride. Anyway, that would probably take longer than the flight, most of it stuck in traffic. She actually found the clattering, slightly juddering tram-like experience of the DLR relaxing, despite the industrial landscape and frequent stops, each bringing with it an inrush of freezing air. Few passengers got on or off along the way.

She wandered along the river embankment for half an hour, getting herself used to the idea of being in London and of life without Rob. Or, rather, personal life without Rob. They'd still have to work together, though they rarely met up under those circumstances. All plans arranged by phone and WhatsApp. Better that way. Her mood improved. Walking in London always helped. She loved the city and especially the river, flanked by history, the Tower and St Pauls, mixed up with the new tower blocks, the Shard, the Gherkin, the Cheese Grater, the Walkie-Talkie. Somehow, it all worked together. What a contrast to Rotterdam; no history there, no impressive buildings. She thought back to Minsk. That had its good points. It was a pleasant city to walk in, too. When one wasn't being followed by the secret police. One day she'd go back. Come the revolution.

She realised she had become a little light-headed and, more urgently, was cold. A coffee shop beckoned. The mid-afternoon lull meant it was empty. She bought a coffee and an almond cake, parked herself in the furthest corner of the establishment, not that it was particularly large, and got out her laptop. Time to catch up with the job. Several emails from Laoban, all along the lines of "where are you?". She realised that she'd not bothered to look at her phone since leaving the airport. Six missed calls from Laoban. Still no reply from Rob.

She checked her other email accounts. The mystery equipment vendor asking for a confirmation of meeting on the 21st. A reply from Fullerton-Price too. Even more egotistical and effusive than his self-description on the web. Yes, of course, his own company, FullFill Ltd, represented all the world's leading medical equipment companies and could sell them anything they wanted, delivered wherever they wanted it, at world-beating prices. He even claimed to be an 'appointed agent' of a certain manufacturer who, Maria knew from her research the day before, was one of two companies manufacturing the robotic equipment they'd enquired about. He was currently in Istanbul, but was only advising that for time zone purposes, please advise exact requirements, etc.

Maria called Laoban, told her about the emails and why she'd been out of contact.

"I know it's a long shot, but I really feel that email to Humphrey was auspicious, and we can get some good business out of it," said Laoban. "But we don't want to get deeply involved unless and until someone hires us. We don't have much time."

"I know," replied Maria. "I feel the same way, which is why I came here to meet Sonia. But it's one thing to make friends with someone I've never met before, even if it turns out we have shared experiences, and quite another to ask her to find out information from her workplace. Especially somewhere like that. Everything will be classified."

"Well, see what you can do. If anyone can, you can." Maria gulped. Yet another example of Laoban being complimentary. A chameleon can change colour, but does that coiled tongue ever lose its poison? Not for long, she guessed.

Still nearly two hours to go, but her phone battery was giving out and there were no power sockets in the café that she could use. She headed for the hotel and got the lift to the top floor. Good idea to get a table early while the bar was quiet. In fact, the bar seemed closed, or at least deserted. Nobody came and asked for her order. She picked a corner table from where she could watch the doors and with a convenient power socket adjacent. She put her phone to charge, opened her laptop and logged into the hotel wi-fi. Helpful of them to display the password on the table.

She composed an email to Fullerton-Price. Trying to be both specific and vague at the same time. 'Our clients are interested in acquiring the latest medical equipment at the best price for their new private clinic in a Central Asian country. CT Scanner, theatre lighting, Robot-assisted surgery, etc. for delivery in 6-12 weeks. A mutual business acquaintance recommended that we contact you first. Can you help us? Should we meet?'

Back on LinkedIn, she quickly found the name of the global sales director of the manufacturer, FutureHealth, based in the States, and emailed him, too. 'Business associates have advised us to work with FullFill Ltd to discuss purchasing some of your equipment for a new private clinic in Central Asia. Please confirm that they are your appointed agents. Discretion appreciated.'

Maria knew that dangling a carrot of millions of dollars of business in front of a sales executive guaranteed a quick response, but even she was surprised to get answers to both emails in less than five minutes.

'Can source all of this,' said Fullerton-Price, then listing some models from the manufacturer of interest. 'Given time scale, any meeting in the next week needs to be in Istanbul.'

'Never heard of them', wrote the manufacturer's sales director, going on to list the contact details for two representatives who were officially appointed.

Interesting, thought Maria.

Half an hour later, she received a second email from the sales director. 'Strongly advise to only use our appointed agents. We have been made aware of fake clones of our equipment being sold in some countries.' He then repeated the details of their official representatives. One with a London number. Well, if it's official, no harm in calling it. Ryan Mallory. She looked him up on LinkedIn. Nice hair. She dialled. He picked up on the first ring. Why had she dialled before preparing what she wanted to say? Extemporise. She more or less repeated what she had written earlier to Fullerton-Price and told him that the sales director in America has given her his number. She could almost hear him salivating at the thought of another big sale. She wasn't yet sure exactly what her clients needed, but she happened to be in London for a day or two. Could they meet so she could get some outline details?

But of course. Meeting arranged in a City office for 10 the next morning. No sooner had they finished speaking than Maria became conscious that the bar was no longer deserted. Indeed, most of the tables were occupied, and more people were arriving. Amongst them, an anxious-looking young woman coming out of the lift and scanning left and right. Maria waved.

"Oh, I'm so pleased to meet you. I worried I was in the wrong place, I know you said it was above the hotel but it doesn't look like a hotel downstairs, does it?" Maria agreed that the high-tech self-service check-in lobby had more resemblance to a Las Vegas casino than a hotel reception. Sonia was tall and very slim, with long and wavy dark brown hair. Long and perfectly manicured nails. What was clearly a designer trouser suit in fawn. Black-rimmed spectacles with an Armani logo on the side. A woman who spent a lot of money on herself. Maria, dressed quite casually, hadn't anticipated that, but Sonia put her at ease. "You look fantastic, so much better than your pictures." Where had she seen any pictures? Oh my god, Instagram of course.

"Well, between ourselves, I don't use my own picture on social media. I've met too many frogs I'd rather not meet again."

Sonia looked nonplussed, but only briefly. "Frogs that don't turn into princes, right?" Maria nodded. "Good idea. I've had more than my fair share, too."

A server arrived at that moment. "Now that your friend is here, can I get you drinks? I didn't want to disturb you before, you looked so busy." Sonia asked for a glass of Pinot Grigio; Maria told the server to bring the bottle. "My treat. It's good of you to meet me so soon."

Nearly an hour of small talk followed, almost as if the girls had known each other for ages. Clothes, hair, boyfriends, all boxes ticked. Maria established that Sonia worked in an office on her own, a sort of glorified personal assistant to a syndicate of ten underwriters (Maria was glad she'd read up about Lloyds earlier, she was fluent in English now, but remembered once getting confused between underwriters and undertakers). She had no friends at work, few friends outside, no current boyfriend, lived in a studio flat somewhere in Docklands, family in Malta, social life comprised going to dancing classes twice a week, volunteering at a food bank on Sundays and teaching herself Mandarin. When she wasn't shopping or having her hair, nails, eyebrows, lashes or makeup done, thought Maria.

Confidences having been shared and the dregs of the first bottle of wine drained, they finally reached the subject of Smith. One that Sonia proved more than happy to talk about, so much so that her tongue had probably not needed loosening with wine. Comparing notes, it transpired that no sooner had Smith pushed Maria out of his bed and into a peripatetic range of projects ranging from the mundane to the downright dangerous in Latin America, he had embarked on a tryst with Sonia, predictably promising her the earth but giving her nothing but chlamydia and an unwanted pregnancy. "Would you believe I worked for him for three months and had to threaten him with going to the press just to get paid my measly salary?" she said. Maria could indeed believe it. He had paid for a termination at a private clinic in Great Portland Street, but when Sonia returned to Smith's apartment-cum-office in Mayfair three days later, he had changed the locks. He'd stuck an envelope to the door with a very short note saying he had gone away on business, and she should email to tell him where to send her 'bits and bobs', as he described them, left behind in the apartment. The only thing she could remember having left was a phone charger. Valueless, but provided the opportunity for her to write Smith a stinging email demanding its return. The package it arrived in also included a set of underwear that she remembered having searched for a month previously, and a £20 note 'for laundry'. Unable to leave it at just that, he had added, 'I am sure you will appreciate this as a thoughtful gesture on my part.'

This sorry tale, which trumped most of Maria's experiences with Smith, played out over the time they took to finish the second bottle. Maria's side of the Smith story hadn't even started yet, and she was conscious enough of coming under the influence to insist they pause for food. Fortunately, they were both hungry, neither on a diet that week, and to the evident surprise of the waiter devoured two portions of spicy chicken fingers and two plates of loaded nachos to act as 'blotting paper' to soak up some of the alcohol.

Sonia had read the story of Smith being revealed as an assumed name, his real name being Arbuthnot, and his arrest, which had given her much glee. She hadn't, however, heard that he had been released from UK custody and fled to Namibia, though that hardly surprised her. The news had been suppressed by means of a super-injunction in the UK, granted under the excuse of 'not being able to report on an ongoing criminal investigation.' Sonia lapped up with great enthusiasm Maria's somewhat over-elaborated story of her part in Smith's downfall and his subsequent re-arrest on different charges and then incarceration in Angola. Maria did nothing to disabuse Sonia of the belief that was all Maria's work and influence, reasoning that in the extraordinarily unlikely circumstance that Sonia would ever meet Ronald Jones, he would be unlikely to lay claim to being the instigator.

Thus, in the space of just three hours, Maria and Sonia were already firmly into BFF territory. However, despite sharing a lot of personal information, some of it true, Maria had still not told Sonia what she did for a living. But then, Sonia hadn't asked. Laoban had laid down the law that none of the partners should ever reveal what they did or who they worked with to any outsider, but Maria decided to take a gamble on opening up a little to Sonia. After all, if the medical project was to succeed, they needed information. Urgently.

"A few of us who worked for Smith have set up on our own now," she told Sonia.

"Oh, how exciting!" she replied. "So you do, what did you say it's called, covert research?"

"Exactly."

Sonia's face clouded over. "Is that legal? Or like what Smith, sorry Arbuthnot, did?"

Maria was quick to reassure her, adopting her most earnest expression and cheesiest smile. "No, that's the whole point. Everything we do now is one hundred percent legal, all above board. Well, we have to be secretive… confidential, of course. But legal. None of us want to go the same way as Smith, do we?"

"God, no," said Sonia. "So, what is it, this covert research? Smith would never tell me what he really did, but it all seemed very suspicious."

"Things he did were risky, but we're the good guys. The last major project was in Africa. We got a team together to search for an illegal drugs factory hidden deep in the jungle."

"I thought the police or army would do things like that. Did the government contract you, then?"

"No, most of our work is for companies. It was a big pharmaceutical company that wanted to know about the illegal manufacture of their product. They didn't trust the police there not to be corrupt." She didn't tell Sonia that, in fact, the team had been hired by a businessman wanting to muscle in on the action and that, rather than close the factory down, they'd left the pharmaceutical company to do a deal with them.

"That sounds so exciting," said Sonia. "Were you trekking through the jungle? Was it dangerous?"

"Not me. I just organise the team, make sure they are in the right place at the right time, have everything they need, that sort of thing. It was dangerous for them. It was a little risky for me, too, at the end." Maria paused. "OMG. I shouldn't have told you all that. Keep it all on the QT, please?"

"Of course, it's just between us." Looking around, she could see that was true at that moment in time. The bar had almost emptied, and the only other occupied table was on the other side of the room. "What are you working on now? Or can't you tell me?"

"I can share a little, I suppose. It's about medical equipment, the high-tech expensive stuff in operating theatres. Stuff that costs millions. Some of it's going missing or ending up in the wrong hands. In remote countries in Asia. Some criminal gang must be making a lot of money."

"How amazing! What are you going to do? Go after the thieves?"

"Well, obviously," Maria paused and tried to look conspiratorial, "I can't tell you that. It's in the planning stages. Remember, just you and me?"

"Secret squirrel, me," replied Sonia. "Heavens, is that the time? I must run. I'll miss the last train." Maria somewhat doubted that Sonia would be doing a lot of running in high heels after downing more than two of the three bottles of wine they'd put away, or that she would stay upright if she tried, but welcomed the evening coming to an end. She was both exhausted and tipsy. With still no reply from Rob, she tottered downstairs to the hotel reception and, after baulking at the astronomic rates, took their last available room.

5 – Waking up in London

One advantage of staying overnight in a five-star hotel is that the bedding is divine and extraneous sounds are insulated out by premium double glazing, meaning one naturally sleeps late, even when sober.

The disadvantage, Maria realised, was this meant not waking until after eleven, and then only because someone from housekeeping was hammering on the door. She discovered first that she had fallen asleep without putting her phone on charge and then, once plugged in, saw that she had more than a dozen new messages and missed calls from Laoban, evidently on the warpath.

Having placated the boss (though expecting an outburst at some time in the future when she saw the bill for the room and the evening's entertainment), she reviewed the other messages. Still nothing from Rob. Well, tough. He wouldn't find anyone else like her.

However, one from Ryan Mallory. Did she want to rearrange the meeting? OMG, that was supposed to be at 10am and she'd slept straight through and then forgotten it. She called him, pretended she had been unexpectedly held up and her phone had died. Could they meet in the afternoon? Of course, and maybe she would like to meet over a late lunch? Excellent idea, she thought, and fortunately, the restaurant he suggested was nearby. 2pm, then.

Nothing else that wouldn't wait an hour or three. She showered and dressed quickly and made it downstairs by ten past twelve. "I really ought to charge you a late check-out fee," the clerk at the front desk said, "though on this occasion I'll waive it." Said with a big grin. As if he was doing her a special favour.

She set up her laptop in the café just off the lobby to read her other messages and emails. First, she booked the last flight of the day back to Rotterdam. No point in staying in London any longer than she needed to.

A couple of messages from Sonia, basically 'we must do this again soon'. Maria sent positive, friendly replies. One from Fullerton-Price pestering her for details of the equipment her people were interested in. A chatty one from Bea, hoping she and Rob would come to Lanzarote soon. Hmm. Nice idea. Probably not together, though. Bea and Laoban were thick as thieves these days. No doubt that's how the boss had found out about them. With nothing else to catch up on, and sobered up by three espressos in short order, she slung her bag over her shoulder and strode off up Eastcheap towards the Sky Garden.

Ryan Mallory looked even sexier in the flesh than in his LinkedIn photo. In his early thirties? A boyish face topped with curly golden hair, tall, slim, wearing a dark blue suit, a dark cerise satin shirt open at the collar. The effect on her was tempered, however, by the chunky gold wedding ring on his left hand. No chance any eligible female would miss seeing that. He was waiting at the ground floor entrance to the tower block she knew as the Walkie-Talkie. She'd never been inside, but remembered someone telling her the Sky Garden was an amazing place to eat. Walking out of the lift on the thirty-fifth floor, she could see why. The bar in the hotel where she'd spent most of yesterday afternoon and evening had a wonderful view, but this was different. Much higher up for a start. Ryan led her up the stairs on one side to the restaurant on the level above, where he had booked a table in a corner.

She opted to drink sparkling water, and, noting that the menu was not as pretentious as she had feared, ordered a hamburger. Ryan chose a Caesar salad. "Do you mind if I order extra fries?" she asked Ryan. "It's just that I missed breakfast and I'm starving."

"Whatever you like, please. If you don't mind my saying so, you don't look like you are one for high calorie food, though," smiling as he said it.

"I eat tons," she told him. "Just have to do a lot of exercise to work it off."

The waiter having been dispatched, they turned to business. Ryan proved inquisitive. "So exactly who do you represent?" he asked. "Your company profile just says 'professional business services'."

Maria had anticipated the question. "That's exactly it. We provide discreet professional help to businesses, usually for one-off projects, where they don't have the appropriate resources themselves, or are based in another country. This time, we're helping a group of investors who are planning to set up a chain of private clinics across Central Asia."

"What do you know about the sort of equipment we manufacture?"

"Nothing really. I've been doing some reading, of course. I was hoping you would help educate me." Maria pouted.

Ryan grinned. "I'd be happy to teach you a little, of course. But we make a lot of different equipment. Did your client say exactly what they are going to need?" His facial expressions indicated to Maria that he wasn't taking her seriously. She pulled herself straight and put on her most serious business face.

"They're waiting for us to provide them with details of what is available and when it can be delivered before drawing up a detailed specification. They understand that some equipment is in high demand and that some might be difficult to deliver to their clinics because of import regulations and other bureaucracy. So that will dictate the order in which they open new clinics and the operations they can offer at them." Maria was making it up as she went along, but was now on a roll. Ryan listened attentively, nodding at the points she made. "I can tell you these are serious people with plenty of money, and they are particularly interested in robot-assisted hip and knee surgery, so perhaps we could start by talking about those?"

Ryan was now all attention. "Absolutely. We are world leaders in robotic surgery. How many clinics did you say that your clients are planning to open?"

"I didn't, but the initial investment is for five or six. Two are already under construction." Well, lie a little, lie a lot. She didn't want to risk him saying to come back next year if the clinics were only in the planning stages. Ryan, definitely interested, started rifling around in a leather folder he had brought with him. He triumphantly extracted a dark blue glossy card folder and pushed it across the table towards Maria, his hand colliding with the server who was just bringing their meals. Fortunately, the only casualty was the miniature basket containing Maria's extra fries, which, shedding its contents along the way, went skimming over the floor.

The little drama over, Ryan and Maria returned to their discussion of medical robots. "So, where are these clinics under construction?" quizzed Ryan. Maria had been dreading this question, but since lying was essential to getting the information she needed, she at least had an answer prepared.

"One is in Uzbekistan, the other in Almaty," she replied. Since the sales document Humphrey had received was in Uzbek and the vendor was in Almaty, it seemed a good way of hedging her bets.

"Kazakhstan, eh? I hope you're not going to tell me your client is Russian. We aren't allowed to do business with Russians." That was something Maria hadn't thought of. Why hadn't she studied the map more closely and at least read up about the countries on Wikipedia before coming to the meeting? More evasion called for.

"Certainly not. The investors we are working for have no links to Russia."

"Chinese, then, I expect," said Ryan. "If investors in Kazakhstan or Uzbekistan were setting up clinics, I'm sure I'd know about it. I was there myself only a fortnight ago. Be careful. There's a huge black market for fake and stolen goods out there."

Maria opened her eyes as wide as she could. "Surely this sort of equipment can't be faked? Or stolen?"

"You'd be amazed. You and your clients need to be careful. Organised crime, too." Ryan nodded as if agreeing with himself.

It was only at that moment that Maria realised that there would be a real opportunity for Laoban to try to do business with Ryan or his bosses in America, to hunt out who was doing the faking or stealing. Had she dug too big a hole for them through the lies she had told in the previous quarter hour, and, in the process, ruined their chances of negotiating valuable business? Why had she drunk so much last night? Well, she'd made her bed. Better lie down in it.

"Assuming it works, how would anyone know if a piece of equipment was fake or stolen?"

"Well, obviously, if it's too cheap. If it's not being sold by an authorised distributor like me. If the serial number is missing or scratched out."

"Or if the salesman is a mafioso holding clandestine meetings in dark alleyways rather than an elegant, handsome man in a fabulous restaurant?" Maria smiled.

Ryan blushed his embarrassment. "That too, of course," he replied, and moving her along without evident encouragement of her flirt. "Have your clients discussed any other equipment we may be able to help with?"

"Not specifically, but now we are in contact, I can email you a full list?" Ryan nodded. Maria chanced another question. "Obviously, we and our clients are only interested in one hundred per cent legal purchasing, but what you said about the black market is fascinating. These are big and expensive pieces of kit, and there's surely not that many hospitals and clinics that would buy them? How do they get stolen? Who are the buyers?"

"Well, I'm not sure how much I can tell you. Or even how much I know. But the sort of people who buy on the black market could be looking to set up a back street medical services clinic on the cheap. Perhaps like your clients?"

"Our clients are not 'back street'. But the crooks who are selling genuine equipment on the black market? How do they get hold of it?"

"One shipping container looks much like another."

"And it's your genuine product?"

"I didn't say it was ours. We know that some of what they sell is legit, some is fake. Our official position is that the black-market equipment is likely to be cheap Chinese copies, but they could be from Vietnam, Cambodia, anywhere like that."

"Mongolia?" asked Maria, laughing. Ryan suddenly looked more serious.

"What made you pick that country?" He sounded accusing. Now it was Maria's turn to blush.

"Nothing, just that I recently read a fascinating article about adventure holidays there. It had a picture of a man sitting on the back of a horse with an eagle perched on his glove. He looked scary, but I can't imagine someone like that selling robots." By now she'd recovered enough to laugh, and Ryan joined in. She decided that saying any more would be pushing her luck too far. Perhaps off the cliff. Anyway, somehow or other during their conversation she had demolished her hamburger and the replacement fries that had arrived unnoticed. She was pretty sure she had done most of the talking, but Ryan had hardly touched his salad.

Coffee and closing niceties done, they descended to ground level, Maria now clutching a bundle of dark blue cardboard folders containing literature for a dozen types of sophisticated medical equipment she hadn't previously known existed. Parting ways with nothing more intimate than a handshake, she walked back towards Tower Hill station to get the train to City Airport. Suddenly conscious of someone running behind her, she ducked into a doorway, twisting her body to trap her bag behind her. Not a mugger, though, but a breathless Ryan. "Sorry, Maria, can I ask you something?"

Her immediate and default assumption was that he had come back to ask her to extend their meeting into the evening and whatever that might turn into. Never mind the chunky wedding ring. But she was wrong on this occasion.

"I hope you don't mind my asking. If your clients get offered any black-market stuff, will you tell me? Please?"

"Of course," she lied. Though this was very useful to know. She hoped Laoban would be impressed.

Another expensive flight and taxi journey got her back to her apartment in Rotterdam in less than two hours. She had hardly kicked off her shoes when two WhatsApp messages popped up. One from Rob. 'Will you still be in London tomorrow?'. Nothing more. Not even a kiss emoji. Doesn't merit a reply, at least not yet. It would probably have made her angry had it not been for the other message. From Sonia. 'Got something to tell you I think you will find interesting. Call when you're free to chat.' Well, even if it's not interesting, at least it'll be someone to share the pain of a breakup with. She got a bottle of wine from the fridge, poured a generous glassful, and dialled.

It took Sonia about half an hour to get to the point in between all the other chit-chat she came out with, but it was indeed interesting. Laoban's theory was right. Sonia had done some discreet research. "You have to understand all of this is highly confidential. There are secret folders I can't get into," she told Maria. "But I did find out that there's one syndicate of underwriters, not the ones I work for, that's suffered big losses on thefts of industrial equipment in Central Asia. Do you think that 'industrial equipment' might include the medical things you are looking for?"

"I certainly do," said Maria. "That's amazing information. Don't take any risks, but if you find out anything else, be sure to call."

"We'll have to be super-careful if we talk about this on the phone, though. I'm not sure I should have said what I already did. They told me about this thing called phone taps in my induction training. I guess that's something you know a lot more about than me."

"True. It's a real risk. Let's use a code. If it's something really important, tell me that the dance club is teaching the tango on Saturday. and I'll come back over as soon as I can."

"Fantastic idea. But let's make it the Charleston, we already spent weeks doing the tango."

A surprisingly successful couple of days, thought Maria. Moving into the room she had set up as her 'control centre', she picked up the scrambler phone and called Laoban to give her the good news.

6 – Now who goes where?

Rotterdam, Netherlands

"It's complicated," said Laoban. "There's definitely a project worth pursuing, but first we need a customer. I see two opportunities. One is the insurance underwriters, though they'll have their own investigators and no doubt want to use them. In fact, they're probably already using them. Then there's the manufacturer. Their reputation is on the line. Insuring shipments must either be costly or impossible, depending how much theft is going on. But they're American, you only have a British contact, and they'll almost certainly want to use the police. Can't imagine the CIA getting involved in theft unless there's some national security threat."

Maria and Laoban stared at each other. Well, each at the picture of the other on their computer screens. A minute or so passed.

"Well, what better ideas do you have, Latviana? Maria, sorry." Laoban, up to now talking like a normal rational human, appeared to be reverting to her default aggression. Maria's phone pinged. "You'd better check that." Laoban got up and walked off camera. Two minutes later, she reappeared.

"So?" she demanded. "Ideas?"

"It's Friday afternoon; we can't do much until Monday. I think I should go back to London on Sunday and meet Ryan on Monday morning. If he's free, that is. I'm worried that he won't trust me after the story I spun him yesterday, so I need to convince him we are bona fide. I'll tell him I was talking to my boss over the weekend and that she has information about

51

black market goods I wasn't aware of. Ask if they want us to help them find the culprits. Agree?"

"OK, that makes sense. Up to a point. But the question to ask is do they want *us* to find the thieves," exclaimed Laoban. "Not *help* them find them. You need to find out who I should talk to about getting hired."

"Do I talk about money?"

"No, that's my job. Find out who I negotiate with. Probably his boss in the States. Do you know where they're based?"

"It says Richmond Virginia on the brochures he gave me."

"Easy. Meet Ryan Monday morning, ask him to make an appointment for me in Richmond on Tuesday morning at 11. Text me confirmation as soon as you've got it. What next?"

"I'll arrange to meet up with Sonia again when she finishes work. I'll chat with her over the weekend and try to convince her to find out what more she can when she's in her office on Monday."

"I need a contact for the underwriters. Someone I can negotiate with. Someone authorised to make a decision. Next?"

"Those pings you heard. That's the vendor pestering for confirmation of the meeting on the 21st."

"Confirm it. We'll be there."

"Both of us?" Maria was surprised Laoban would consider taking her with her. "Not us. I'll plan a team. Humphrey knows about medical stuff. Probably Robert, in case things get difficult. He's good at getting people out of tight spots." Maria tried to control her facial expression, stay neutral.

"Neither of them speak the language. I know the message the guy sent was in English, but what most people speak out there is Russian."

"I just told you, you're not going!"

"I didn't mean that. Just making the point. The team might need someone who can understand Russian, that's all I'm saying."

"Fine. Noted. What was the other message?"

"The other one?"

"I heard two pings."

"Ah. That was the salesman from Istanbul. Again. He messages three or four times a day. Shall I get rid of him, tell him we've got what we want elsewhere?"

"Certainly not! He could be very useful to us. Depends on what he's like, what he knows, and so on. Arrange a meeting with him on Monday."

"Who's he going to meet? I'll be in London. You'll be on your way to America."

"I'll have one of the other members of the team fly to Istanbul. Just arrange the meeting. We can fill in the details later."

7 – A very anxious sales director – Laoban

Richmond, Virginia, United States

Walking down the corridor towards me, he looked exactly as I expected him to. The stereotypical all-American salesman. Mid-forties, at a guess. A shade under six feet tall. Sandy-coloured crinkly hair. A somewhat sun-beaten freckled face. Navy blazer. Tan slacks. White shirt with a discreet check, open collar.

"You've come all this way from where?" Interesting way to open a conversation. Good morning to you too.

"It doesn't matter where I came from, Mister…?"

"Sorry, Jennick. Bob Jennick," he said, smiling broadly and proffering a business card with both hands. Used to dealing with Asians, then.

I reciprocated, bowing, taking it with both hands and examining it as if some deep import might lie within it. "So, there are three of you? Clones?"

Bob Jennick looked mystified for a moment, then his face cleared. "Oh, Robert Jennick the Third. That just means that my father and grandfather were both Roberts before me. It's an American tradition. And you are Ms Laoban, right?"

"Correct. There is only one of me. And it's just Laoban, not Ms or Miss or Mrs." Jenrick raised his eyebrows but made no comment.

"So, what's this all about? Ryan told me you have very important things to tell me, and that I needed to drop everything to meet you today."

"Can't we go somewhere more private?" I asked. Up to this point, we had been standing in the middle of the reception area of his company, FutureHealth.

"Of course, I'm sorry. You won't mind if we use my office? They only told me an hour ago what time you were coming in, and all the meeting rooms are booked up." Bob led me through a large open-plan area, cubed off with low partitions, a hive of activity, eventually reaching a corner office. Glass walls. Bob pressed a button near the desk and the slats of venetian blinds snapped shut. I surveyed the office. Photographs covered most of the wall behind Bob's chair. Happy family. Sporting scenes. Certificates too. On a table in the corner, a clutch of trophies. "Mostly golf," Bob said proudly, seeing me studying them. "Do you play sports?"

"Ju-Jitsu. Black belt. But we are not here to discuss me. Or sport. Is golf actually a sport?"

Jennick looked worried, as if he must have said or done something wrong already. Good. I needed him docile. "Ha ha, well we like to think so," he responded. "Before we get to business, coffee or tea?"

"Black tea would be appreciated."

He picked up the phone and placed an order. "Now, tell me, what is this all about?" he asked.

Time to get straight to the point. "You have shipments to Uzbekistan that are going missing." Robert Jennick III's cheery face turned serious.

"How do you know that? And what business is it of yours?"

"Never mind how I know. Would you like the problem to stop?"

"We don't pay ransoms. Or bribes."

"Of course not. I would not expect a company like yours to do so. But you admit the problem exists?"

Jennick looked pensive. Perhaps a minute passed before he spoke again, cautiously. "It is true that one shipment did go missing recently."

"Not just the one," I retorted. "My information is that you have lost several shipments en route to Central Asia."

Now he looked seriously worried. "Where have you got this information from?"

"A source of ours told me you can no longer get insurance at normal rates. Your company is on notice. If you lose another shipment, you will be uninsurable." My bluff had hit home. We stared at each other, stony faced. I had no intention of being the first to break eye contact. Or the increasingly uncomfortable silence. Eventually, Jennick spoke.

"What business is this of yours, and what exactly do you do, Laoban?"

"My company undertakes covert research. We uncover secrets. Things our corporate customers are eager to know but are unable to find out for themselves. Or maybe where they have tried and failed. For example, who do you believe is stealing your shipments?"

"We don't know. That's a job for the police. Not researchers, or whatever you call yourselves."

What a simple-minded man, I thought. "Which police force were you thinking of?" I asked. "Between here and Uzbekistan, your latest missing shipment travelled in a Danish container on a Panamanian flagged ship to Dubai, and was then driven by truck through Saudi Arabia, Kuwait, Iraq, Iran and Turkmenistan. The container that arrived in Uzbekistan had all the right documentation but proved to be packed with plush toys made in China. It could have been switched in any of those countries. Which of those police forces are you relying on?"

"All of them, obviously. And the CIA and FBI. Interpol. The whole darned lot of them."

"How is that going for you? Are any of them doing anything? What results have you seen?"

I had him in nervous discomfiture now. Sweating. As planned. "It's a work in progress. It all takes time," he snapped tartly.

"Which means you know nothing. All the time you wait, more shipments, more containers, more equipment of yours will go missing. All the police agencies will simply pass the buck, from one to another. Nothing will get done. You lose your money and your reputation." I sat back and waited for a reaction. It didn't take long.

"So, Laoban, what is it exactly that you are proposing?"

8 – All over the place – Robert

London, England

What a fortnight. The last few days have been fun, though. Thank goodness things have improved. If you'd asked me at the start of the month, I'd have been sniping at Laoban for landing me with that woman. Three weeks of dawn to dusk 'close protection', as she liked to call it. With no more interesting projects in the pipeline after the African adventure, it was back to the mundane. Not so much covert research as covert boredom. I know we need to keep the business active and generating money. I just wish we had the resources to hire some foot soldiers to do what I was doing. Guarding an extremely wealthy octogenarian widow from Estonia. A tiny country with a border with Latvia. That kept me thinking of Latviana, sorry, Maria. I admit to missing her dreadfully. I couldn't fly over to Rotterdam. In fact, I couldn't fly anywhere – talk about being grounded. Couldn't even call or text; Laoban had read me the riot act about total radio silence on this body guarding project. Apparently, nobody else could know. I discovered later that Laoban had told everyone else on the team that I was delivering a three-week intensive flying training course to some rich young model. Not a word of it true. Almost certainly intended to drive a wedge between me and Maria. Laoban can be a bitch sometimes. Most times.

The widow in question went by the name of Inessa. Female, rich, but no model. She was about four feet high and about the same wide. With assets alleged to be of the order of four billion dollars, inherited from her oligarch husband, who had no doubt robbed them from the former Soviet Union. She was a smart cookie, I have to give her that. One evening, after several vodkas too many, she confided she had packed everything small and movable, gold, jewellery, stuff like that, into a cabin trunk, taken the ferry from Vilnius to Helsinki and stashed it in some place of safekeeping there. "I'd have to kill you if I told you where," she chortled. Now she was in London to arrange transfer of all her paper assets to a web of offshore trusts so that her four children, nine grandchildren and forty-year-old toy boy could go on reaping the benefits. She had contracted us to guard her because she feared that other greedy oligarchs had hired men to kidnap her and extract her wealth before she could finish the job.

Laoban had rented what she told Inessa was a 'safe house'. A newish terraced town house in Maida Vale, backing onto the railway and with hard standing in the front. I was required to live in. We'd also hired a car, one of those station wagons adapted for wheelchair users. Inessa didn't need one, but it meant that the car came with a rear door she could use, so it would be very difficult for anyone to see her getting in or out. Even someone with a telescope in the house opposite would think that it was just me living there. Well, that's what we hoped.

Thus, I was a bodyguard, butler, chauffeur and chaperone. Inessa was thrilled to have a relatively young man to accompany her and wasn't afraid of being seen as long as we were in busy high-profile locations. We went to the Ritz for afternoon tea, Alain Ducasse for lunch, places like that, you get the picture. Arranging to get her in and out through service entrances was nightmare enough, but accompanying her to flashy venues was downright embarrassing, as I was sure the staff assumed I was her 'escort'. She'd left the real thing back in Vilnius, minding the shop.

The only thing that made those few weeks worthwhile for me was that the dear old lady was indeed at risk. She certainly wasn't making it up. Almost from the first day, I spotted operatives monitoring places we went to, and we were followed several times. One time, in a car park under Canary Wharf, where she was meeting with her bankers, a black Bentley tried to hem us in, and I was forced to reverse at speed up the down ramp. Just as well we met no cars on the way.

I was relieved when, business done, I could drop her off at Northolt for her flight back to Vilnius or wherever she was headed (I suspect somewhere warmer and sunnier). For once, I was quite happy not to be piloting the plane as I watched it take off. Thinking that I now deserved some R&R, I lost no time in calling Maria. To say she was not best amused at my not having been in contact for three weeks is an understatement. I'd describe it as an icy reception. No, I could not come over to see her. She had new instructions from Laoban to give me. Do not pass Go. Do not collect £200. Do not take a day off. Do not go to Rotterdam.

The good news she shared was that Laoban had landed a valuable new international project. The details so far were sparse, something to do with black market medical equipment. It was going to be complicated, but very lucrative because she had sold the project to two different organisations. Everyone in the team had a role to play.

My first task was to carry out some surveillance on a sales executive based in London. Maria had met him and thought he was legitimate, but Laoban wasn't sure. On her instruction, Toshio had hacked his phone and email, which had apparently been easy, as he mostly worked from home and rarely remembered to fire up his VPN. The only suspicious thing he had uncovered was that his American sales director was flying to London to meet with him and two men with Russian-sounding names. Laoban smelt a rat. Following and watching the two salespeople was easy enough. The routine was the same for three days running. The American was staying in a Park Lane hotel close to the office. The British man, Ryan, travelled up to London from his home in Putney by underground, alighting at Hyde Park Corner station. The men started the day over breakfast in the hotel, not eating much but downing cup after cup of coffee until nearly eleven. Interestingly, their phones never rang, and I never saw them checking messages or email. They were neither being discreet nor bothering to look around, so it was easy to eavesdrop from an adjacent table.

After breakfast, they went to their office for an hour or two. There was a café right opposite with a table where I could sit giving me an unobstructed view of the front door. Nobody else came or went. Around one o'clock, they went to an upmarket restaurant on Brook Street and gorged on steaks. After that, the American went back to his room in the hotel and Ryan caught the tube home. The same routine every day.

In both restaurants, they mostly discussed financials. Essentially, the American telling the Brit that he wasn't selling enough and the Brit complaining about how long it took to get the health service to agree to buy anything. Along the lines of "the surgeons don't want robotics because they think it will put them out of a job, the health service doesn't want to pay for the machines and most of the people waiting for a joint replacement will be dead before they get to the top of the list." Repeated frequently over three days. Ryan, the Brit, was, however, promising what he described as a "hot new prospect." I guessed he was probably elaborating the lie that Maria had spun him.

It wasn't until breakfast on day three, the day of their meeting with those suspect men, that the topics of conversation changed. The American was concerned that "the business with the Russkies" (so at least I now had confirmation of their nationality) could prejudice Ryan's new prospects, while Ryan did his best to reassure the American that both deals could be done. What they agreed about was that nobody else in their company should know anything about the 'Russkie Deal' until it was done and dusted. And probably not even then. By 9.30 I'd learnt that the meeting would be at 10 in a private meeting room they had booked in a co-working space nearby, so I had only half an hour to put on my false beard, the one I once used at the reading group, go there, park myself in reception, hold up my phone as if I was checking messages and use it surreptitiously to snap any likely arrivals.

Ryan and the American arrived ten minutes after me, and the 'Russkies' ten minutes later. Just as well I got pictures of everyone who came, as one arrived dressed as a motorcycle messenger and the other was a young woman with a scarf over her head and wearing big dark glasses. No point after that in waiting inside; I'm sure the receptionist wouldn't have cared if I'd sat there all day, but I told her my friend wasn't coming and left, staying in the street until the visitors exited, forty minutes later, each one separately at one-minute intervals. The woman had obviously called an Uber as she went straight from door to cab. The man already had his helmet on before he left the building, got on his bike and sped away. I noted its number, but doubted that would help us; the bike had almost certainly been nicked. I sent the pictures and registration to Maria, and followed the American back to his hotel, where he checked out and got in a cab, no doubt back to the airport and home. And I went back to mine, cursing all the way that I had been too lazy to shave that morning – it would make removing the beard much more painful.

Still no rest for the wicked, or at least not for the covert. I'd hardly had time to get back to my hut and remove my disguise before my phone went into a fit of beeping. WhatsApp messages from Maria. Not the romantic ones she used to send me up to a few weeks ago. These were instructions on behalf of Laoban. In summary, go to Almaty and make sure that Humph and Ronald don't get into any trouble. That might be fun. She could book me on a flight from Gatwick to Istanbul at 21.00 with an airport change and eight-hour layover before the connection. Should she go ahead and get the ticket? Sod that, I thought. Gatwick, other side of London. Never mind the rest. I knew that wasn't Maria's fault. The boss always insisted on the cheapest possible option. If only Laoban had invested in a private jet. The only aircraft I had access to was a twin prop at Elstree. Even if the owner didn't miss it for a week or so, it would be no good for such a long trip. I didn't need to be in Kazakhstan for a couple of days, so I had a few hours to think and plan.

A sudden inspiration led me to phone Gavin, an old mate of mine from before when I worked for Smith. We used to fly business charters together from Biggin Hill. Not only was he on the ground and picking up calls, something of a miracle, he was up at Stansted. Much better. In little more than half an hour we were reliving old times over coffees in the private aviation terminal there, and in an hour more we'd been joined by a couple of other pilots I hadn't seen in years who were booked to fly a Gulfstream 650ER to Abu Dhabi. Not where I needed to get to, but arguably on the way, as I could get a commercial flight connection from there. They had space in the rest area for a third pilot, and in return for a few bevvies in the hotel bar on arrival they might let me co-pilot for part of the way. I tried calling Maria to tell her I was making my own arrangements and was on my way. No answer. I sent a message. Instant 'OK' back. So, still not talking to me. Upsetting, but I couldn't hang around to mope. My plane was leaving.

I got lucky in Abu Dhabi too, as a big 747 freighter was leaving for Almaty only an hour after we landed, and, since I was in uniform, the pilots agreed to letting me stow away. I got to sit in the navigator's seat. Fascinating. Shame I'm not licensed to fly those big beasts.

I had a bit of hassle at the airport in Almaty. I didn't need a visa, but I wasn't on the flight manifest and the immigration guy was enjoying his moment of power. Those ex-Soviet state officials can be a bit scary. Fortunately, his shift was ending within ten minutes, so after making his point forcefully, he checked his watch, stamped my passport and waved me through.

I was glad I'd been to Almaty before. Although the city is quite compact, it still takes some getting used to, and all the signs are in Cyrillic script. Luckily, most of the younger people speak passably good English. It's very pretty as Soviet cities go. Lots of trees. I'd visited twice, both times about six years ago when I flew oil company executives coming to do gas deals. They'd spend a couple of days and nights there before flying back, so my co-pilot Gavin and I got time to explore.

I arrived to a slew of encrypted messages from Maria and, unencoded, a hotel reservation. Which meant I could check in and then sit in my room for a couple of hours translating all the messages into words I could understand and then plan how I was going to babysit a couple of unpredictable men entering an unpredictable situation with unknown and probably dangerous criminals. The hotel I was booked into was different from the one Maria had arranged for the guys, but more or less just around the corner. They didn't know I would be there, and I needed to do my best to disguise myself any time that they might see me. That's how we always work; it's important I'm not recognised as a member of the gang. I wouldn't be able to protect them if I was.

I had two days to get myself organised, which was pretty generous by our usual standards. Normally I'd be lucky to have two hours. First, I needed wheels. Which meant I'd have to get back to the airport, since that's where all the car rental offices were. I got lucky with a young taxi driver who spoke English well. Bogdan. After his initial surprise I wasn't going to catch a plane, we had a bit of a bargy about what a rip-off car hire companies were, and I tried asking if he knew of any cheap local places, especially ones that might rent older cars at a bargain price. Long story short, Bogdan ended up renting me his own taxi for a week for five hundred euros. He was happy getting a month's fares upfront and a week's holiday. Despite probably paying twice what an airport hire company would charge, I was happy having an ideal car for the job with no paper trail. If a bright yellow twelve-year-old badly maintained Hyundai Elantra could ever be ideal for anything. Bogdan assured me that as long as I didn't put the 'for hire' sign on the roof, nobody would try to stop me, and I'd have no problems. I crossed my fingers, hoping he was right.

In the market, I bought the sort of cheap clothes I thought a Central Asian taxi driver would wear and a woolly hat. Dressed like that, and without shaving for a couple of days, I was confident that Ronald wouldn't recognise me, especially as he wouldn't be expecting me in Almaty, even less as a taxi driver. I wasn't so bothered about Humphrey, as he had rarely seen me without my book club beard.

At a hole-in-the-wall cell phone shop, the owner, more Chinese than Kazakh, recited a long list of bureaucratic prerequisites before I could buy a local phone and SIM card, but a few hundred dollars worked just as well.

Bogdan, my new best friend in Almaty, told me that his father was an "English teacher and tour operator." He brought him to my hotel next morning, and over coffees I learnt that Stanislas ("but you can call me Stan") indeed taught at the university, but because it didn't pay very well, he incremented his income when he could by transporting and guiding tourists. Perfect. The guys were coming by different routes, as usual. Ron was arriving in the evening from Dubai, Humph the next morning from Istanbul. Stan was delighted to get the business of picking them both up and being their 'wheels' while they were in town.

9 – Almaty – Humphrey

I confess I passed most of the flight from Istanbul to Almaty in a state of trepidation. Surprisingly, in all my years of military manoeuvres, where most of my flights were spent sitting on the floor of a Hercules and my landings were parachute-assisted, I don't remember ever feeling nervous. It was all just part of the job. But this time, still doing my job, though now as a well strapped-in passenger in a moderately comfortable seat on a regular flight, I spent four hours feeling on the verge of a panic attack.

Changing planes in Istanbul, rushing from gate to gate, may well have been the trigger. That airport is VAST, and the airline's official minimum connecting times are quite unrealistic. My flight coming in from Madrid reached the gate twenty minutes late, which allowed just forty-five minutes before the Almaty flight left. "You'll make it," smiled the girl who checked my boarding pass at the foot of the ramp at gate A15. She must think I'm a professional athlete, I thought as I arrived panting at gate F20 thirty minutes later. Six thousand three hundred and fourteen steps according to my Fitbit. I wonder how the elderly or those unfamiliar with airports cope. I suppose they miss their flight and catch the next one. Not something I could afford to do. There are just two flights a day on this route, and the next one was in twelve hours. I had a 10 am meeting and little time to spare.

Staring out of the window didn't help. At first it was night, with nothing to see apart from my own reflection (and that definitely did not lighten my mood). About two hours into the flight, dawn broke. An eery landscape appeared beneath me, so strange that it took some time to work out what it was I was seeing. Desert, I decided. Not golden sand desert like the Sahara, but a drearily unpleasant grey-green colour. Occasional darker rectangles that might be ploughed fields. No rivers or lakes. No roads or tracks, at least none I could see from my vantage point thirty-five-thousand feet up above. Were they fields? If so, what grew there? With no roads, how could a farmer – or anyone else – reach them? As the sun rose further, a faint white line on the horizon slowly grew in intensity until it revealed itself as a wide ridge of snow-covered mountain peaks. I pulled the inflight magazine from the rack in front of me, searching for a map at the back. Kazakhstan. I'd never realised the country was so enormous. If the scale was correct, it was as big as the whole of continental Europe. Most of it desert, though.

As the plane descended towards the mountains, the landscape below changed, first to green fields, and then adding roads, houses, villages and cars before finally touching down. Other than the ancient couple seated next to me, who had slept all the way, swaddled in coats that appeared made of carpet, I'd taken no notice of any of my fellow passengers. Now, trapped in my window seat until the elderly couple slowly regained consciousness, I observed the others as they made their way down the gangway, pushing and shoving each other in their hurry to reach whatever joys Almaty held in store for them. Most looked like businesspeople, suited and ready for their morning meetings. Something I was not. Sweatshirt and jeans were probably not appropriate attire for a medical professional negotiating the purchase of robotic surgical equipment. Even if it was black market stuff.

Last off the plane and through passport control, I surveyed the baggage hall. Deserted. Both of people and luggage. Strange. Was I the only passenger with a checked suitcase? Where had the others gone? A head popped up behind a little hatchway in the wall in front of me. I approached. The man didn't speak English, but went and found someone who did. A little.

"My suitcase isn't here," I said, waving my hand at the empty carousel.

"All the baggage has gone, Sir. You are the last." Telling me something I knew. "Perhaps your bag was not on the flight. You have the baggage check?"

I handed over my boarding pass with the bag check stuck to the back. He studied it in more detail than it deserved.

"You changed planes in Istanbul, correct, Sir?"

"Yes, I did."

"How long between the flights, Sir?"

"About forty-five minutes."

He nodded fiercely, having seen the light. "Not enough time, Sir. Your bag will still be in Istanbul. It will come on the night flight, do not worry. Many people with this problem."

"Will you send it to my hotel? Do I fill up a form?"

"No, no, Sir, you come back here. Tomorrow morning. Bring your card," pushing my boarding pass back at me. "Do not worry, Sir. It will be safe."

Strange that I didn't have to fill in a form or do anything else, just come back. I'd expected a lot of bureaucracy in a country that until twenty-five years ago was part of the Soviet Union.

At least I had my laptop and paperwork with me.

I'd taken only one step out into the arrivals hall before I was accosted by a tall, slim and rather elderly man, wearing a tweed jacket and looking for all the world like my Uncle Albert. Rest his soul. "Mister Hunter?" he enquired. "I am Stanislas. Your driver and guide. Follow me." Maria hadn't told me she had organised a driver. She probably just assumed I'd expect it. She's efficient like that.

Taxis and cars lined the kerb outside, and a large car park was visible beyond it, but Stanislas led me away down a side road between two old buildings and lined with trees to a small parking area. He unlocked the rear doors of a dark blue minivan, and only then asked, "Where's your luggage?"

I explained my predicament. Stanislas ("it's OK, you can call me Stan, I don't mind") was not in the least fazed by this revelation, and took only seconds to come up with a plan. He would drop me at my hotel, wait while I had a shower ("but you will have to be quick") by which time the shops would be open. He would then take me to buy some new clothes ("don't spend hours browsing like my wife does") that I should change into in the shop. Assuming no delays, he was confident we'd make the Ritz-Carlton by ten.

It was a pleasant drive into the city along wide, tree-lined avenues. Lots of trees. Two million, according to Stan. Many different species, but the important ones are apple trees. Stan told me that the city's name, Almaty, means 'apple orchard' or something like that. Rising beyond the trees, snow-capped mountains. Nestled between the trees, quite attractive city buildings. I'd expected Soviet architecture but could see nothing of the kind. Instead, a modern, spacious city. I was enjoying the ride so much that I completely forgot my earlier nerves.

The hotel was tucked away in a back street and approached by a narrow road that went through an arch under other buildings. It was nothing special, but better than I had expected, and there was no problem checking in at 8:45 in the morning. The room was spacious and modern, and there was a powerful shower with hot water. Exactly what I needed. I put my clothes back on, ran down the stairs and jumped into the waiting minivan to approving nods from Stan. Ten minutes. I'd have done it in less if the form I'd had to fill in on arrival had only been one page long.

The clothing store was literally just around the corner. Marks and Spencer? In the middle of Asia? Well, good, I knew my size, so I could be sure whatever I chose would fit. Stan pulled up outside on the stroke of nine, but we had to wait five minutes while the security guard we could see behind the glass doors figured out how to open them.

Duly attired in new smart casuals and a blazer that felt one size too small (I really must diet one of these days), and three hundred euros poorer, we drove off towards the rendezvous. Stanislas extracted a card from his jacket pocket and handed it to me. "Programme the number into your phone now, then call me to check it is working." I did as he instructed. "When you finish, call me. I come and pick you up." I nodded understanding. "If they take you back to your hotel, still phone and tell me." Then, dropping his voice and adopting an almost threatening tone, "Unless I hear from you by five, we will come searching for you." Excellent way of getting my nerves back on edge.

The Ritz-Carlton was a mirror-glass tower block reaching into the sky and reflecting the majestic mountain range it faced. Inside, the lobby exuded opulence. Rather too much of it for my liking; I instantly felt completely out of place. But I was there only for a few seconds; a smartly uniformed young man propelled me straight into a lift that, moments later, deposited me in the hotel reception thirty floors up. 9:56am. Four minutes early, so not much time to take in my surroundings. I don't remember what wowed me more, the decorations or the view through the floor-to-ceiling windows. The spacious lobby was silent and almost empty. Spoiling the effect was Ronald Jones, sitting on a sofa, dressed in a tweed suit and looking mightily pleased with himself, with an empty coffee cup and a plate full of crumbs on the table in front of him.

"You made it! Good to see you, Huh…" Suddenly remembering we mustn't use our own names, or possibly just choking on the remnants of his demolished pastry, he succumbed instead to a fit of coughing.

"You too. You need a haircut, by the way." Though I supposed that since he was playing the role of translator, the mad professor look might be credible.

He ignored the jibe. "Try the hazelnut croissants! They're remarkable!"

"I don't think we have time," I replied. True, though I rather wished we had. Either there hadn't been an inflight meal, or I'd dozed through it. Probably the latter. Anyway, it was now ten, and a tall, slim and extraordinarily attractive brunette materialised in front of us. "You are here for the ten o'clock meeting arranged by email?" she enquired in almost accent-free English. I nodded. "Do you speak Russian?"

"No, but my associate here is my translator."

"Good." She turned to Ronald and rattled off something, obviously in Russian. He'd told me back in Lanzarote that he was just learning the language, so I wasn't expecting him to be up to much, but he clearly understood what she was saying and replied to her.

"We are to go with her. The meeting will be elsewhere. She has given me a code word to use when we arrive." She nodded with some satisfaction to show that Ronald had translated correctly, and we followed her over to the lift. It seemed my experience of the Ritz-Carlton was to be limited to less than five minutes in the lobby.

Instead of returning to the main entrance, we descended to a basement level, and were then led down dark grey painted corridors into a loading bay. Functional. Far from the luxury of the hotel lobby. I was nervous again, but Ronald was remarkably calm. "Story of my life," he said, "I always end up leaving by the tradesmen's entrance." Another minibus awaited us, this one with blacked-out windows, the logo of a holiday company emblazoned down the sides, the passenger door wide open. As we approached, the driver got out and came towards us. He was very Russian in appearance, just as they look on TV spy thrillers, though I suppose he was Kazakh. Probably in his fifties, with a weather-beaten face, dirty green anorak and a maroon woolly hat pulled down over his ears. He barked out some words in Russian. "He wants us to put our arms out and legs apart. He's going to search us." He scanned all around us with a device that looked like a spare hand for Captain Hook. Or rather, in this case, since it was a round loop, Captain Eye. It buzzed, then the noise escalated to a shrill whistle as he brought the device down the side of my jacket. He reached in, pulled out my phone, and gave it to the girl. Did the same for Jones. Took our wallets, our passports, packs of paper hankies. The lot.

Still not satisfied, he growled another question. "He's asking where our guns are, I think," Ronald translated. The driver had obviously not believed Ronald's denials, as he now put down the electronic scanner and resorted to using his hands, giving us very thorough patting-downs. Another guttural order. "He's telling us to pull down our trousers," translated Ronald. We did as instructed, in my case feeling embarrassed that I hadn't changed my underwear when I put on the new clothes in the store earlier. The man walked round us, patting our waistlines, and eventually satisfied, pointed to show we could pull our trousers back up.

Now the brunette gestured we should get into the van, and as soon as we had boarded, she closed the door, remaining outside, and the driver, who I hadn't noticed getting in, fired up the engine and pulled away. Silent concentration. Ronald tried to engage him in conversation. Not a dicky bird in reply.

The drive took about half an hour, though I'm sure it could have been done in ten minutes, as we were weaving back and forth through the city, passing the same landmarks two or three times. Eventually, we stopped outside a modern glass-fronted building. The driver alighted and opened our door. Getting out, we were greeted by a short, stocky, sixty-something-year-old woman. "Welcome to Kok Tobe," she announced in English. Her expression looked anything other than welcoming. "Your tour starts here. Follow me." Inside, after climbing two flights of stairs, we entered a waiting room packed with people, most of them elderly and looking morose, though there were a few younger couples trying to control hyperactive small children. Our guide pointed to the rows of benches on which everyone was sitting, indicating that we should join them. She sat herself down next to Ronald. I think he asked her what we were waiting for, but she was by now as uncommunicative as the bus driver.

At the far end of the room, three ancient men sat against the wall, two of them beating small drums held between their legs, the third plucking at some mournful-sounding instrument. Can you play a dirge on a banjo? It may have been music to his ears, but not to mine. A racket. But one we were forced to endure, at least for ten minutes. Every minute or two a man would appear from a doorway behind the musicians and summon a group of about ten from the waiting room. We would then all shuffle along the bench or, reaching the end, move to the row below. New people kept arriving in ones and twos and joining us. Eventually, it was our turn to be summoned through the doorway, and the reason for our wait became clear. We were going to board a cable car.

This was all unexpectedly touristic. The cable car duly ascended the mountain in front of us, and as we turned around to look behind, we had a panoramic view of Almaty beneath us. "You are lucky to come in autumn," the guide said. "No view in winter, just smog." She pointed out buildings with tall chimneys that she said housed district heating boilers. All of them coal fired, in a country that is one of the world's biggest producers of natural gas. I tucked away the information. Quite irrelevant to the task at hand, but an interesting fact.

Outside the cable car station at the top, incongruously, was a fun fair. Pride of place was given to a big wheel resembling a giant and rusty Meccano construction. I hoped we would not be expected to go on that. Though just as stony-faced as before, our guide had now switched to full tourist mode, spouting out information as if it were pre-recorded. Presumably the same verbiage used for every group of visitors she brought here. "Very popular with families at weekends," she announced. "Very quiet at this time of day." Then, pointing at a monstrous bronze statue, "Raging Bull!" No explanation as to why, or whether it symbolised anything other than what it looked like (a raging bull). Unless we were going to be told a load of old bull, of course. But our guide was marching on, and we hurried to follow. More statues. "Beatles!" she barked. She did not explain what a bronze statue of the Beatles was doing on the top of a Kazakh mountain, but it was clearly the number one tourist attraction. A queue of people snaked along the path, waiting to take their pictures with the Fab Four.

She marched us onward past a long row of aviaries. "Birds!" she exclaimed, waving her hand at them. I asked what kind, but she ignored me. Well, we weren't there for the guided tour, but if we had been, her commentary would have proved most unsatisfactory. Personally, I wouldn't have minded lingering by the aviaries. But we were marching on, and had left the genuine tourists far behind us now. Here all we saw apart from trees were solitary young men, standing at forty or fifty metre intervals, none taking any notice of the birds, but all watching us and looking vaguely threatening.

We walked for maybe ten minutes before reaching the end of the path. A small concrete hut, probably a café, but closed now, with the shutters down. A few tables and chairs on the terrace outside. One was occupied. Our guide pointed towards it and left us on our own. Sitting at the table, a man in a black anorak. I registered a bulge underneath it, in the same place as my former military colleagues carried their firearms. Despite the warmth of the autumn sun, he had his hood pulled up, partly covering a royal blue baseball cap with a colourful flower motif. His face was largely obscured by a medical N95 mask. Meaning that we would neither catch Covid from him nor learn what he looked like.

For a shady salesman about to negotiate a high value sale of black-market equipment, his attitude was more than vaguely threatening.

10 – A meeting in Istanbul – Beatrix

Istanbul is a city I'd always wanted to visit. Never managed it, though. Until now. Work never took me there, and those I went with on holiday always wanted sun and sand. Just kept it on the bucket list. Maybe Humph and I can plan a trip, now that we're together. I certainly saw nothing of it this time around.

Oh yes, I flew to Istanbul Airport. Astronomic in scale, the biggest monstrosity of an airport I have ever been to. God help anyone who has to change planes in a hurry here, though that seems to be what most of the passengers are doing. It's proudly claimed to be the biggest airport in Europe, and I believe it, but not because all those millions are going to visit Istanbul or even Turkey. Sorry, I have to call it Türkiye now; I read the inflight magazine. Anyway, arrive late evening after a long journey via Madrid, walk miles through arrivals to the taxi rank, fifteen-minute drive in the dark, seeing nothing, told by the driver that we're actually going in the opposite direction away from the city, and finally reaching a hotel that seems to be set in the middle of a park. Meeting in the morning, drive back to the airport, catch another flight, this time to Barcelona, miss the connection and decide to sit it out in the terminal overnight since the next flight is at 7am. Lanzarote is a lovely place to live, but not exactly handy for espionage activities. Laoban agrees a private jet would be a good idea, but she says we can't afford it yet and she doesn't want to pull Robert off whatever mysterious project he's on at the moment. I didn't get involved in the discussions before, but I'm going to pester her now before she lines me up for any more sixty-hour trips for a two-hour meeting.

To add to my irritation, Humph was flying to Istanbul too, en route for Kazakhstan, but for whatever reason, presumably because Laoban always has her under pressure to save a few pennies, Maria booked us on completely different flights. We did fly from Lanzarote to Madrid on the same plane, though the budget airline seated us about ten rows apart. Then I had to rush to another terminal to make my connection, so we had just five minutes to kiss goodbye and wish each other good luck before I left him to kick his heels for a couple of hours before his flight.

You're not interested in all of that, though. I need to tell you about my meeting with Ben Fullofhimself-Price. Grandmothers delivered anywhere, all legal shipping documents included, airfreight, land or sea, best prices guaranteed. Imagine the most oleaginous double-glazing salesperson you've ever met, blended with a hefty dose of doorstep preacher, all packaged into a fifty-year-old overweight man of average height, reeking of cheap cologne, brylcreemed combed-over hair, dressed in a brown tweed jacket and dark red tartan trousers. That's him. I hardly registered the first words he spoke, so taken was I with his outrageous outfit. Who wears tartan trousers in Türkiye? Or anywhere? Golfers, perhaps? As soon as I told him I was British, he told me he was Canadian. I've met quite a few Americans who've done that. Do they think we might be less prejudiced? I simply shrugged.

He was waiting for me in the hotel lobby when I came out of the breakfast room. Half an hour early.

He obviously thought he was doing me a favour, after postponing our meeting originally planned for a week earlier ("but you know how it is in business, always at the beck and call of the customer!").

I was annoyed, as I'd been planning on having a little time to brush my teeth and go over the paperwork that Maria had scanned over to me one more time.

All in all, my first impressions made me think I was on a wild goose chase before we even started our meeting. But Laoban and Maria had said that it must be worth talking to him because he'd been on the contact list of that man called Smith or Arbuthnot. Someone I had only met for a few minutes in Windhoek before Ron contrived to get him re-arrested. Nasty character, but the girls said Smith wouldn't have Fullerton-Smith in his address book if he was a waste of time. They admitted they didn't know what he could bring to the table, but insisted he had to be worth an hour or two's conversation. Plus, in my case, about sixty hours of travelling.

Maria told me she hadn't mentioned Smith to him, and I should only bring up his name if I thought it was worthwhile.

Fullerton-Price ("Benjy to my friends" – yuk) presented his business card with arm outstretched, as if it were an item of some value. I think I was supposed to study it and reciprocate, maybe even bow, but I didn't have any cards, so I simply tucked it into my folder. He had booked a meeting room, already set up with notepads, water, and a jug of coffee. I had four talking points prepared. What I prefer to call 'missions of discovery.' I had them listed out on paper in front of me to make sure that I went through them formally and didn't go off on a tangent. Something Humph is always accusing me of doing.

Mission One. How much did he know about medical equipment? Answer, elicited very quickly, not very much, but he could certainly talk the talk. I suspect he had googled 'what sort of equipment would a private clinic want to buy' and memorised the answers. I suppose I looked cynical, as he quickly added, "The doctors give me the list of what they need. I just get it bought and delivered. I don't need to be an expert," accompanied by a sort of nervous titter. He claimed to have procured operating theatre equipment ("you know, those couches that the patient lies on and the floodlights over the top") for clinics in Iraq and Malawi and I can't remember where else. He promised references if we signed a letter of intent.

Mission Two: What equipment could he source? I was interested in what he would claim, knowing that he wasn't an authorised representative for the robotics company that Maria had met up with. Answer, just about anything. "You name it, I arrange it." When I said that I'd been told that the manufacturers only sold through their appointed agents, he pooh-poohed it. "Dangle a carrot in front of them, they'll bite your arm off." This turned out to be one of his favourite and most irritating expressions, as he repeated the same words at least ten times in the course of two hours. He claimed it was his amazing negotiating skills that got faster delivery, lower prices, and (tapping his nose) "no questions asked."

Mission Three: What pricing could he offer, specifically for robot-assisted prosthetic surgery? Answer, not as good as the mystery vendor in Kazakhstan, or Mongolia, or Uzbekistan, or wherever he was hiding out. As I'd expected, Call-me-Benjy was prepared for this. He offered ten per cent off list price. "I only get twenty per cent max, darling, I split it fifty-fifty with you, can't say fairer than that, can I?" I laughed, partly because it was a laughable offer, but more because he had now dropped his fake American/Canadian accent and gone pure cockney. Without realising it! It was the 'dahhling' that gave it away. Something he must have said thousands of times to women equally as infuriated by it as me!

Mission Four: What insights could he provide into importing equipment into Uzbekistan? Answer, a surprising amount. For the first time in our meeting, he sounded like he really knew what he was talking about. He claimed to have sold industrial machinery and air compressors and things like that to Uzbek companies, and I have to say I believed him. He explained that, being a land-locked country, everything heavy and bulky had to be delivered overland, which meant crossing at least one or two other countries along the way. Different paperwork needed for each one. Containers transferred from one truck to another. The neighbouring countries weren't all as developed or friendly. Guards needed bribing. Shipments went missing or got substituted. "It's like the Wild West out there," he told me. "Except it's the wild east, if you see what I mean." Accompanied again by that little boy laugh.

It wasn't until this point that he commented I hadn't taken any notes. I realised that he'd been writing almost nonstop, not on the pad provided but in a thick and obviously well-used notebook of his own. I'm not much of a note-taker myself. I tend to rely on a better-than-decent memory and just jot down things I can't risk getting wrong, like new prescriptions for our care home residents. I thought I had better demonstrate I had been paying attention, so I told him to wait, and promptly jotted down everything I remembered he had said that seemed to be useful information. I read it back to him.

"I'm impressed," he said. "Whenever anyone says to me they have a photographic memory, I immediately assume they mean that I'm talking bull. I'll have to rethink."

"I wouldn't claim my memory was photographic. I prefer to think of it as near-perfect recall."

"Whatever, darling. I wish I had that skill."

Time to get to specifics, then. Sticking to the scenario that Maria had created, I asked Fullerton-Price (sorry, I just can't call him 'Benjy' without cringing – it's a name for a cuddly puppy) what robotically assisted prosthetic surgery equipment he could offer for delivery to Uzbekistan in, say, two months. He pulled a sheet of paper from his case and presented it to me with a flourish.

"Two different manufacturers, full details and model numbers. The first one is a little cheaper than the second, but it'll take about four months to arrive. I can get the second one in two." The first was the one that Maria's sales executive friend had given her literature for. The second one was a manufacturer I hadn't heard of.

"This first is American, correct?" I asked. "I don't know the other one."

"German company, but built in Czechia. Very high quality. The big hospitals in London prefer it," he added, reeling off the names of a few.

"Obviously I will have to ask our clients and they will consult with their surgical teams," I extemporised, "but can I tell them they do the same thing?"

"Yes, more or less, though each is designed to work with original replacement parts and customised software." I established that the parts he was referring to were the metal and plastic hips and knees that got inserted into needy patients. It was also explained that the biggest single reason for the difference in delivery dates was the logistics used. Despite its weight and size, the Czech equipment would be delivered by airfreight direct to Tashkent. "Expensive, but makes sure it doesn't fall into the wrong hands along the way of the Silk Road," he said conspiratorially. Seeing me raise my eyebrows, he explained that the American equipment would come by sea and road. "Containerised. Shipped by sea to Dubai, then by road from there," he explained. "What I was telling you earlier. That's how the Uzbeks get most of their stuff, but there are lots of risky borders to cross. There's no other way since the routes via Russia and Afghanistan got closed off."

"So, what are the prices?" I asked. His reply almost made me fall off my chair. The first was indeed cheaper than the second, but what's ten thousand dollars when one is talking a million?

"That's the price it is, luv," he said, continuing to patronise me. "It's the manufacturers that set the prices, not me. Don't forget your clients will need a compatible CT scanner as well, and have to purchase software and installation. None of that is included in the price."

I told him that our mythical clients had been quoted about half his price (in fact, it was nearer a tenth if we'd got our Bitcoin exchange rate right, but I didn't want to sound absurd). "They have it in writing," I confirmed.

"Then, even if that price excludes shipping and taxes, it's black market. Sorry, I thought you were after original, fully documented equipment. My business is one hundred per cent legitimate."

"Well, of course, our clients only want legitimate equipment too, but expect us to research and negotiate the lowest possible price for them. What they've been offered elsewhere is very attractive. Tempting. I know you understand." Sweetest smile time.

Fullerton-Price then treated me to a five-minute lecture on only ever buying direct from the manufacturer to ensure it was guaranteed, to get after-sales service, software updates etc etc. Obviously rehearsed and repeated many times before. Eventually I interrupted.

"Because we were given your name by our mutual acquaintance, Mr Smith, we assumed we would get better prices than going direct to the manufacturer. That you were a man who could…" At the mention of Smith's name, his face immediately clouded with suspicion.

"Smith, you say? I know dozens of Smiths. It's a very common name."

"Well, Smith was the name he used for business. Based in Mayfair. His real name is Arbuthnot."

Now Fullerton-Price looked seriously worried. "That Smith? I thought he was out of business nowadays? I only ever met him the once." I could tell that was definitely a lie.

"Correct. He is no longer in business."

"So how did he give you my details, then?"

"We have taken over some of his business interests. The legitimate ones."

"Well, well. So, you're in bed with that other smarmy bastard, are you? He always bangs on about 'legitimacy'. Load of bullshit, he's crooked as they come."

"Sorry, I don't know who you are talking about."

"Youngish, curly hair, uses a couple of letters as his name, AA, BA, something like that."

"EA?"

"That's the one."

"I've only met him the once, briefly. He's a

freelance, nothing whatsoever to do with us. We are an entirely above the board business." Fullerton-Price didn't look convinced. "What was he talking to you about, anyway, if I might ask?"

"Wanted me to sell some dodgy aircraft parts that he'd got a supplier for. Landing gear, engine cowlings, stuff like that. Probably copies made in China or somewhere. I wouldn't do it."

"Why not? He obviously has you down as a super salesman."

"Well, I am, though I say so myself." He was back in a cheery, self-congratulatory mood now. "But my job means I do a lot of flying. I wouldn't want to think that a plane I was in might crash because the airline had saved a few quid on some part or other."

11 – Evading pursuers in Almaty – Humphrey

Talk about bizarre. We were on the terrace of a deserted and closed café on the top of a mountain in a remote country, ostensibly here to purchase expensive equipment from a black-market dealer who looked more likely to kill us than negotiate a sale.

We pulled up chairs and sat opposite him. Ronald spoke the code word, and the man nodded, then spoke a few words to him in Russian. "Yes, we would actually," Ronald replied in English, turning to me and adding "he asked if we would rather talk English."

"It's better anyway," the man said, speaking perfectly fluently. "There are no secret police up here, but if there were any around, they'd probably not understand English."

"What about him over there?" I moved my head towards a tall man about fifty metres away, with his back to us, apparently staring down at the panorama.

"My assistant. He keeps watch. So, tell me what you want?"

That seemed a stupid question. "We are interested in the equipment we saw in the document you sent us," I replied.

"Of course," he tutted. "But what equipment?"

"Robotic surgery. Oh, and a CT scanner, of course." Just in case he thought I didn't know it was a necessary adjunct.

"You are a doctor?" he asked me.

"Yes. An orthopaedic surgeon."

He looked sceptical. "OK, prove it. Tell me the names of the components of the knee."

At least this was something I knew like the back of my hand. Or front of my knee, of course. "Tibia, Femur, Patella, Cartilage, Ligament, Tendon, Meniscus," I trotted out.

"You missed one."

"Sorry. Synovial membrane."

"Hmm. OK, you pass that test. What about your friend?" pointing to Ronald.

"I am the translator. And in charge of business matters," said Ron. I wouldn't have thought of Ronald as having any business knack, but it seemed to go down well. The mystery man nodded in acknowledgement.

"Where is your clinic?" I wasn't ready for that question, but fortunately Ronald was.

"Khiva." I did my best not to look as if I didn't know where that was, but the mystery man answered immediately.

"Uzbekistan. Good. But you are a British company? American?"

"Neither. Our company's official headquarters are in Tonga. But we represent a group of foreign investors."

"You mean Russians." He spat. We didn't respond. "When?" The man was only paying attention to Jones now, ignoring me.

"Three months. Perhaps four. We are still building. Can you deliver?"

"It is very little time. It will cost extra."

"Will you install it too?" A brave question from Ronald, but one that the man found highly amusing.

"Very good joke! No, of course not. It will be delivered to the country. You will be given the papers and you will need to collect."

"How? From a warehouse?"

The man shook his head. "You never did this before, did you?" he sniggered. Clearly thought us a pair of fools. "You have a truck pick it up from a container park." Seeing incomprehension on my face, he added, "you have the container picked up. Then you bring it back it empty. You understand now?"

"In Uzbekistan?"

"Correct."

I thought it about time I asked some more detailed questions. "Is the equipment American, Swiss or German?"

"It depends on what we can source. We get all kinds. Those ones. Japanese, Korean, Chinese too. I will talk with my people. Tomorrow, we will tell you what we can do."

"How much?" Ronald asked.

"Depends on what is available. You pay in Bitcoin. Half up front, half when we give you the collection document."

"Twenty-five per cent up front, twenty-five per cent when we get the papers, the rest after we examine the merchandise and confirm it is what we ordered." Wow! I hadn't expected that. Ronald Jones the negotiator! The man was unimpressed, though.

"We talk price and terms when we confirm the order. Tomorrow. You remember the pretty girl at the Ritz?" I nodded. "She will meet you at your hotel. Nine o'clock sharp. Check out of the hotel and bring your bags with you."

"Where will we be going?" I asked.

"You'll see." Obviously registering the concerned looks on our faces, he added, "Don't be afraid. You are safe with us. We want happy customers. Now, go off and be tourists for the afternoon. I think you have never been to Almaty?" We nodded. "Good. You will like. Very nice city. The cathedrals are interesting. The music museum also."

"What about our things?" asked Ronald. "Phones, passports, wallets?"

"You will find them in your rooms in your hotel." Odd. We hadn't said where we were staying. The man, evidently finished with us, picked up his phone, turned to look the other way and made a call. Moments later, the old woman guide reappeared, gesturing for us to follow her. No running commentary this time, just straight back to the cable car and down the mountain to the street below. There she hailed a passing cab, gave him some instructions and a bank note, told us to get in and slammed the door behind us.

"She told the driver to take us to our hotel," said Ronald. "I suppose they followed us. Or that Stan character works for them." That didn't seem likely, since his transfer services had been arranged by Maria. She'd probably found his details online. There must be lots of drivers in Almaty, surely?

"What if…" I started a question, but Ronald put his finger to his lips and pointed to the driver with his other hand. Wise. Although it had looked as if the 'guide' had hailed a random taxi, we couldn't be certain. Ronald whispered in my ear. "I just realised. That woman told him to take us to our hotel, but didn't say which one. Which means he must be working for them, and they really do know where we are staying – and maybe who we are."

Ronald then spoke to the driver in Russian. I was becoming quite impressed by him. For someone who claimed to be no more than an elementary student of the language, he was remarkably confident.

"I asked him to drop us at the cathedral instead. He seems to be refusing." As if we needed any further proof, Jones tried opening the door when the taxi next stopped at a red light. Locked. A loud and unintelligible reprimand from the driver, who sped away from the lights and turned the next corner on to a much wider road, driving as fast as the traffic allowed and weaving from lane to lane. Fast and furious.

"*Vamos en camino equivocado*," muttered Ronald. Despite my best intentions, I'd not picked up much Spanish in my few months in Lanzarote, but it was pretty obvious that he meant we were going the wrong way. No doubt assuming the driver wouldn't understand. This was worrying. If the vendor really wanted happy customers, why would he try to abduct us? But then after a sharp right turn, then right again, we were heading back on the parallel road, a narrower but equally leafy avenue. Only then did the driver speak, to say that he thought we were being followed. In English. I'd totally lost my sense of direction by then, so it was much to my surprise when, just one left turn later, we drove through the archway and up to the hotel entrance. "Bye bye, Englishmen," said the driver, unlocking the doors, still staring straight ahead.

"Shower, then walk to the cathedral," announced Ronald in a loud voice as we stood at the desk waiting for our keys. Intending to be overheard. I thought Laoban expected me to call the shots, but Jones was assuming command. No longer the mad professor. But I had no objection. His proposal was logical. In the lift, we both attempted sign language to tell the other not to bring their phone with them, making such a hash of it we reached the third floor in fits of laughter.

The hotel corridors were dim and depressing, but the room was bright and bog-standard. Two single beds, both rock hard. A counter-top along one wall, a TV on it, no English language channels. I switched to a news programme with a fierce-looking presenter and coverage of some conference of men in military uniform. I could not understand a word, but it was better than the view out of the window onto a yard littered with waste. I searched for hidden microphones, lying on the floor, running my hands under the counter and the beds, climbing on the chair to check the top of the wardrobe. In the smoke detector, perhaps? Probably. Better not disconnect it though.

As the man had said, my phone was lying on my bed along with my wallet and passport. What surprised me, though, was that my suitcase was there too. They'd told me at the airport that it wouldn't arrive until midnight, and I'd have to go there to pick it up. How had it got here? All the possibilities were unnerving.

I had my shower, more than welcome after that somewhat stressful day, never for a moment forgetting that I was probably being watched by some spy camera I hadn't found. I hoped whoever was watching was enjoying my honed physique. And the background noise from the TV of all those military men who were now singing a turgid anthem at the top of their voices.

As far as I could tell, nobody had tampered with my case. The combination was still set at the number I always put it to when I lock it, and the black thread was still poking out from the zip, set in the third tooth, counting from the combo lock. Not that I'd been expecting trouble on this trip. Just force of habit. Training. Once learnt, never forgotten. I lie. It was something I read in a spy novel when I was a teenager. It seemed a good idea then, and it's something I've been doing ever since. This was the first time I'd actually found it reassuring. Though was it?

12 – Going Orthodox in Almaty – Ronald

Maybe, like me, Humphrey had his showering habits instilled in him by Laoban, but he really takes it to the extreme. I must have been changing feet for twenty minutes waiting for him to appear. The wait did, however, give me the opportunity to wander and observe. The hotel has a little restaurant leading off from the reception area. Closed. According to the sign, only open for breakfast. By the way, that was a miserable affair. I walked out this morning as soon as I saw the so-called buffet offerings, and instead found a nice patisserie just around the corner that did me a scrumptious frangipane tart and excellent coffee. Anyway, here, at four in the afternoon, there was a man sitting awkwardly at a corner table. Positioned so that he could monitor all the comings and goings in the lobby. Lurking. And almost certainly not waiting for a coffee, since that would not be served until six the next morning.

The area outside, in front of the hotel, would be better described as a yard than a forecourt. Quite a contrast from the Ritz-Carlton. A couple of cars that couldn't have been moved in months, covered with caked-on filth and blocked in by about twenty big waste and recycling bins. What I didn't expect to see was the taxi that had brought us back to the hotel standing there. Unlikely that the driver was waiting for a fare; I'd seen a rank in front of the patisserie, just fifty metres away.

I didn't need to be a spy to know that we were being watched. What I didn't understand was why. Surely the only people who knew we were here were the black marketeers. To them, we were simply customers, interested in purchasing medical equipment of dubious provenance at bargain prices. I'd thought the vendor might invite us for dinner, or at least a drink. Isn't that what salespeople do? Not have us watched and followed. What were we going to do in a strange city? I supposed they might think we would shop them to the police, but that would mean they thought we weren't bona fide – and surely we'd done nothing to make them think this?

While I was having these unsettling thoughts, Humphrey joined me. "No phone?" I asked, just to make sure. He shook his head. "We have company," I added, nodding towards the taxi, where the driver was slumped in his seat, apparently asleep. But probably not, as I could see the blue light of the dashcam flashing. He'd be watching that. A useful device; Bea has one in her Mini. That's how I know about them.

We walked towards the archway at one end of the yard and turned left. "I assume you know where we're going?" asked Humphrey. I just nodded. I thought I'd already said we'd go to the cathedral. Well, one of them. Perhaps both. Crossing the main avenue, we entered a park and followed a wide path flanked on both sides with bronze busts, presumably Kazakh heroes. The names on the plaques meant nothing to me. But it was rather impressive, and a pleasure to walk in the warm autumn afternoon sunshine. The park was well-kept, full of trees as we'd come to expect, expertly mown verdant lawns, flower beds full of blooms. And there, facing us, a most impressive cathedral painted in yellow and white, and topped with three onion-shaped domes of assorted sizes, each decked with colourful tiles. Humphrey commented it could be mistaken for a stately home.

I'd have liked to have gone inside, but the doors were locked. The morose beggar sitting on the steps told me it closed at four. Ten minutes ago. That's what comes of taking too long with one's ablutions, Humphrey. We sat on a bench and looked around. There were very few people walking in the park. One man was sitting on another bench, looking at us. The same man as in the hotel restaurant? He certainly looked familiar.

Humphrey and I had a meeting of minds. It seemed safe enough; we knew we weren't wearing or carrying any bugs, so felt confident the man on the other bench wouldn't be able to overhear us. We agreed we needed to report back to Laoban, but had to find a way of doing so without using our phones or the hotel wifi. Not only did we not know why we were being followed, they hadn't told us where they were going to take us the next morning. Disquieting, but that's life as a covert researcher sometimes. And this was just a bit spicier than usual.

Resuming our stroll, we reached a busy shopping street. Humphrey nudged me and pointed to the department store on the opposite corner. "That's where Stan brought me to buy clothes this morning," he said. Followed, after he pulled his hand from his mouth, by "Oh damn, I forgot he told me to call him." Well, nothing for it. He didn't have the phone with him, so he'd have to call when we got back to the hotel.

A tiny money exchange office was tucked between the department store and another clothes shop. The list of exchange rates on the door was written in English, but there was also a sign over the door in Russian saying 'Internet'. Inside, there was barely room for the two of us to stand in front of the glass-fronted counter. I practised my Russian with the smiling youth on the other side of the counter, and was rewarded by a reply in perfect accent-free English. For five dollars (he didn't want the *Tenge* I'd changed money for at the airport) we could use his computer for half an hour. Knowing we were probably being watched, Humphrey stayed in the front office acting out the pretence of a particularly long-winded exchange transaction, while I squeezed through a narrow door to get to the back of the office and the solitary computer. We'd left our phones in the hotel, but I'd quite unintentionally but very usefully brought the special USB stick Maria had given each of us a few days before (the tiny thing had fallen through a hole in my jacket pocket into the lining). It had been most interesting learning about Virtual Private Networks and how one was embedded on the memory stick so that the origin of any message that was sent from any computer would be completely hidden. I do love information technology and mucking about with computers.

I duly plugged in the USB stick, opened up Gmail and emailed the company address that Maria had set up for our fictitious private health clinic. Hunterhealth again, but with a different extension after the dot. I assumed she would retrieve it and pass it to Laoban, and trusted what I'd written would be clear to her but appear meaningless or innocuous to anyone else who might intercept it. Without our current book club novel handy, I had to resort to plain language and, where I remembered them, a few numerical codes for words. I hoped they wouldn't take the one for 'kidnap' too literally.

Writing and emailing took only five minutes. Back in the front office, Humphrey was deep in conversation with the foreign exchange clerk. "Go back there," the young man said, motioning Humphrey to follow. He punched numbers into a keypad that unlocked a door at the back labelled 'Fire Exit'. "Good luck," he said, thrusting us through it into a back alley and slamming the door behind us.

"Ivan, the guy in the office, is almost certain the man following us is secret police," said Humphrey. "Escaping this way won't stop them finding us again at the hotel, but should buy us a little time to ourselves." Good. We needed it, if only to try to figure out the situation. So, the secret police. Were they after the black marketeers? Or were the black marketeers themselves police? And, if so, were they seriously offering to sell equipment or had they set up a sting for us?

We needed food to get our brains working. Well, I did. It felt like a long time since that frangipane tart, and Humphrey admitted that he hadn't eaten all day. "I know just the place," I said, "but without the phone, I don't know how to get there."

"How on earth can you know 'just the place' when you only arrived here today?" asked Humphrey.

"You know me," I replied. "Always looking out for the next good meal. I searched restaurants on my phone."

"Would a map help?" Humphrey waved one that he had picked up in the exchange office. We worked out where we were fairly easily, or, rather, located the parallel street where the front entrance was. We were in a long narrow alley, the back entrances to shops and offices, strewn with all kinds of detritus. There was only one way out. We just had to hope the police officer, if that's really what he was, wouldn't be waiting to pounce on us there. He wasn't. But the taxi we'd seen before was now hovering on the opposite side of the road.

It didn't look like a long walk to the restaurant. By dint of turning right and right again, we reached the city centre pedestrian precinct. The taxi wouldn't be able to reach us here, but no doubt the driver would tell his colleague and we'd be followed soon enough. If we weren't already. Well, nothing we could do. Except eat. We strode off in the direction of the restaurant.

The interior was quite impressive, sort of Ottoman style, carpets hung on all the walls, carmine red and gold ceiling hung with enormous chandeliers. No problem finding a table in the late afternoon, too late for lunch, too early for dinner, and we chose a booth by a window. Not that we could see out, as the glass was frosted. Humphrey liked that the menu had pictures of all the dishes; me less so, as it reminded me of a chain pizza restaurant. Never mind. He was happy to leave the ordering to me.

A delicious spicy soup with meatballs arrived in no time, and we slurped away for a few minutes before saying another word. "The meatballs are delicious," said Humphrey. "Beef or lamb?"

"Horse," I told him.

Humphrey dropped his fork and spoon, only narrowly avoiding splashing soup everywhere.

"It's very popular in this country," I confided. "I've been reading about it. I thought we should try it. And, as you say, it's delicious." I went on to tell him about the health benefits of horse meat, high in Omega-3, lower in cholesterol than beef, high iron content, how the French gave it to sick children, but to no avail, Humphrey wouldn't touch the rest of his soup. I was happy to finish it for him. Fortunately, the kebabs that arrived next were of lamb. Even though the waiter confirmed it, I'm not entirely sure that Humphrey believed it.

At that point, the doors behind him sprung open and our meal was interrupted by a furious-looking Stanislas. "I told you to call me," he shouted.

"Calm down," I said. "Our phones were taken off us. We'd have called once we were back. We were hungry."

"You haven't been kidnapped, then?"

"Not yet. That's our plan for tomorrow."

13 – Discreetly helping the team – Robert

Almaty, Kazakhstan

The front desk clerk at Ron and Humph's hotel turned out to be a regular drinking companion of Stan's. (I got the impression that Stan knew people at all the hotels in Almaty, and probably every business of any kind). He had tipped him the wink that there were a couple of secret police making enquiries about our spies. He'd even seen one of them hovering around the lobby, not bothering to make any effort to blend into the background.

After dropping Humphrey off at the Ritz-Carlton in the morning, he'd parked up opposite in a bay next to some tour buses where he could watch and wait in case they needed a quick getaway. Smart thinking, except he saw nothing, because they left by the service entrance at the back. Which, fortunately, is where I was parked, since that's how I've always extricated people I didn't want to be seen. I took some photos of the girl with Ron and Humph before she disappeared back inside. Very nice. When I showed the pictures to Stan later, he immediately recognised her as the daughter of a well-known local gangster. He was fairly sure that Daddy was currently locked up somewhere cold, remote and spartan.

I set off in pursuit, calling Stan as I drove. He was obviously enjoying this undercover stuff and was good at it, as I saw his minibus quickly fall in behind me in the mirror. I let him overtake, as I figured the abductors wouldn't take much notice of a dark blue minibus following them. Much less conspicuous than a bright yellow taxi. At the cable car terminal, Stan parked his van and followed them up the mountain, since his tourist guide pass let him jump the queue, while I hovered on a yellow line in sight of the exit so I'd see them when they came back down. Stan called me from the top to tell me what was going on. To start with, I'd assumed Ron and Humph were in no danger. Only needing to be discretely monitored. Just in case. To my mind, choosing a funfair at the top of a mountain ridge for a clandestine discussion between black marketeers and prospective customers made perfect sense. Somewhere I might have chosen myself. However, when Stan told me they had finished their meeting and were now being followed by thugs with what looked like machine guns, I started to get worried.

As soon as I saw Ron and Humph come out of the terminal and stand on the pavement with the woman guide looking around, I chanced my luck and drove over to where they were waiting. I lowered the window. "Taxi?" I shouted. It seemed that was exactly what the woman was looking for, as she shooed the men into the back and barked incomprehensible instructions at me, thrusting money into my hand. Neither Ron nor Humph recognised me. I overheard Ron telling Humph that the woman had told the driver to take them to their hotel. Good, because that was where I was planning on taking them, anyway. Maybe she hadn't passed on the message to the black Audi that had screeched to a halt behind me. Presumably the official transport, but maybe they were the secret police? They followed as I drove away, but it wasn't hard to lose them.

The guys didn't spend long at the hotel. I had to trust they were keeping their wits about them, as I couldn't follow them across the middle of a park. The only thing there was a cathedral. I'd never thought of either of them as the praying sort, but one learns something new every day. I figured they would head back to the city centre later. There was nowhere to park on the street, so I cruised around slowly, stopping whenever I could for a minute or two. Eventually I got lucky, seeing them sneaking out of a very narrow back alley. Good. They'd clearly cottoned on to the fact they were being followed.

Maria passed on Ron's message to me as soon as she received it, so I knew they were having another meeting with the crooks in the morning. I reckoned they were safe until then, even though Ron's message had used the code word for kidnap. I guessed he meant that they were taking that risk. If they didn't get arrested by the secret police in the meantime. Since the two assets I and Stan had seen following them were acting about as discreetly and professionally as the cops in silent movies, I doubted that. Nevertheless, I followed our guys to the restaurant in the evening, just to keep an eye from a distance.

I was surprised when Stan pulled up in his van, rushed into the restaurant, and then came straight back out again. What was he doing there? I got my answer by text message within moments. "Your men never called me today to say they were safe. I found them in Pasha restaurant. All OK." I was too embarrassed to reply and tell Stan that I already knew and was parked opposite.

14 – An abduction to Bishkek

The girl from the Ritz-Carlton was waiting for them in the lobby, dressed in a smart blue uniform with matching hat, the kind air cabin crew wear, and clutching a clipboard, looking totally innocuous. Had the covert researchers been aware that she was the daughter of a local mafia boss, they would have been even more nervous than they already were. "I hope you are ready for your tour," she said brightly, after introducing herself as Anna. "Bring your passports with you, but leave your cases in the room over there," she told them, pointing to a door behind them. "We will collect them later."

The forecourt of the hotel was dominated by a big coach, black paintwork, black windows. They climbed aboard, Ronald noting that although the tinted windows prevented seeing in from the outside, from inside they had a completely clear view of the taxi, still parked on the other side. No sign of the driver, though. "Where are we going?" he asked Anna.

"First, we go up in the mountains. If it is safe, you will change to another car there."

"Safe?"

"You're being followed."

"We know. We thought it was your people."

"No. Could be police, might be our competitors. Either way, we need to go somewhere safe. Trust us."

Ronald and Humphrey doubted it was safe for them to trust anyone, but nodded, accepting their fate. They had no choice, after all, especially now the coach was driving out of the city down a highway at a speed way above the limit.

After a while, the traffic highway narrowed into a minor road winding upwards, flanked by mountains on both sides. Half an hour later, they reached a vast parking area. The end of the road. From there, they could see wide paths leading up into the mountains in several directions. Right in front of them, there was also a large stadium, a concrete monolith. Incongruous in that idyllic setting, and the first construction they had seen that was without doubt Soviet architecture. Anna, in tour guide mode, gave them an unnecessarily loud lecture on all the international ice-skating competitions that had been held there, and insisted on leading them inside to see the scale of it for themselves. Neither Humphrey nor Ronald had the remotest interest in ice skating, or any other winter sports for that matter, but duly followed their leader, assuming this was all part of the theatrical subterfuge, if an unusual approach to selling medical robots.

A large ice stadium with no ice (it being summer) looks remarkably like a grey concrete football pitch with no grass, and Anna ran out of interesting things to say about it after about twenty seconds. Seeing nobody else around, they returned to the coach, the electric doors sliding open as they approached. No sooner were they aboard and those doors closed behind them than a matching pair of doors on the opposite side slid open to reveal they were parked next to a minibus with its side door open. "Change bus," instructed Anna, who shut the coach doors behind them as soon as they had done so. Humphrey and Ronald watched the coach drive away with Anna on board.

They weren't in the minibus on their own. There was the driver, a man so wide that his body rested on the gearstick, dressed in a grey woollen jumper that had seen better and cleaner days and a matching hat. He sat there, hunched over the steering wheel, slowly moving his head from side to side, scanning the few parked cars and vans, neither saying a word nor acknowledging their presence. For a minute or two, he stared at a couple as they got out of their car, donned backpacks, got out walking poles and strolled away towards one of the mountain paths. Then, suddenly, uttering something in Russian, he started the engine, and they drove away. "He said it is now safe," translated Ronald.

"Hellooooo!" came the unexpected, shrill and very high-pitched voice from the front passenger seat. A woman, so short that neither of them had noticed her from their seats behind.

"You gave us a shock," said Humphrey.

"I'm so sorry!" she shrieked. "I was so busy I couldn't talk before. Look, it's complicated!" She held the end of a scarf she was knitting proudly above her head to show them. Ronald looked down into the footwell of her seat, where her earlier handiwork lay coiled like a very long python. She'd obviously been knitting for a long time.

She twisted in her seat so they could see each other. At least seventy years old, with a thin wizened face topped by unkempt grey and black hair resembling a snow-dusted bird's nest. She wore a bright red and green patchwork coat and, around her neck, an enormous necklace of what looked like children's wooden building blocks. "I am Katerina! Tell me your names! Let us be friends!" Delivered in ascending volume and pitch.

Humphrey and Ronald duly introduced themselves. "Humphrey! What a handsome name! For such a handsome young man!" And, after a short interlude for cackling, "and Ronald! So handsome too! I am a lucky lady! Two handsome young men!" A compliment lost on Ronald, who feared he was only a few years younger than Katerina, and knew he wasn't handsome.

"You have an important meeting in Bishkek! We go there now!" All spoken at a pitch that could shatter glass. Painful and nerve-wracking enough for Ronald and Humphrey to pray that the journey would be short, and she would not say much more.

It was not to be. "How far is that?" asked Ronald.

"Quick journey today! Very fast driver!" came the reply.

"Yes, but how long? Ten minutes? Twenty?"

Katerina engaged in brief conversation with the driver, then turned back to them. "Boris says two hours. Maybe two and a half to the border."

The border? Where were they going? Why? Maybe 'kidnap' had been right. Thoughts and fears passed through their minds before they could express them, but Katerina seemed to know what they were thinking.

"Bishkek is in Kyrgystan. It is not safe for you in Almaty. You know you are being watched. Better we go to another country. There, you will be safe and do serious business. Police there are stupid, not clever like the ones here in Kazakhstan."

"What about you? They might be after your people."

"Bishkek Tours and Travel?" Katerina cackled with laughter, collapsing in her seat. "Why would the police be after a tour guide?" She obviously thought this was wonderfully funny, as she carried on tittering for several minutes. Since her laughter wasn't as irritating as her voice, the men left her to it. When she stopped, Ronald asked a question.

"I meant the man we came to see yesterday. They may be after him."

"I know nothing about that. I don't know who you met. I'm just your tour guide. My job is to take you to your big meeting in Bishkek. We do some sightseeing along the way, yes?"

At first, they bowled along at a good pace. The highway was wide, and they sailed past convoys of trucks, the only other traffic on the road. The landscape was barren, undulating grassland, stretching to the horizon in every direction. The driver and guide focused on the road ahead of them and remained silent. Humphrey, always the inquisitive one, eventually popped a question.

"Why are there no animals? I'd have expected to see sheep or goats, at least with all this grass."

"What a very good question!" A screech trailing off into another fit of the giggles. "What you see is the Kazak steppe." Seeing Humphrey look uncertain, she added, "steppe with two p's!" Only a short burst of laughter this time. "The ground is salty. No farm animals can graze for long." Now she had started, it was impossible to stop her. She went on to explain that there were few permanent villages, and the people who lived there were nomads, moving around and living in yurts, which were big cylindrical tents that they carried around with them. They herded goats and horses and camels, and as soon as those had eaten all the fresh vegetation in an area, which didn't take long, the nomads and their herds moved on to new pastures.

Humphrey and Ronald thought the information all very interesting, just wishing it were delivered in a normal voice at a lower frequency. Now they had shown some interest, there was no stopping Katerina's flow. Spotting a graveyard at the top of a hill near the road, she gave them a lecture on Kazakh Muslim funeral practices and the forty-day mourning period, then somehow they got onto childbirth which meant the mother and baby were secluded for forty days, the forty day Ramadan fast, even the need to cut one's nails every forty days. Humphrey, prepared to tolerate Katerina in return for facts, asked what the significance of forty days was. She didn't know, but, unsurprisingly, thought the question hilarious. Realising that they had stopped moving, or rather that they were now in an almost stationary queue of traffic, Ronald ventured, "I hope we don't have to spend forty days in this minibus." Katerina enjoyed another laughing fit. "No, this is the end of the highway," she told them. "They are still building the rest. Now the road will be slower."

What an understatement. They were now negotiating a deeply rutted dirt track, following a procession of extremely slow trucks, twisting around a succession of little islands on which stood marooned and neglected mechanical diggers and suchlike equipment. The truck in front gave every sign that it might tip over in one of the ruts, and a few minutes later, they were forced to manoeuvre around another one that had already suffered such a catastrophe.

While they were crawling along like this, Katerina decided to change seat. "I am coming back to sit with you handsome men!" she announced brightly, implying that they would be pleased. "It's so much more fun when we are together, yes?" Climbing between seats didn't prove an elegant process, and as the van suddenly moved forward, she lurched headfirst into Humphrey's lap. Hilarity for her, discomfort for him. "How wonderful! To be in the arms of such a lovely young man. At my age!" She steered herself in between the two men on the bench seat, turned to Ronald and started stroking his shoulder. "Don't feel left out, my friend, you're handsome too!" Ronald would have been quite content to be excluded from this tactile encounter. Less than two years earlier, he would have recoiled at any close proximity to another human; touch was a complete no-no. Katerina clearly sensed rejection. "Sorry, sorry, are you two... what do they call it, an item?"

"I beg your pardon?" said a stunned Humphrey.

"You know, gay?" She made an obscene gesture.

"No, we are not," he replied emphatically. "We are just two businessmen going to a meeting. Which you say is in this place, Bishkek. So please, can we just go there? Quickly?" Ronald had never seen Humphrey angry. He was quite impressed by the outburst. Not that it did any good.

"Are you both married, then? How many children do you have?"

As if they'd agreed by telepathy, both Humphrey and Ronald stayed silent and turned their heads away from her to stare out of their respective windows, concentrating on concrete pillars that might one day support something, new bridges going nowhere, lots of machinery, but not a single worker. Bits and pieces of a highway never to be completed. Onwards the dirt track wound, and in half an hour more they reached asphalt, but to little improvement of the journey. The road now was two ways, so relatively slow. The driver achieved sporadic bursts of speed, overtaking a dawdling truck only to get find himself behind another one belching black diesel fumes. Ronald checked his watch. So much for two or two and a half hours to the border. Nearly four hours so far, and no sign of it. An opportunity for Katerina, who had been silent for nearly an hour and was bursting to say something. "Very close now! Maybe ten minutes. Are you both enjoying the sightseeing?"

Ronald couldn't resist a riposte. "We're taking it steppe by steppe." Katerina didn't react. She only likes her own jokes, he thought. But then, a bend in the road around a hill, and there in front of them was the border. A low building bridging the road, soldiers everywhere. "We must get out here and take our luggage. We need to walk through the checkpoint. Then Boris will meet us with the van on the other side. You have your passports ready?"

"Yes, but we don't have our luggage. They said we would go back to get it." Ronald was surprised he hadn't given it a thought until now.

"No, no, no. Don't look so worried. Your bags are in the back of the van. We got them for you. After the men watching you had gone." So that was the reason they'd been told to leave the bags. So that whoever was following them wouldn't think they were leaving town. "Stay with me when we get to the Kyrgyz side, remember I am your guide and you are on a Silk Road tour." Humphrey and Ronald nodded. It wasn't their first covert research project where they'd had to pretend to be tourists.

"Don't we need visas?" asked Ronald.

"No, you are free to visit as tourists. But please look like friends on holiday. But not gay ones! They will shoot you!" She cackled again. "You look angry. Be happy! Follow me."

Getting through the border was quicker than they had expected. Two checkpoints, one to leave Kazakhstan, one to enter Kyrgyzstan, a fifty-metre walk between the two. Disinterested officers stamped their passports and waved them on. A longer walk on the Kyrgyz side that led to a small parking area with a little cafe and some money change kiosks.

"Welcome to Kyrgyzstan!" exclaimed Katerina. "Now you are safe!" Humphrey and Ronald felt no safer now than a hundred metres back in Kazakhstan. The long road journey in the company of an irritating guide had shredded their nerves.

"We wait for Boris here," Katerina told them. A few dozen others were waiting too, all holding on to suitcases and bags, all looking back at the border post behind them where they could see many vehicles, none of them moving. Katerina went to exchange a few words with another woman she recognised. "We arrived at a bad time," she said when she returned. "Now the border is closed for lunch. We have to wait here one hour."

Waiting by the side of a road in blazing sunshine for what might be ages was not a welcome prospect. "Let's eat," said Ronald, always prioritising his stomach. "I suppose they serve food here?" pointing to the café.

"Of course, very tasty food. Many Kyrgyz specialities!" pronounced Katerina. The three of them were just in time to secure the last table. A faded and chipped brown plastic laminate top, sticky from spillages by earlier visitors. Old metal chairs. Not a fine dining establishment then. The menu was a plaque on the wall where only the prices changed, attested to by the number of labels stuck over each other. Katerina translated. "Hamburger, Cheeseburger, Hot Dog, Chicken sandwich…"

"What about those Kyrgyz specialities?" asked Ronald, interrupting.

"Oh yes. You like to try hoshany?" Seeing that the name meant nothing to them, adding "they are like meat pies. Oh, and they have oromo too! Delicious!" Seeing uncomprehending looks, continuing "like stuffed pancakes. You will see."

"Fine, we will try both of those," said Ronald, still eyeing the menu. "The one at the bottom. Is that shish kebab?" Getting confirmation, they ordered one of those as well.

The hoshany and oromo were obviously regular orders, as they arrived within moments, and the men got ready to tuck in. "Are you not eating anything?" asked Humphrey, seeing that Katerina had pushed her cutlery away.

"No, I am not hungry. My health is very bad, everything disagrees with me. Old age!" Humphrey and Ronald weren't the only ones who found her screeching and subsequent hysterics disturbing; everyone else in the café was turning to look at her.

"The hoshany are delicious," said Ronald. "I prefer the oromo," replied Humphrey.

"Both should be delicious!" exclaimed Katerina. "Let me try just a little bite of each." Without waiting for an answer, she pulled their plates towards her and cut off and ate a piece of each. "How marvellous! So delicious!" Ronald didn't think they were that special, but agreed they were quite tasty and filled a hole. He certainly couldn't reach the enthusiasm of their guide. "Just a little more!" she trilled. Humphrey, suppressing the urge to get up and throttle her, took her plate, put one of each on it and pushed it back towards her. "Oh, thank you, but I couldn't possibly eat that much!" she exclaimed, proceeding to demolish both pastries in short order. She refused one of the skewers when the kebab arrived, though. Perhaps she knew how tough and gristly the meat was going to be.

By the time they'd finished and changed some money to pay the bill, Boris had arrived with the van, and in only half an hour more, they reached the outskirts of Bishkek. Not long enough to get much of an impression, but the housing and the people they saw were clearly much poorer than their neighbours in Kazakhstan. Katerina had stayed quiet – and, thankfully, in the front seat – until now. "Look to your left!" she instructed in her shrillest voice, waving her left hand. Presumably slapping Boris in the face was unintentional. "The Central Mosque!" Huge, white, with blue-tiled arches, an enormous domed roof and three minarets, set in a park. "We stop here!"

Humphrey had had enough, both of the interminable journey and of Katerina. "I'm sure it's very interesting, but we're not here for sightseeing. Can we go straight to the meeting?"

"But your meeting is here! Not in the mosque, of course!" Collapsing with laughter as usual. "Come, you will see." Chatting all the while with someone on her phone, she led them through the gate into the gardens, then along the side of the mosque and out through another gate behind it, then through another park and across the road at the end, where in front of them stood a rather uncared-for four-storey office block with a convenience store on the ground floor. "Top floor," she told them, pointing to the main entrance. And with a "See you later, alligator!" she left them and went into the shop, cackling like a maniac all the while.

15 – Doing a deal in Bishkek

Ronald and Humphrey traipsed up the stairs. No lift in this office block. No tenants on the first or second floors either. The third was a different story. Sliding plate glass doors at the top of the stairs, and a sign in gold lettering. 'Kyrimpex Import and Export Agents'. A desk with a smiling receptionist, another attractive brunette. Ronald thought she might be a younger sister of the girl in Almaty. "You can go straight through," she told them, indicating the door on her right with a gold metal plaque on it saying 'Director' in English, presumably the same above it in Cyrillic script. "You are expected. I will bring tea."

As indicated, they walked into the adjacent office. Utterly unremarkable. Plain white painted walls, windows on two sides, all with filthy venetian blinds. Only one desk, though the room had space enough for ten. It didn't look like much importing or exporting was getting done here. Getting to his feet from behind the desk was a man, silver-haired, though probably only in his fifties, smart three-piece suit, white shirt, pink tie. "Good afternoon gentlemen, welcome. I hope you had a pleasant journey?" Extremely well spoken.

"Not really. It was very long," replied Humphrey, now extremely tetchy. "And a good afternoon to you. I am Doctor Humphrey Harrington, and this is our business manager, Ronald Jones. And you are?"

"I know who you are. You do not need to know my name. First, let us see if we can do business."

"We don't deal with people who don't have names," said Ron. A ploy that seemed to work, as after a momentary staring match, maybe lasting as long as ten seconds, he relented.

"Kulov, since you insist. I apologise for having you come here, but it was not possible to have a safe meeting in Almaty. So, tell me. Why are the Kazakh secret police following you?"

"We don't know. We thought they were sent by you. Or following you?" said Ronald.

"Certainly not me. I have been in Bishkek all the time. And my clients, the ones you are interested in doing business with, have always been very discreet."

"Do you mean you are not selling the equipment we are interested in?" asked Humphrey.

"Not us. We are just the shipping agents. If you purchase equipment from them, we will arrange the delivery. But they have asked me to represent them on this occasion. You are free to discuss everything with me, and I am authorised to make you a proposal. But first let us drink tea."

The receptionist was hovering with a tray with glass cups and a glass jug full of light golden tea, the leaves floating in it. "Have you tried Bishkek tea?" she asked.

"No, we've never been here before," Ronald replied. If given the choice, he would have asked for coffee instead, but the floating bits and the floral smell of the tea were intriguing.

"I am sure you will like it." The tea was indeed delicious, infused with ginger and honey. The three men, contentedly sipping, stayed silent for a minute or two.

"So now, tell me why you are here and what you want," said the shipping agent.

"I thought you knew," replied Humphrey. "We told the other man yesterday."

"Tell me again so we can be sure of each other."

Humphrey was doubtful over this but duly explained, torn between elaborating the story to make it sound more convincing and worrying that he might have said something different the day before and therefore contradict himself. He just had to trust that Ronald would interject if he said anything wrong. He didn't. The shipping agent sat, his hands clasped in front of him, his face straight, betraying nothing. Humphrey, on the other hand, was sweating, trying to control his nerves. After a long day cramped in a minibus and now suffering from the acid reflux of some very indigestible Kyrgyz roadside snacks, he had to push himself to go on. Even to get out the few sentences it took to explain what they wanted and why.

"I don't believe you," said the shipping agent when Humphrey had finished. Ronald, conscious of his colleague's state of mind, took over.

"What do you not believe? We have come all this way. We are serious businessmen."

"If you are who you say, I cannot believe you would want to buy equipment that would be of, how shall we put it, dubious provenance. I assume you will want proper invoices, guarantees, certificates of origin? Our clients cannot provide any of those things."

Ronald smiled. "But perhaps you can?" The man smiled back, but said nothing. "For an additional fee, of course."

The man nodded, appearing reassured. "These are things we might discuss. But it does not matter what I think. Our clients have made their own enquiries about your business and tell me they will sell to you. I think they have already told you their terms of business?"

"Yes, those were made plain yesterday. Today we were expecting to be told exactly what can be delivered and the asking price."

"The robot and the scanner you asked for can arrive in Uzbekistan in seven weeks."

"We were also told we would learn the origin of the equipment. Germany, Switzerland, China?"

"I am not certain, but I believe they told me America."

"That is good," said Ronald, thinking that Laoban would be happy since the most likely American manufacturer was their client. "And the price?"

"The price, not including any documentation, will be twelve bitcoin. Firm and fixed."

"No. That's more than double the original price," said Ronald. "The terms are also quite unfavourable to us. The most we will pay is six bitcoins."

"I think you should consider this carefully. Twelve bitcoins is less than half the official price. You will pay very little import duties. And I am told it is original brand-new top-quality equipment, not a Chinese copy."

"I am glad to hear that, but no, our best price is six bitcoins." Humphrey was impressed that Ronald seemed so confident with his negotiation skills.

"I am instructed there can be no negotiation. The price is fixed, twelve bitcoins."

"Then I am sorry that we have wasted our time, your time, and that of your clients." Ronald stood up and tapped Humphrey on the shoulder to join him. "Can you ask Katerina to come here with the van? We left our luggage inside."

"Katerina's work is finished. My clients have arranged a hotel for you and your bags have already been delivered there. In the circumstances, I suggest you should pay your own bill. Svetlana will get you a taxi. I am sorry we could not do business. No doubt my clients will be in touch with you. If you change your mind, I will look forward to arranging the transport and delivery." He pressed a button on his desk phone and Svetlana, the receptionist, appeared within seconds. "Good night, and enjoy Bishkek." Then, seemingly as an afterthought, "You should eat dinner in Navat restaurant." A recommendation or an order?

Svetlana, having confirmed that they had *som* to pay the fare, issued rapid instructions to the taxi driver. Soon they were stuck in heavy traffic. When he found out that Ronald spoke some Russian, the driver became talkative. Ronald humoured him. When they reached the hotel, the driver said, "that's unusual. That yellow car behind us. A Kazakh taxi. Must have brought a fare from Almaty. I've seen it a few times in the mirror, like it's been following us."

16 – An interrupted dinner – Humphrey

Bishkek, Kyrgyzstan

The hotel the black marketeers had booked for us was basic, though perfectly adequate. It was modern, the rooms were big, but it was spartan. Plain brick walls, a window with a view onto a high concrete wall, hence little natural light, and minimal furniture. It reminded me of my university hall of residence back in the 90s. Maybe that's what it was built as. But since all we needed was a bed for the night, it served that purpose. Now we were on our own in a city and country we had never planned to visit. What we were going to do in the morning, where we would go next, how we would travel, were all questions that preoccupied us and needed urgent answers.

Obviously, it was a priority for Ron, but I agreed with him that we both needed drink and food. Lubrication and sustenance to discuss and make decisions. All the hotel had to offer was a vending machine for cans of fizzy drinks, but nothing stronger, and no food. Thus, leaving Ron in his room to deploy his encoding skills and email Maria and Laoban to update them on the day's events, I engaged the dozy young man behind the check-in desk to get directions to the Navat restaurant.

"I can call you a taxi," seemed to be his stock reply to any request for directions.

"We prefer to walk."

"It is a long way. You may get lost. I will call you a taxi."

"We don't want a taxi. We want to walk."

"It will be dark soon."

"Is it not safe to walk at night in Bishkek?"

"No, it is safe. Very safe here."

"So please, can you give me a map and show me how to walk to the restaurant?"

Grudgingly, he printed off a fuzzy and not very legible map from his computer and marked up the walking route from the hotel.

"Where can we find a nice bar?" I asked.

"No bars," he replied.

"There must be bars, surely?"

"No bars. We are all strict Muslims." Having seen the size of the Central Mosque and the dozen or so others that we'd passed in the taxi on the way from Kulov's office to the hotel, that was easy to believe.

"So, there are no bars at all in Bishkek?"

"No bars in Kyrgyzstan. Many coffee shops." Then, as an afterthought, adding, "but you are tourists. You can get beer and wine in the restaurant." Good. That would do us.

The hotel was central, and the walk to the restaurant provided us with a little unplanned sightseeing, despite the fact that it was almost dusk. A park with a big statue of Lenin in the middle. Some massive floodlit white marble-faced buildings. Ron, who had found a Russian-language tourist leaflet in the hotel, said that the bigger ones were the National Museum and the Parliament. Both impressive white marble structures with big courtyards in front of them, one with a long ascent of steps. As our stroll had coincided with the 6pm changing of the guard, we enjoyed ten minutes' entertainment watching soldiers goose-stepping up and down.

Navat was indeed an attractive restaurant. A busy one too. Ron ordered a small mountain of kebabs. I was afraid they were going to be horse meat again, but he assured me they were lamb or beef. He didn't seem to know which. In any case, they were spicy and delicious, made even more pleasant by being washed down by two bottles of Russian red wine, though that was of questionable provenance and quality.

Over dinner, we discussed our options for the following morning. Would the shipping agent summon us back and propose a revised deal? Somehow, that didn't seem likely. Should we return to Almaty? We had open return flight vouchers, but it didn't seem a smart idea to go back with the police waiting to pounce on us. Anyway, the thought of the interminable drive alone put us off that idea. Were there others after us? If so, why? We'd come with the sole intention of finding out who was selling what. We'd known that dealing with black marketeers wouldn't be straightforward, but we hadn't planned on it being dangerous.

We needed to get out, anyway. We resolved to go to Bishkek airport at first light and see what flights were available. Not that we were very optimistic. Ron had an app on his phone that he insisted showed every flight, and all except one of the ones listed for the next day were either back to Almaty or to various airports in Russia. One country we definitely didn't want to go to. Anyway, we'd have needed visas. The odd one out was to Dubai, which would have been ideal, but the airline website showed it being sold out in both economy and business class. Maybe there would be some no-shows. We could only hope.

Nourished and lubricated, with nothing else to discuss, and now unfit to walk in a straight line, we tumbled out of the restaurant, intending to hunt down a taxi. We saw one parked a hundred metres away. Then we saw concrete.

17 – Doing what I do best – Robert

Almaty, Kazakhstan

That morning, when I followed the bus up the mountain and I saw the guys going to the ice rink, I'd assumed that was where they were having their second meeting. I was surprisingly lucky with where I'd parked to watch, as if it had been a few metres to the left or right I'd have missed seeing the switch from the side door of the bus to the side door of the minivan. Clever move. And the last thing I expected when I followed them was that they would be headed for Kyrgyzstan.

I was a bit worried about how I was going to get through the border post with a taxi. Since I didn't speak Russian or Kazakh, or Kyrgyz for that matter, I couldn't answer questions or bluff my way through. Luckily, while the van carrying the guys got stuck in a queue behind two big buses, I was directed into a separate lane for cars. The border guards showed no surprise at seeing an Almaty taxi being driven by a man with an Irish passport, probably because they wanted their lunch. I was simply waved through, and the barrier came down behind me. Like the guys, I then had to wait an hour before the minibus came across. I watched them tucking in to what looked like tiny Cornish pasties, ignoring me while I was lining up to pay for my crisps and chocolate bars.

While I was waiting, I called Stan. Thought maybe it was a good idea to tell him where I was taking his son's taxi. He was horrified. "They're all mafiosi in Bishkek!" he exclaimed. "Very dangerous country!" I wondered if this was simply the sort of prejudice against the people of neighbouring countries one often encounters or was based on facts. He rang back a minute later to tell me he was coming too. "You'll need my help," he insisted. I wasn't sure I would, but I couldn't talk him out of it, so took advantage by asking him to pick up and bring my things from my hotel room. Correctly, I assumed I wouldn't be going back.

By the time that Ron and Humph emerged from the office building in Bishkek, Stan had already crossed the frontier and was on his way to the city. Made a lot faster time than we did. Perhaps there were no trucks on the road in the afternoon. And by now I'd changed my mind and was glad he was coming, as I could see that reinforcement might be useful. Something to do with the bulges under the jackets of the two unsavoury characters who had appeared out of the shop under the offices and climbed onto hefty-looking motorbikes parked close behind the taxi that Humph and Ron had just boarded. More threat than protection, from the look of it, as one bike moved in front, the other behind the taxi as they drove away. I followed, keeping as much distance as I could without losing them.

There were plenty of empty parking spaces opposite their hotel, a good vantage point to sit and watch. The bikers were watching too, but from a position higher up the road in front of a fast-food restaurant. They'd picked well, as they blended in with the couriers around them waiting for orders for home delivery. Interestingly, as soon as Ron and Humph emerged from the hotel, presumably going for dinner, the bikers sped away, making no attempt to follow.

Stan had arrived half an hour before they left and, as arranged, had parked a couple of spaces away from me. He'd brought Bogdan with him, who seemed to be enjoying the escapade and our covert surveillance as much as a ten-year-old schoolboy might. Not quite the A Team, but good that there were three of us. Ron and Humph turned straight into the park, making it clear they were going to walk. Bogdan volunteered to follow them and report back to say where they'd gone.

Stan correctly predicted that their destination would be the Navat restaurant and promptly drove off in that direction. "That's where all the tourists go," he assured me. I had to assume he was right. If there were any other tourists in Bishkek, that is. All the other people I'd seen going in or out of the hotel looked like locals to me. Bogdan called twenty minutes later to confirm that they were now out of the park and on the main road, headed that way.

By the time I'd navigated a byzantine one-way system and reached the Navat, Ron and Humph were already inside. Bogdan came over and told me that the bikers had also arrived about ten minutes earlier. They had conferred with two men in a dark-coloured van that had been hovering outside, and then bikers and van had driven around the block. They were now parked on the street just around the corner from the restaurant. Pole position for abduction, if that was their plan. Whoever these guys were, they obviously weren't planning to let our men go back to their hotel that evening. Not without a bit of help from us.

I'd expected Stan and Bogdan to be scared of ruffians twice their size and armed with guns. Especially Stan, who had to be well over sixty. Not a bit of it. "Three years of military service," they both pronounced proudly. "Makes us ready for anything." I later found out that they both frequented a boxing club, too.

Two hours passed. Either Ron and Humph were having an unusually good time or the service was very slow. I wouldn't have been surprised to be told that Ron had ordered a seven-course tasting menu, or something like that. Once they finally emerged, not quite staggering but not quite vertical either, a motorcycle screamed around the corner, mounted the pavement in front of Ron and Humph, and screeched to a halt. The rider and pillion passenger leapt on top of them, pinning them down on the pavement while pulling their arms behind them and securing them with cable ties. They kept turning their heads and looking up the street like they were waiting for backup. I put the taxi in gear and revved the engine, ready to move. Ron later told me they'd been arguing about when a truck would arrive and whether they would get paid. Then, more screeching of brakes as a van turned the corner. I was reassured to see Bogdan at the wheel and Stan sitting beside him. They'd successfully disarmed and disabled the van's driver and his mate. Stan proudly told me they'd found a pair of body bags in the back of the van (confirming that they didn't mean well) and he and Bogdan had zipped each of them inside and then carried and dumped them in an alleyway.

I immediately drove over in the taxi to help incapacitate the heavies. Not that Stan and Bogdan needed any help. They were definitely enjoying themselves, making some very inventive use of cable ties as well as some real handcuffs they'd found somewhere. Getting those brutes out of all that would hold up their backup team for quite a while – once they got themselves out of those body bags. Bogdan got back in the driver's seat while Stan and I manhandled Ron and Humph into the back, leaving them lying on the floor and slamming the doors. Rather impolite, but we didn't have the luxury of time.

Once we were on our way and Bogdan slowed down enough for me to be able to stand up and move, I went back and cut the cable ties. "Get up," I told them. They sat on the back seat, perspiring and trembling. Saying nothing for a minute. Then, Ron twigged. "Mr Pilot! Sorry, Rob. You've come to rescue us again!" Talking to me like this was something quite normal. "Are we going back to the hotel now?"

"No, we need to get you out of here," I said. "Those guys were sent to neutralise you. Mafiosi. I'm guessing that if you would not do business with them, you had to be taken out of the equation."

"So, what are you doing here?" Humph asked.

"I was sent by Laoban to keep you out of trouble," he replied. "It's what I do."

"And very good at it he is too," Ron said to Humphrey, who was sitting there shaking. "Thank you for getting us out of that. So what's the plan?"

"Airport. Then work it out from there."

"Will I be travelling in a coffin again?" asked Ron. As if it brought back some nostalgic memories for him.

18 – Debrief in Dubai

The following morning. 8:20 am. Terminal Two, Dubai. Ronald and Humphrey staggered down the steps of the plane. The effects of their over-indulgence at dinner had worn off long ago, but those were as nothing compared to the accumulated effects of the last twenty-four hours. As Ron said, it had been a long and stressful day. A master of understatement.

After the 'incident' at the restaurant, they had been driven first to the hotel, where Stan took less than two minutes to collect their cases and passports. Then on to the airport. By then it was nearly midnight, but there were still two flights scheduled to leave in the early hours. One to Dubai at 3am, completely full. The other to Ekaterinburg in Russia at 4am. Plenty of empty seats on that one. Rob told Humphrey and Ronald to sit on a bench in a far corner of the check-in hall and not to move. Half an hour later, he and Stan returned and handed them back their passports together with boarding passes. To Ekaterinburg.

"Don't say a word," instructed Rob, as Humphrey opened his mouth. "Go through security now and wait somewhere near Gate 12. The gate for Dubai. Be patient. It may take a while for me to catch up with you there."

Patience proved difficult for Ronald and Humphrey. It felt like hours, sitting on hard moulded seating in a departure lounge patrolled by police with guns, a constant reminder of the risk of imminent arrest. Nothing else moved. Then a sudden a burst of activity as airline agents arrived at the gate and started boarding the flight. Not enough activity on its own to wake Ron or Humphrey, who had both dozed off. They were restored to consciousness by a nudge from a man in uniform. Not police. Rob, once again dressed as a pilot.

"Give me your boarding passes," he whispered. Taking them with his right hand and putting them in an inside jacket pocket, he produced two others from another with his left. "Now, quick, get on that plane before they close the gate," he whispered, swiftly moving away.

The new boarding passes were for Dubai, but weren't in their names. That clearly didn't matter, as the airline agents weren't checking passports, eager to get the aircraft away (or perhaps just get home to their beds) simply tearing the passes in two and propelling passengers down the jet bridge as quickly as they could.

Humphrey, with his long legs, thought that the budget airlines that served Lanzarote were uncomfortable enough, but being crushed in the back row of this plane, with no recline and no legroom whatsoever, rated as the worst flight he had ever been on. However, looking on the bright side, he and Ron had escaped kidnap or worse and got out of Bishkek alive.

On landing, they'd briefly wondered where they were meant to go next, surprised when no instructions popped up when they turned on their phones immediately on touchdown. In Humphrey's case this rapidly changed to panic when an airline employee met them at the foot of the steps, telling them to follow her. Dressed in the light fawn uniform of a major airline, wearing a hat with a face veil hanging in front, clutching a folder. Humphrey was nonplussed that Ronald didn't seem in the least concerned. In fact, he appeared more than happy. "It's Laoban," he whispered, hurrying Humph along into the terminal building by grabbing his elbow. "I told you she's a chameleon. Never know when she's going to turn up or what she's going to be dressed up as."

He obviously wasn't whispering quietly enough, as their leader turned on her heels to face Ronald. "You will not compare me to a lizard! Understood?" Aggressive. Resuming their walk, she led them through a door labelled 'no entry'. At the end of the corridor in front of them was a white buggy, with a big red cross and crescent painted on the front of it. She extracted four crutches from under the back seat and handed the men two each. "Get on board, and make it look like you need these!" she said, jumping into the driver's seat, still angry.

In his previous day job as a qualified and experienced trauma surgeon, Humphrey would certainly not have approved of the way that Laoban was driving two supposed invalids, almost tossing them out of the buggy at every corner she negotiated. But today he was a covert researcher, and a very exhausted one at that, and the only thing that mattered was getting out of the airport without hassle and then, at the first opportunity, into a bed. The first objective was easily met, as, bypassing the queues, they zoomed through immigration, abandoned the buggy and crutches on the kerb outside and piled into the first taxi in line. The second objective would have to wait, as, after pulling up at a rather wonderful looking airport hotel just a few minutes later, Laoban insisted on a debrief.

"Can we get breakfast? Or do you need me to shower first?" were Ronald's first questions on arrival.

Laoban eyed him critically and sniffed. "Debrief is urgent. But we'd better sit outside."

They commandeered a table on a terrace overlooking an enormous pool fringed with palm trees.

The men were pleasantly surprised when Laoban summoned a server and told them to order what they wanted. Full English for Humphrey. Full Arabic for Ron ("only to see what delicacies they bring me, you understand"). Just a Lapsang Souchong tea for her. While they waited for the food, she returned to the lobby, reappearing only minutes later dressed in a pale blue voile trouser suit with matching wide-brimmed hat and sunglasses. As if she was a film star, ready to walk the red carpet. "How on earth can you change so quickly?" asked Humphrey, much more used to the ages it took Bea to get dressed. Laoban offered only a knowing smile in return.

"Why are you here in Dubai?" asked Ronald.

She explained that their arrival was an unexpected coincidence. Her reason for being in Dubai was because Toshio, who seemed to be hacking everyone's emails, had found out that the Istanbul-based sales executive and the British sales manager for the American medical equipment manufacturer were both coming to a conference, ostensibly about robotics for manufacturing. They had registered for the conference independently, but within an hour of each other, and were also booked to stay in the same hotel, which wasn't the official conference hotel, though it was nearby. Enough coincidences to get Laoban's antennae twitching. In case they went off on their own and had to be tailed independently, she'd brought Beatrix to join her.

"You mean Bea is here? In Dubai?" asked Humphrey, now wide awake and excited.

"She is. But she's here to work, remember?" Humphrey sucked in his cheeks. "You can stay in the same hotel room, though. For tonight. Saves the company money." Not because it's nice, of course. Laoban being tight-fisted as usual.

"And after tonight?"

"That depends."

Over the next hour, Ronald and Humphrey recounted every detail of their time in Almaty and Bishkek, sometimes in rather more detail than Laoban wanted. She recoiled from Ronald's enthusiastic description of the gourmet delights of horse sausage. "I thought that you Asians ate anything that moves," he commented, receiving a withering stare in return.

Laoban told them that the photos that Rob had taken had been shown to a 'friendly' contact in Interpol, who had identified the men who attacked them in Bishkek as relatively junior members of a well-known organised crime gang. The office they had visited wasn't let to a 'shipping agent' or anyone else. Stan and Bogdan had gone there barely an hour ago, and found the offices locked and empty. The shopkeeper downstairs told them the top floor of the building had never been occupied by any business, and the ones on the other floors had closed down at least a year previously.

They were interrupted by a 'ping,' on Ronald's phone. "The man who says he's a shipping agent," he said. "Kulov. Wants another meeting today. Says he has a new deal to offer. What do I reply?"

"You don't," said Laoban. "At least, not yet. He's fishing. Must want to know if you're still in Bishkek."

"Anyway, it would be too dangerous to go, even if we were able to. Shame we couldn't get a picture of him," remarked Humphrey.

"Can we get to one of those photofit artists?" asked Ron. "I can pretty much remember what he looks like."

Laoban was immersed in her phone and appeared to be ignoring them. But no. "We can do better than that. Tell him you had to leave on urgent business but can meet at the Kazakh border post in an hour. Tell him to look for a dark blue Toyota Hiace with this registration," pushing a slip of paper over to Ron.

"Is Rob going there, then?"

"No, he's already on his way here. Bringing your luggage. Landing in just over an hour." Ron and Humphrey looked at her enquiringly. "Rob is coming on a freight plane. I'm sending the men that he recruited in Almaty, Stan and Bogdan. They'll take pictures and find out what the deal is."

"But those people we're dealing with are dangerous."

"Rob tells me his new friends like danger and can look after themselves. My idea is that it will be safe to meet there by the border. I assume there'll be police everywhere."

"Aren't Stan and Bogdan scared of being arrested?"

"It seems not. After all, they're just drivers who dropped off tourists to Bishkek and are on their way home."

Ron tapped away on his phone, happy as a small boy. "These eSIMs are so clever! Fancy being able to have lots of numbers on one phone!" "He's answering. Just a mo. He's asking to meet somewhere else." He looked up at Laoban, who was shaking her head, and started tapping again. "I've told him the border or nowhere. Outside that wonderful restaurant." Humphrey shuddered.

They all sat in silence, waiting. A few minutes passed. "I suppose he's not going to bite," said Humphrey.

"Hold on," said Ron. "He's typing again. He's on his way there."

"Excellent," said Laoban. "Now I need to get back to the airport before Mr Mallory arrives, but first we'd better get you to your hotel."

"We're not staying here then?" said Humphrey, a note of resignation in his voice.

"No. Too expensive. And not covert enough. I'm calling you an Uber."

19 – Watching and Waiting

Dubai, UAE

Bea stood in the arrivals hall of Terminal One, transfixed. How could anyone travel dressed up like that? How could any man, travelling solo, coming to a three-day conference in Dubai, have so much luggage? What on earth could he have in those two enormous trunks? Well, presumably nothing illegal, since she knew customs x-rayed every bag on arrival. Ben Fullerton-Price, a proud and considerably overweight peacock in the glossy teal blue plumage of a three-piece suit, pushed his trolley onwards towards the terminal exit, perspiring under the effort. Nobody there to meet him. That was really what Bea was interested in; otherwise she could simply have waited for him to arrive at his hotel, sitting in comfort in the lobby there rather than having to stand for an hour in a crowded and noisy concourse, being continuously jostled by a milling crowd of others come to meet arrivals, haggle for fares or, like her, simply observe. Covertly.

She doubted he would notice her in the crowd, or recognise her if he did. Nevertheless, after her long meeting with him in Istanbul, she did her best to make sure, first applying foundation in a darker shade than usual, and lots of mascara, and then covering her head with a dark maroon hijab. Earlier, after half an hour of vain efforts to don that correctly, she had begged help from a woman passing in the hotel corridor, whose expert hands had taken less than twenty seconds to complete her disguise.

Thus camouflaged, she could walk right behind Fullerton-Price and overhear him telling a taxi driver to take him to the hotel, and then watch the two of them struggle to get his luggage into the boot. Every day needs some amusement in it, she thought.

Meanwhile, over in Terminal Three, Laoban awaited the arrival of Ryan Mallory from London. His flight was delayed, only for half an hour, but long enough for her to regret having changed back into her airline flight attendant uniform. It felt like the whole world was lining up to ask her for information, and the need to keep her default fiery temper in check was becoming intolerable. Still, she could hardly risk being impolite, as that would unmask her disguise. Fortunately, Ryan was travelling light, and emerged through the doors into the arrivals area just fifteen minutes after the flight touched down. He made a beeline for a young man dressed in white flowing robes and a traditional red and white checked *keffiyeh* headdress, who was brandishing a tablet with a travel agency logo and 'Mallory' displayed on it. Laoban followed the two of them outside, where a gleaming white Mercedes was waiting, engine running, chauffeur standing to attention. She waited for the car to drive away, then followed the young man back into the terminal and accosted him. "Where has the car taken Mr Mallory?" she asked. "He left this behind on the plane and I need to take it to him." Waving a phone.

"No worries, I'll call the car back," he said, getting out his own phone.

"No, please don't do that. He said he was in a great hurry because the plane was late. He is one of our very important passengers, and my supervisor insisted I take it to him personally."

The travel agent shrugged. "OK then. JW Marriott Marquis hotel."

Good, no change from the original plan Toshio had discovered. Not bothering to thank the man, she turned to leave. He called after her. "Shall I call a car for you?" Now that was a good idea. In the few moments it took to go back outside, another Mercedes was hovering, ready to whisk her off in hot pursuit of Ryan Mallory.

To say the hotel was impressive and opulent would be an understatement. It was also tall. Very, very tall. Over seventy stories high. As Laoban entered the lobby, she could see Ryan's back as, accompanied by a bell boy, he disappeared into a lift. She watched the indicator. It stopped at floor 42, and then moments later started to descend. Her flight attendant uniform would be a liability rather than an asset here, so first checking that nobody was watching, she dived into an adjacent disabled toilet. The woman who emerged two minutes later appeared unmistakeably Arab, dressed in a gold-trimmed navy blue shalwar kameez with matching headscarf. Laoban once again justified to herself her astronomic investment in an extra-large Hermes bag. Big enough to carry several changes of clothing discreetly. Flamboyant enough to blend in at five-star hotels. And what a wonderful invention the hijab was! Ideal disguise for a woman. Of course, she understood that others didn't wear it for that reason. Though she wasn't the only one. A western woman taking similar advantage of the costume was sitting in a far corner, intent on her phone, but glancing up and looking about her every now and again.

A few minutes later, not through coincidence, those two women found themselves in the same clothes boutique, just off the lobby, critically eyeing evening wear. "Excuse me," said Bea, maintaining the pretence that they did not know each other. "How much is fifteen thousand dirhams in euros?"

"About three thousand," said Laoban. "You can't afford it, and you'd look terrible in it. Made for much taller, younger and slimmer women."

"And richer ones," retorted Bea. "As we're the only ones here apart from the girl behind the till, can we talk… discreetly?" Laoban nodded.

"Fullerton-Price is in 4701. Big suite. One of the room boys showed me 4801. He says it's the same. He'll be sleeping. He told the check-in clerk to set an alarm call for six, as he has a meeting at seven."

"How did you manage to hear that?"

"He's very loud. You can hear him from miles away. Anyway, I have other news." Laoban raised her eyebrows questioningly. "You remember that curly-haired man we saw in Windhoek? Used to work with your old boss? Smith?"

"His assistant? The one who calls himself EA?"

Bea nodded. "He's here. I'm sure it's him. He was sitting in the lobby drinking coffee for a while. Disappeared just before you came."

"What's he doing here, I wonder? Message Maria and see if she or Toshio can find out anything about him. We have still never found out his real name."

"I already did. I sent Maria a photo too. I took quite a good one. She didn't reply yet." Laoban nodded. "So, what do we do next?" asked Bea.

"It's nearly six now, so let's go to the lounge."

"Lounge?"

"Executive lounge, for all their regular customers and those who pay extra. Floor 37."

"OK, but what's six o'clock got to do with it?"

"Free drinks and snacks," replied Laoban. "However drowsy they may be, that attracts business people like moths to a flame. You'll see."

"Will this help?" asked Bea, pulling out a plastic key card from her bag. "Fullerton-Price dropped it when he was looking for money to tip the porter."

"Perfect. We won't need to bluff our way in."

The lounge occupied the whole floor. Laoban dragged Bea away from admiring the panorama of Dubai and its harbour, choosing a strategically placed sofa from where they could monitor guests that came and went. "I thought you said it would be busy," said Bea, looking around.

"It's only ten to. You'll see." They sat quietly, sipping herbal tea.

On the stroke of the hour, and in the space of just one minute, two remarkable things happened. First, hitherto empty counters were decked with countless dishes of food by a small army of servers, and a shutter was lifted to reveal a well-stocked bar. Alcohol might be prohibited outside in cafes and restaurants on the street and to local people, but here in the hotel there were no limits. Second, people started arriving. At first a trickle, then a tsunami. Every one of them, as Laoban had predicted, making a beeline for the food and drink. Bringing up the rear, looking for all the world like he was the last in a race panting to get over the finish line, was Fullerton-Price. "Stay here," instructed Laoban, getting up and gliding over the room towards him.

"Mr Fullerton-Price, please take a seat and permit me to bring you a drink," she intoned. "A glass of wine? Something a little stronger?" Her quarry, whose instant assumption was that Laoban worked there and was recognising his premium status, assented willingly, requesting a large Scotch and heading off to a window table, while the crush at the bar parted as Laoban approached.

Drink duly delivered, she returned to the sofa. "Shall we move?" asked Bea. "We can't see him from here." Shaking her head, Laoban delved into her bag, pulled out two small black boxes and handed one to Bea. "Earbuds," she said, unnecessarily as Bea was already putting hers in, checking around that nobody was looking and rearranging her headscarf over her ears.

For five minutes or more, all they could hear was the occasional cough and burp and a clash of glass every time he put his drink down on the table. "Where did you put the mike?" asked Bea. "Under the table?"

"No, in the little flower vase. Wait, he's talking to someone." Leaving Laoban to concentrate, Bea went to see who was with him.

"Not someone we've seen before," she reported back. "Mid-fifties at a guess, silver grey hair. Drinking sparkling water."

"They're waiting for someone else. It sounds like they're discussing logistics. I heard mention of containers and Baku." Registering Bea's incomprehension, adding, "it's in Azerbaijan." Bea nodded.

Whilst they continued to listen intently, nothing was said in the following hour that related to black market medical equipment. "I've drunk too much tea," said Bea. "I hope they finish soon so I can go to the loo." At which point, Ryan Mallory appeared in the doorway, now casual in jeans and sweatshirt. A few moments later, the women heard Fullerton-Price greeting him, and introducing the third man. Now they had a name. Felix. Not that it meant anything to them. Then.

Beatrix was glad that she didn't have to wait long, as all Ryan said was that he'd come to get a bottle of water and was going to bed. Fullerton-Price and Felix said they would do the same, and in less than a minute, all three of them were gone from the lounge. Laoban scuttled round to pick up the remote microphone, and they too bid their goodnights.

"Aren't you staying in the same hotel as me?" asked Bea.

"No, we don't want to be seen to be together. Better we leave here separately too. And before you ask, I'm not staying here. We'll meet at the conference hotel tomorrow at nine." As Bea walked towards the lift, Laoban called after her. "There's a surprise waiting for you at your hotel. One you'll like." And a moment later, the food and drink having disappeared at 8 as quickly as it had arrived at 6, and it now being ten past, the lounge was empty.

20 – Making an exhibition of themselves

Dubai, UAE

Once she had overcome her shock on learning of the dangers that Humphrey had faced and hearing he had nearly been kidnapped, or worse, Beatrix and her surprise had spent a very happy night together. All good things must come to an end, though, and dawn saw them preparing for a day's surveillance at the robotics conference in Dubai. They found Ronald already installed downstairs in the basement breakfast room. Not looking happy.

"All they have is Weetabix and tea," he moaned. "I hope they have croissants in the conference hotel. I got the message that the boss is roping us in to help, but what does she expect us to do there?"

"In your case, not spend all day feeding your face, for sure," Humphrey replied. "I wouldn't be surprised if she picked this hotel specifically for its meagre breakfast. Anyway, today. The usual. Watch. Listen. Report. At least, that's what I suppose?" Beatrix nodded. "We'll find out when we get there."

"Stan messaged to tell us what happened yesterday," said Ron. Seeing the reception clerk coming into the room, adding, "I'll tell you all when we meet up with the boss."

"Mr Appleby?" asked the clerk. Humphrey had to be jabbed in the ribs by Beatrix. He was always forgetting his *nom de guerre*. "This envelope was just delivered for you."

Inside were 'exhibitor' badges and lanyards for Humphrey and Ron. No doubt needed to get into the conference hotel. "I assume you already got yours yesterday before we arrived, Bea?" he asked.

"Yes, and I'm a delegate," she replied. "I'm better than you!"

"The boss just messaged to say to meet in room 2018," Ron interjected. "We're to get the lift to floor 21 and walk down the emergency exit stairs to floor 20. I suppose she's got her reasons. Everybody got that?". Humphrey and Bea duly nodded. "I'm off. See you there," he added, pulling the lanyard over his head.

"Hold on," said Humphrey. "What about Robert? He must be here somewhere as our suitcases arrived."

"Don't worry about the Pilot. Perhaps not in the same class as the chameleon, but he's definitely a phantasm of sorts. He'll be around. Rely on him popping up as and when and where needed." Ron waved a cheery hand behind him and walked up the stairs.

Humphrey thought their taking three separate taxis at three-minute intervals to go to the same place was needless, especially if none of the people they were going there to watch had ever seen them before (admittedly one of them had met Bea, but in her attire of hijab and abaya she was certainly unrecognisable as the same person). His colleagues, who had done a lot more covert surveillance, thought it essential, though, so he went along with it.

The conference hotel appeared to be even more ostentatious than the Marriott, though at a mere thirty stories it was more a blip on the cityscape of Dubai. Humphrey wondered if all the hotels in the city, except for the fairly basic one they were staying in, were like this. There was no luxury on show in room 2018, however. Totally devoid of any furnishings. Laoban said the floor was being refurbished, but the workers were busy on another floor that day. Room 2018 was at the end of a short corridor opposite the lifts, the approach covered by only one security camera. Currently pointing at the ceiling.

Ronald and Humphrey's unexpected arrival in Dubai meant the expanded team could now be allocated to trail one person each. Beatrix was to continue to follow Fullerton-Price and Humphrey was assigned to watch Mallory. Ronald was more than happy not to have to do any footslogging. His role was to sit in a coffee shop with a laptop and try to identify other people the two of them met up with from photos that Bea and Humph would send him and research their background. "You can start with this man," said Laoban. "He was talking with FP for more than an hour last night. Goes by the name of Felix."

"But we already know who he is," replied Ron. "He's Kulov. Or, at least, the man we know as Kulov. The shipping agent from Bishkek."

"Wasn't he going to meet Stanislas at the border yesterday?" asked Laoban.

"Stan told me last night that he didn't show up. He sent his men instead. As soon as they saw Bogdan and Stan walking towards them, they simply drove away."

Kulov being in Dubai was an interesting development, but also concerning. Whilst Ron could hide away in a café, Humphrey was going to be in and around the exhibition hall, and Kulov would certainly recognise him.

"Is Robert still here in Dubai?" asked Beatrix.

Laoban eyed her curiously. "Why?"

"Well, if he has his false beard with him, perhaps we could borrow it? There must be a drug store in the mall next door, so I could get some bits of makeup there? I can make Humph look like someone else in ten minutes." Laoban nodded and tipped her head sideways, indicating dismissal, while tapping away on her phone.

Even though the mall was directly linked to the hotel, it took nearly half an hour for Bea to locate the pharmacy, choose what she wanted and get back to the lobby, where, hurrying on her way to the lift, she bumped into a uniformed airline captain. Robert, wearing his favourite outfit. Apologies exchanged, he passed her an envelope, and turned away.

The combined effect of the false beard on Humphrey's jaw and the makeup applied to the rest of his face added at least ten years to his appearance. Thus disguised, said covert researcher entered the exhibition area of the conference in a state of mild paranoia, no longer worried he might be spotted but that he might rub his eyes or scratch at his nose or do something else to smudge Bea's handiwork and thereby reveal himself as an imposter.

The exhibition, such as it was, comprised about thirty small stands, ranged along three walls of a large and high-ceilinged rectangular room. The space had clearly been designed as a ballroom, given the red and gold flock wallpaper and a somewhat odd mixture of chandeliers and mirror globes suspended from the ceiling. Each stand comprised three panels, each a metre wide and two metres tall, hinged together to create a recessed space. Each such alcove was populated by one or two individuals whose role was to lure in any delegates foolish enough to linger in front of them for more than a second or two. At that moment in time there were no delegates to entrap, all of them being in the adjacent conference room, possibly enthralled by the presentation or, more likely, half asleep.

Humphrey wandered around. None of the bored stall holders took any notice of him; his 'Exhibitor' badge was disguise enough. Just another one of them. Humphrey knew nothing about robotics for manufacturing, and after looking at the panels on all the stands, decided that he now knew even less. Machines to drill, to weld, to assemble. Nothing related to surgery. He now realised that despite being badged as an exhibitor, he had no stand to be located at. And his false beard was itching.

His musing was interrupted by a sound like a gathering wave, developing in volume and reaching a crescendo as a tide of business people washed outwards from the conference hall, almost all men, most in suits, some in flowing white robes, all babbling to each other, pushing and shoving their way towards a row of tables ranged against the far wall of the exhibition area, on which stood steaming vats of tea and coffee, bottles of water and countless cups and saucers.

Cups and glasses in hand, the delegates dispersed around the exhibition, where stallholders who had materialised from the shadows endeavoured to attract their attention. Now Humphrey needed to locate Ryan Mallory. Not so easy amongst so many. Unlike Fullerton-Price, who was easily spotted, being substantially bigger than most and dressed flamboyantly, conceivably in the same outfit he was wearing when Bea met him in Istanbul. But F-P wasn't Humphrey's quarry. He checked the picture that Maria had sent him for the hundredth time; surely Mallory couldn't be that difficult to find? And then, suddenly, there he was, walking towards him from the direction of the bathrooms, clearly headed for one of the stands. One that Humphrey hadn't noticed on his walkabout tour earlier. 'Silk Road Import Export Company'. Standing in front of it, wearing an exhibitor badge, was Kulov.

Humphrey's phone pinged. A message from Ron. "Kulov really is a shipping agent. Runs a company called Silk Road Impex. Based in Tashkent." He tapped in a quick 'I know and he's right here' reply and moved closer to the stand, taking up a position just around the corner from it and pretending to be immersed in his phone. No chance of planting a bug on the stand now. Maybe later. But he did have his high-tech hearing aids. He didn't admit to needing them for day-to-day use, but they proved very helpful when, like now, he was engaged in covert surveillance. He had an app on his phone to adjust them, so he could not only increase the volume of each aid selectively but also indicate the direction from which the sound he wanted to listen to was coming. They'd be no good if Kulov and Mallory whispered, but with all the chatter going on around them they needed to speak up to be heard by the other. Nobody else but Humphrey was taking any notice of them.

While he couldn't hear all they were saying, he caught enough to confirm that Ryan's company was a regular customer of Kulov, who was being asked to quote for two shipments that would shortly be arriving in Dubai from the States. One was 'kosher' and going to Uzbekistan, but there was some complication with the other. The name of the place where the shipment needed to be delivered eventually was drowned out by background noise, but he heard Kulov telling him to get the paperwork issued for delivery to Baku and that Kulov would make sure it went on to the right address. Baku? Azerbaijan? This was getting complicated. Humphrey would have to swot up on the geography of Central Asia.

Perhaps there was nothing more to discuss, or maybe Ryan was desperate to attend the next presentation, as he joined the crowd returning to the conference hall without bidding any farewell to Kulov. Humphrey, having noted that the badges for delegates and exhibitors looked almost identical, turned his around, tucked it behind his lapel and followed, nearly losing his quarry in the melee. There must be a thousand people here, he thought. Never knew robotics could be so interesting. An hour later, he decided he'd been right all along. It wasn't. As for Ryan, in Humphrey's sights in the row in front of him, either he was so enthralled that he was taking copious notes or he found the presentation as turgid as Humphrey and was busy catching up on his email and messages. Engrossed in his phone, anyway.

Humphrey's pursuit of Mallory meant he missed seeing a stylishly dressed woman who had been hovering, waiting to catch the attention of Kulov. Laoban, clutching a clipboard and with phone open and ready in recording mode.

"Mr Kulov?" she inquired. "I'm a reporter for the Abu Dhabi Business Times." Whether there was such a publication, she didn't know; it was a spur-of-the-moment disguise. Anyway, she thought it less than unlikely that Kulov would know if the paper was real or not. "I wondered if you could spare a few moments to talk to me and tell me about your shipping business?"

Kulov was flattered. "But of course, I would be delighted to, especially for such an attractive young lady, if I may say so." Laoban kept a straight face. "Perhaps I might invite you for a drink in the bar while the exhibition is quiet and all the delegates are in the conference?"

"That would be perfect," replied Laoban. "I trust you won't mind if I record our discussion?"

Never mind whether he harboured any unprofessional intentions, any thoughts he may have had that this would be an easy conversation in which he could impress her by simply reeling off his usual sales patter were quickly quashed. He also realised his lack of discretion when Laoban said that she had overheard him when he was talking to his last customer, and how exactly did Mr Kulov deliver the goods from Dubai to Baku? And what type of goods were they? Where did they originate? How were they packaged? What other countries could Mr Kulov deliver to?

Laoban was enjoying herself. Getting into her stride. Surprising herself by how much useful information she could extract from this dodgy businessman. Although maintaining a smile and frequently fluttering her eyelashes was proving to be hard work. While employed by Mr Smith, Laoban had never had to do any actual spying. She was just a facilitator, a fixer, what Smith liked to call a 'Project Coordinator', and she had been very happy not to get directly involved on the front line. Safer to stay behind the scenes. Not that she'd not thought she could do better than the agents she facilitated. Most were a waste of space, in her opinion. As for her last charge, that Ronald Jones – well, she'd had no words to describe him. Though now he was her employee, and an enthusiastic, diligent and reliable one, who had conquered a lot of his bad habits. Thanks to her.

Laoban belatedly realised that Kulov was no longer paying her the rapt attention he had before. Instead, he was focusing on something over her shoulder. He lifted his right hand and clicked his fingers, as if to order more drinks, and she relaxed. Wrong move. She felt a firm hand on her shoulder, and a gruff voice asking for her documents. Not a waiter at all.

21 – What's in a name? – Ronald

Dubai, UAE

I have to admit that following shady people and sometimes confronting them, pretending to be something I'm not – IT technician, Civil Engineer, CFO of a private health clinic, whatever – can be thoroughly entertaining and provides a frisson to life, but, on this occasion, I was more than happy to be consigned to a café of my choosing with a laptop. I enjoy a close relationship with my friend Mr Google and can happily immerse myself in online research for hours on end.

I didn't have to wander far into the mall adjoining the conference hotel before I found the perfect spot, a coffee shop fronted by an enticing pastry counter and with a long, deep dining room behind it. It had what people call 'mood lighting', in that it was slightly less dark than (though reminiscent of) a cave, and I had no competition for a corner table against the back wall. In fact, the café was almost empty when I arrived, but quickly filled with 'Arab Ladies Who Shop' partaking of tea and cakes. This was good, because it meant that it was highly unlikely that anyone walking past in the mall would see me, though possibly bad, as I was the only male and the only westerner there. I ordered a cappuccino with an extra shot and an extremely large and luscious-looking *pain aux raisins*. Now that's what I call breakfast. Sustenance sufficient until elevenses. I could survive the hour.

Sadly, I was not allowed to enjoy the succulence of that Danish pastry. No sooner had I placed my order than Laoban materialised and sat opposite. "What did I tell you about dieting?" she hissed at me. "There is no place in our team for a fat owl. You already had breakfast in the hotel. You are not young. You will develop diabetes and possibly much worse. And you have an important job to do. Control yourself." With which, she picked up the pastry that had just been placed on the table by a waitress and disappeared as quickly as she had arrived. I knew she had a point. Fat Owl? I couldn't imagine Laoban reading Billy Bunter books, but then she always is full of surprises. I know I eat too much. But it was a very magnificent-looking and most irresistible confection.

As the boss said, I had urgent research to do. It took no time at all to establish that Silk Road Import Export was a legitimate company, and that Felix Kulov was listed as Director. Presumably he was also the owner, as I found no other names associated with it. By the way, online translation tools have improved to be wonderful things these days. They still occasionally throw up howlers, nothing like as many as before, but when one is researching online information written only in another language, in this case mostly Russian, being able to copy, paste and instantly translate back to English makes sorting the wheat from the chaff quite an efficient process. And much quicker than me struggling to make sense of things with my very limited Russian skills and a paper dictionary.

So, without scratching the surface very deeply, I established he had a company based in Tashkent, that according to his rather sparse website specialised in transporting valuable and delicate cargos across Central Asia. Just the one office, though. Nothing in Bishkek or Almaty.

Because I'm pedantic, rather than be satisfied with the first hit, I kept on looking. As so often happens, the 'truffles', as I call them, or hidden treasures if you prefer, are often found on page three or four or five of an online search. Which is where I discovered that Silk Road ImpEx had 'exclusive' sales agents in Bishkek and Almaty, and also in Baku, Baghdad, Kuwait and Ashgabat. What's more, digging a bit deeper, I found that the Baku and Ashgabat companies had branches in Moscow. The former listed its General Manager as a Mr K. Feliks. K for Kulov? Felix spelt differently?

This was becoming fascinating. There was lots more to research. But the clock had already moved on by an hour. Time for elevenses. I needed another coffee. And, if I could be sure Laoban was not watching, perhaps a slice of cherry cheesecake.

Returning from the counter to my table with my victuals, my phone began to vibrate in my pocket. A new message from a withheld number. 'Stay off grid until further notice.' Odd. I wondered what might be going on. And deleted the message that I had been in the process of typing to the boss to update her.

I'm not sure I possess a sixth sense, but the message preoccupied me. Did it come from one of our team? If so, being so curt - and especially withholding the number – had to mean that something had gone wrong. If it came from someone else, then they knew of my existence and had discovered my number. Since it was an unregistered 'burner' SIM, that would be extraordinary. Whoever it came from, it was unwelcome and worrying. Without further ado, I rapidly typed up my notes on Kulov and, after checking the VPN was connected, encrypted the file and uploaded it to the cloud. Even if I was compromised, at least the company wouldn't lose the value of two hours' work sustained by only one extremely tasty piece of cake.

I kept sneaking a look at the others sitting around me in the coffee shop, but without exception they were small groups of women and children, either all local or dressed that way, none appearing to be a credible threat. At the far end where the café was open to the mall, however, I spotted a tall man dressed all in black who stopped, peered in, walked away, returned, peered inside again. Back and forth every minute or so, same procedure. Looking for me? One of Kulov's men? Humphrey was in disguise, but I wasn't, and there had to be a risk I'd been seen. Maybe we had passed each other in the mall.

The safest bet was to assume I was the man's target, and he would be waiting to pounce on me when I left the coffee shop. Trusting that the phone message had come from one of the team, I sent our group chat a message. Just the code number '601'. Meaning I was in danger. Meaningless to anyone else. As soon as the stalker moved out of sight, I gathered my things, cleared the empty cups and plate on to another nearby table, and ducked into the adjacent bathroom. I hoped that on his next pass of the frontage the man would see I was gone and assume I'd given him the slip while he wasn't looking. Then, maybe in another ten minutes, I could leave without being seen. I locked myself in the furthest cubicle and stood on the lavatory seat. I was just tall enough to peek over the top of the partition and observe anyone who might come in, trusting they wouldn't see me.

I admit the plan was far from perfect. I'd only been there for two or three minutes when the door opened and the tall man came in. As I should have anticipated, of course. Swarthy features. A bit of a bruiser. White skin, but black hair, black tee-shirt, black trousers and black tattoos all down both arms. I held my breath and crouched a little, clutching the top wall of the cubicle and concentrating on not falling off the pedestal. The man entered the cubicle next door and rattled the door of mine. I thought he'd kick it open – the latch didn't look very secure – but, luckily, he was disturbed by someone else coming into the bathroom and, from the sound of it, washing their hands. Then a phone rang. I heard loud swearing in Russian, the door banging, and both my pursuer and whoever else had come into the bathroom had gone. Leaving me alone.

Well, I couldn't stay there all day. I gave it another two minutes before I left, looking left and right and left again. I had no doubt the man would be back, and I was wasting time. I needed to find somewhere else to hide myself away. And by now, it was lunch time.

There was no shortage of restaurants in the mall. In fact, every other unit was occupied by one, probably between them representing the cuisines of every country in the world. Had I felt relaxed, I'd have enjoyed lingering over the menus and choosing something interesting based on what tickled my fancy. But I was being hunted and needed to keep out of sight. Unfortunately, none of the restaurants I passed satisfied that need. Either they were full, or the tables were inside hidden behind a wall, or the only available tables were in places I couldn't help but be seen.

The mall opened out into an enormous atrium, and I could see two floors above me. Never stopping looking around, I took escalators to the top floor. That left the crowds behind. If anyone was following me up here, I'd certainly see them. And them me. Unlike the ground floor, the second was quiet, indeed almost deserted. To one side of the escalators, there was a parade of bridal shops; on the other, baby wear and accessories. Some logic in that. Didn't help me, though. No restaurants. However, further on, beyond the children's shops, a flashing illuminated sign invited me to a

'Games Alley'. I'm no games enthusiast – in fact, probably the antithesis of one – but some inner sense drew me to investigate.

At first, I thought it was just an amusement arcade, a dark space lit only by an army of those electronic wheel-of-fortune type slot machines. The heavy beat music throbbing out of loudspeakers combined with the whirring and tinkling of the machines created a version of Hades. Nobody was playing the machines. Beyond them, a neon sign promised 'Paintball Heaven'. Below it, a glass cubicle ticket office. The occupant, a young Asian man playing with his phone, raised his head when he saw me reading the price list and long list of terms and conditions displayed on the wall. And admiring the array of guns clipped to it.

"We've only just opened," he said, "so you'll have to come back later if you want to play with others."

"Can't I play on my own?" I asked. I had no wish to, but I'd had an idea.

"Sure, if you want to practise. Nobody else will be here until two, so you'll have to pay for an extra hour. There's also a hundred dirham deposit for the gun." A bargain for what I wanted. I'd never picked up a gun in my life, so I simply selected the one I thought looked most realistic, a sort of pistol with a long barrel and a silencer, like I'd seen in films. Although those ones probably aren't made of plastic. The cashier took payment, handed me the gun and a plastic bag of 'ammo', pointed to the double doors at the end of the wall and went back to looking at his phone. Checking he was taking no notice, I banged the doors but instead of going in, stuffed the gun into a pocket inside my jacket and ducked behind the row of fruit machines. Now I was armed and dangerous!

I thought I probably had an hour before the cashier might check up on me, but didn't want to risk my luck too soon. While there was no restaurant as such up here on the second floor, there was a fried chicken place at the end of the arcade. It was set up for takeaway service, but had three red plastic tables and chairs for waiting customers. With nobody else around, apart from the two guys behind the counter, I could take my pick. Not a gourmet establishment, I grant you, but a piece or two of poultry encased in a dozen herbs and spices is always a mouth-watering snack. If rather greasy. No finger licking was required, though, as the server presented me with a handful of wet wipes along with my order. I sat at the table that gave me the best view down the mall. In case there was anything interesting to see. A group of three women arose into view at the top of the escalator and disappeared into one of the shops. Another woman came out and went down the escalator. Nothing to worry about. Until, while I was calmly munching a thigh, a uniformed man materialised, as if by magic, walking determinedly towards me. Reflective yellow jacket, so probably a security guard, but I couldn't be sure. Police? Hired assassin? I had nowhere to escape to, so I choked down the chicken, wiped my fingers and positioned the end of the gun barrel poking out from under my jacket. Just like I'd seen in films. Not that I knew how to use it, even to threaten someone. Just a covert researcher, me. A nervous trembling one.

I prayed he wasn't coming for me.

22 – Pilot to the rescue again – Robert

Dubai, UAE

It was just as well I hung around the conference venue after passing Beatrix the envelope with the false beard in it. I had no badge, but nobody was checking, at least not at the door of the exhibition area. As soon as it got busy in there – I think the conference was taking a break – I swanned in and looked around. Loads of people, mostly in small huddles, holding cardboard cups of tea and coffee, all concentrating more on trying not to burn their fingers or spill the contents than on whatever their companions might be saying. Very few of them were paying attention to the stands ranged around the room. Hardly surprising, in my opinion, since all that most of them displayed were pictures of robotic arms. Seen one, you've seen them all. Just pictures. No actual physical robots. Well, some of the guys manning the stands might have been, I suppose, judging from the expressions on their faces.

I found it easy to spot Humphrey, even though Bea's disguise was excellent. My beard definitely looked better on him than on me, and I doubted most people who knew him would see through the disguise. I was sure Kulov wouldn't. Seeing my false beard on someone else reminded me it's got a bit too long and wispy. Not that it actually grows! I must get a new one.

Humph was lurking by the only stand that didn't have pictures of robots. Since it was for a shipping agency, it was easy to conclude that the silver wiry-haired man, at a guess in his early sixties, must be Kulov. I supposed the young one was Mallory. Humph had his back to them, the best angle to eavesdrop and stay unnoticed. Standing three metres away and watching all three of them was Laoban, disguised in a dark red silk floor-to-shoulder number and matching headscarf. As Mallory left to return to the conference, Humphrey on his tail, she moved in to talk to Kulov. Why? What on earth was she doing? The others are the spies. Sorry, researchers. She's the boss. She's supposed to stay in the background, managing everything, not get involved at the sharp end.

The exhibition hall slowly cleared as the delegates went back to their conference. Two tall muscular men I hadn't seen before remained, standing watching. They didn't look like exhibitors. One was positioned near the conference room entrance, the other by the lobby doors. The first one resembled one of the thugs we'd encountered in Bishkek a couple of nights before. Dressed in a black suit, it was difficult to be sure. But that was irrelevant. He was certainly watching Kulov and Laoban. Talking into a headset. He could have been venue security, but from his body language, I doubted that. I stepped into a stand abandoned by its resident salesman, made a show of tidying up a stack of leaflets and watched from the corner of my eye to see what would happen. As Kulov and Laoban left the stand and walked towards the hotel lobby, the first man followed them. As did I. Now I had a rear view of Kulov, I could see that he too was wearing a headset, not for a mobile phone, but the kind that security people use. He was tapping it with a finger of his right hand, I assumed not noticed by Laoban, who was walking on his left. As they exited the exhibition, the second man left too, taking a different direction.

Something was up, for sure. Whatever Laoban had said must have raised Kulov's suspicions. But here, in the busy lobby of a big hotel, she was safe. They crossed into a bar on the opposite side of the lobby. A room just as big as the ballroom-cum-exhibition, but this one was thickly carpeted, dimly lit, with lots of sofas and armchairs arranged around low tables. No other customers, as far as I could see. A solitary bartender. Kulov pointed to a table at one side, and Laoban, who appeared relaxed, took a seat. Kulov sat opposite her, facing the door. The tall man hung back until they were settled and had placed an order with the server, then entered and found a vantage point in the shadows at the back where he could sit and watch. I could see only one other doorway, more or less behind Kulov. Marked as a fire exit.

As quickly as I could, I moved around the lobby, trying to work out where that rear door might lead to. Nowhere obviously accessible from the ground floor that we were on, that was for sure. On the verge of giving up, I walked headlong into a cleaner, pushing his trolley towards the bar. He happily accepted my apologies and a one-hundred dirham note, and although he spoke little English, he quickly got the drift of what I wanted. Still pushing his trolley, he led me to the lifts, up one floor, along several corridors and finally pointed to another fire exit door. Trusting that he'd got the right one – well, he kept giving me thumbs-up signs – and that the door wasn't alarmed, I pushed through it and ran down three flights of stairs to the next landing. Hopefully, if I'd calculated right, the fire door here would be the one into the bar.

I had my pilot's uniform on, so looked official. I'd put away the peaked cap in the satchel I was carrying earlier. Now I pulled out a fluorescent yellow jerkin. I carry it for walking across airport aprons, and it's one of those thin lightweight ones, not the kind that emergency services guys wear, but I figured it would do the job. Fake security guard Rob to the rescue. I pulled the door open.

My gut feel had been right, and I was literally just in time. Kulov's minder was facing me, standing behind Laoban with his hand on her left shoulder. Kulov was also on his feet, but had his back to me, talking into his headset. Time to assume command. I strode forward.

"I'll take it from here," I announced. "Madam, you are to come with me."

Kulov spun round to face me. "And who might you be?" he asked.

"Security. I am instructed to conduct this lady to our offices. But first I need to see your ID."

Kulov shook his head. "That won't be necessary. We are leaving now." Grabbing the opportunity, Laoban moved her right arm behind her, grasped the arm of the tall man and tossed him over her, landing him on the low table, and right on top of the tea, or whatever they'd been drinking. He must have been at least 50cm taller than Laoban and twice her weight. I'd forgotten how skilled she was at jiu-jitsu. At the sight of that, Kulov practically ran out of the bar back towards the lobby, hotly pursued by the bartender waving a bill.

No sooner were we out of the bar, back in the stairwell, Laoban pulled off her headscarf and unwound her dress, stuffing both into her enormous handbag. In the black stretch jumpsuit she was wearing underneath, she looked a completely different person. And quite a scary one. It's that chameleon effect.

The exit signs on the stairwell pointed downwards, but I didn't know where they would lead. Safer to go back the way I came. Our luck was in. Nobody in the corridors on the next floor up. Cameras, yes, but we couldn't do anything about them. Just keep our heads down and walk normally. Laoban and I have worked together for years now, so using a little discreet sign language, we agreed she would go back to our hotel while I rounded up the others.

So, where to start? I checked the local phone I'd picked up from an airport kiosk when I'd arrived. One message. From Ron. 601. How had they targeted him? Kulov, or one of his Bishkek-based heavy mob, must have spotted him earlier in the lobby. Older white almost-bald overweight male with a predilection for tweed suits. Not exactly inconspicuous in a shopping mall in Dubai. Trusting that Beatrix and Humphrey could look after themselves, I texted them 'RTB' messages, hoping they'd understand that Base meant our hotel and not the room Laoban had found on the 21st floor. And then I went in search of Ron.

I could establish his rough location using my regular phone – as long as his was switched on and he hadn't disabled the tracker function, which he'd succeeded in doing a few times in the past (heaven knows how or why). Last known location in the mall. Somewhere. The problem with these trackers is that they're not precise and don't discriminate on altitude – he could be on any level. I'd just have to wander around to see where the tracking signal got stronger. A bit like those rangers you see in the wildlife programmes on TV following big cats they've collared earlier. But without the need to brandish a huge aerial.

The yellow jerkin proved an effective disguise. The real security guards were all Asian, but the ones I passed nodded, and one even saluted. Maybe they thought I was the boss checking up on them. Rather than a covert research facilitator searching for a retired spy repurposed as a schoolteacher repurposed as a covert researcher. The mall was long, and although I walked the length of the ground floor, the signal stayed the same. Ron was around somewhere, but not close. I tried the next floor up. Towards the far end, the signal got stronger, but I couldn't see him. What I could see, however, was Kulov's other man, standing by the escalators and talking into his headset. No doubt waiting to pounce if Ron was spotted. With no time to waste, I ran up the escalator to the next floor up. A much stronger signal now, but a very unlikely place for Ron to be found. Baby clothes and wedding dresses? But there he was, down beyond the shops at the far end. Sitting at a red table by an amusement arcade. As I strode towards him, he fidgeted, obviously seeing me and pushing what appeared to be the barrel end of a gun up from under his jacket. Ron with a gun?

Fortunately, he recognised me before he attempted some false bravado and pulled the trigger. Just as well, since being splattered with red paint would hardly have made us less conspicuous. I had to admit, the gun looked convincing. But not in his hands. I relieved him of it and pushed it down under my belt. A visible deterrent.

Instructing Ron to walk in front of me, as if he was my prisoner, we made our way back along the second floor of the mall, passing the escalator well, where Kulov's man was still waiting on the floor below. We turned left into a short corridor with lift doors on both sides. Ignoring them, we opened the emergency exit door ahead of us and ran down the stairs. Two floors down, we reached a deserted lobby, from which a glass exit door led to the hotel and mall drop-off area outside. I removed my yellow jacket, donned my captain's cap, and discarded the gun; then, on second thoughts, pushed it into my bag, which just about concealed it. To avoid the risk of Ron being spotted waiting for a cab, or more likely his forgetting the name of the hotel he was staying in, I ordered an Uber for him. A posh XL one, since having him climb into an ancient, battered saloon would be more noticeable than getting into the gleaming black Merc that was even now pulling up to the kerb. I waited a minute to see if either of our pursuers showed up before I left too, walking out purposefully and taking the regular taxi that was conveniently hovering by the kerb. But I wasn't returning to our hotel, at least not yet. It was good that I was wearing my Captain's uniform. I wanted to beg a favour.

23 – Meanwhile, in Rotterdam
– Maria

Children who grow up in Minsk, even those with fathers in the KGB like me, learn to keep their wits about them all the time as soon as they start to walk. I had the added benefit of my father teaching me spying techniques when I was still in primary school, and as I grew older, I often helped with a little moonlighting when he thought a teenage girl would be a better watcher than one of his spooks. So, coming out of the supermarket in Rotterdam, and without even thinking about it, I knew at a glance that the couple standing on the opposite corner, ostensibly studying a guidebook, were no tourists. That said, I wasn't expecting to be the focus of their attentions. Home was just around the corner, but, just in case, and from force of habit, I walked in the opposite direction. After turning two street corners, I knew for sure I was being followed. Just a few hundred metres away from my apartment and burdened with two bags of groceries, the last thing I needed was to have to evade pursuers. Presumably they didn't yet know where I lived, or they'd have staked that out.

I didn't need a coffee either, but my regular haunt was just a few metres ahead. I could hardly claim that Hans the barista was a friend, but at least he always said hello and was open to a little gentle flirting. He was very tall, very slim and dreadfully shy. Lonely too, I guessed. His job couldn't have helped, spending all day on his own behind the bar. I'd never seen anyone else working there. Most of the time there weren't any customers either, today being no exception.

"The usual?" asked Hans.

"When I come back," I told him. "I've got to go back to the shop for something important and these bags weigh a ton. Can I leave them here for ten minutes?" I didn't wait for a reply, but seeing a tram pulling in at the stop opposite dashed out of the café again and across the road, just in time to leap onto it before the doors closed. I didn't want to go to Willemsplein, but it would do. It was easy to blend into the crowd getting off there, and there was a big cheap clothing store right by the terminus. Five minutes later, I emerged dressed in a brown smock that looked absolutely revolting. All the other girls in Rotterdam must have thought so too, as it was marked down to 3.99. Coupled with a two-euro pair of black rimmed reading spectacles, I'd managed a very quick and cheap disguise. Enough to put my followers off the scent for a while. The glasses made me a bit disoriented, so I pushed them up on my brow. Like a fashion model. Easy to pull them back down if I spotted my tails again.

Why was I being followed, though? Who had found me? And how? It had to be Mallory. I remembered I'd told him I was based in Rotterdam when we had that lunch in London. Stupid mistake. At the time, I thought he was squeaky clean. I'd probably been off my guard too, after the tipsy evening with Sonia and relaxed chatter over lunch. But why would he have me followed? He had the number of one of my work phones and an email address. Much easier ways of finding me. But if not him, then who?

There was no sign of the odd couple who had been following me, so I caught a tram going back towards my apartment, and alighted where I'd got on, opposite the café. No sign of my pursuers here, either. The café door was locked, but I could see Hans inside, crouched over so presumably cleaning up his espresso machine. I hammered on the door, and he quickly came over and unlocked it.

"You said ten minutes," he said. "It's been two hours."

"I know. I'm sorry. Do you still have my bags?"

"Of course. I put your milk and yogurt in the fridge. I hope you don't mind me looking in the bags," he added, now looking sheepish.

"No, it's only my groceries! Thank you so much!"

He shook his head. "I'm sorry. I can't make your coffee now. I've just cleaned the machine."

I wasn't sure it was a good idea, but I felt like taking pity on him. "If you've finished work, how about a beer at the bar next door?" He looked like I had just asked him to jump off a cliff. "Just a quick one? I have to go soon." I put on my sweetest smile.

"I... I... I can't tonight," he eventually stuttered. "But... it's very nice of you."

"Perhaps tomorrow then? I owe you a thank you for looking after my bags." He nodded hesitantly and went to unlock the door to let me out. I ventured a question. "By the way, did anyone ask about me this afternoon?"

"There were a couple of tourists. They spoke English, but they didn't sound or look English. Maybe Turkish? The man said he had seen you drop something in the street and then come in here. He wanted to give it back to you. I said he could leave it with me, but he wouldn't. They just went. They didn't buy coffees." Apparently, the ultimate insult in Hans's opinion.

Who were these people? The question preyed on me all the way home. As I waited for the lift in the lobby of the apartment block, I got my answer. Mevrouw Beek, the nosy neighbour from apartment 1C, always in her pink housecoat, had seen me coming and opened her door. She who probably devoted her entire day to watching who came and went. "You know that couple who've been loitering outside for the last two days?" she called over to me. What? Now I felt really bad. They'd been there all that time and I hadn't registered it? "They left a note for you." She pushed a piece of paper into my hand. "I didn't let them in." She turned and went back into her own apartment without another word.

Just four words. Russian words. 'Report to Embassy. Tomorrow.'

So that's what it was. A simple message that brought on a sinking feeling of dread. Made worse by the 'Tomorrow' on a separate line, emphasising the urgency of my fate. Nothing to do with Ryan Mallory or the current project at all. Just my past catching up with me.

Five years ago, my father had waved me off from the airport in Minsk, Belarus, expecting me to return a fortnight later from the course in London I had convinced him to let me register for. But I had no intention of doing that. Instead, I had left London for Amsterdam, and through a combination of design and accident quickly become involved with a certain Mr Smith, applying my charms and the espionage skills my father had taught me when I was a teenager, and in the process acquiring a remarkably well-faked Latvian passport and becoming a key player in his shady empire of covert research. There I met and worked with Laoban and Robert (though all three of us studiously followed Smith's corporate mantra of never using names, even between ourselves). Three years later, unpaid and largely abandoned, we conspired to have Smith incarcerated for his crimes and took up the covert research business for ourselves, enjoying some satisfying initial success. Five years, in which I have never contacted, never missed, and not even often thought about, my parents. Now, without any doubt, my father, a Belarusian KGB colonel, wanted me back and had applied his rank and influence to finding me. After everything I had done to avoid ever getting found. He had succeeded. I had failed.

So, they knew where I lived. I opened the door to my own apartment with trepidation, though I was confident they wouldn't have got in, even by climbing up the drainpipe (was there a drainpipe?) and through a window, without Mevrouw Beek knowing all about it. No, it all looked the way I had left it. Untidy, but my own untidiness. Now what? I wished Rob was with me. He'd know what to do. Or Laoban. Perhaps I should call her? No, that would mean explaining my history. Things Laoban didn't need to know. I'd have to make my own decisions.

Not to go to the Belarus Embassy, that was a given. If I did that, I'd simply be shipped off to Minsk. Possibly in a box, like we'd sometimes used to ship Ronald Jones around South America. But if I didn't go to the embassy, they'd certainly come and get me. In fact, I was quite surprised they weren't waiting for me outside. Perhaps they were. Perhaps Father had told them to be gentle. Better not count on that, though.

The only possible decision was to get out. As soon and as discreetly as possible. The time was seven o'clock. Still time to fly out that night. If there was a flight. I checked the airport information online. 21:55 to Lanzarote. That would be nice, except all the team were in Dubai. No doubt Josefina would make me welcome, which would be nice for a holiday, but the team needed me to be useful, and so that just wasn't practical. 21:45 to London. There, I could be useful. I'd just have to be even more careful than in Rotterdam. Lots of my countrymen and women there, all trained since birth to keep their eyes on others. Another expensive last-minute ticket; but that couldn't be helped. I'd make up some story for Laoban tomorrow. It took me only five minutes to pack, and in five minutes more I had changed the safe combinations, turned on intruder alarms and set timers for the living room and bedroom lights to suggest to any outside observer that I was in residence. I carried my unopened shopping bags back downstairs and approached Mevrouw Beek's door. No need to knock, of course. The door opened as if it was automatic. She really does never stop watching.

"I have to leave urgently. My mother is ill," I lied. "I'll be a few days, and I just bought all this shopping. It'll go off if I leave it, so I thought you might like it? There's a packet of that lovely ham you told me about somewhere in there." I'd never seen Mevrouw Beek smile before. Scuttling back to my flat, I took out a bottle of malt whisky that I'd bought for when Rob next came, which he hadn't (bastard), and crossed the landing to the apartment opposite. This time, I had to knock quite a few times before its occupant came to the door. "Pieter, how are you? Can I ask you a favour?" pushing the bottle at him.

Pieter was well over fifty, and lived on his own, though I knew he frequently had much younger overnight visitors. "My toy boys," he had once proudly told me, using the English expression. He was also the only resident I knew in the block who had a car, an Audi he was very proud of and kept in the underground garage.

"My mother is sick and I need to fly out tonight, but the flight is very soon and I can't get a taxi. Could you take me to the airport?" My sweetest smile was getting a lot of use that evening.

"For you, anything, Maria," he replied. "Even without this very welcome bribe! But I have a friend coming in an hour, so it needs to be quick. Are you ready to leave right now?"

"Packed and ready to go," I replied, crossing to my apartment door and pulling my suitcase and backpack out onto the landing. Within minutes, we were driving up the car park ramp and out on to the street. While I couldn't see any unlikely tourists or anyone else loitering around the block, I was glad I hadn't had to risk leaving by the front door and taking a cab.

There was no love lost between me and my mother, or at least not when I had left Minsk, but even so, by the time I had spent the fifteen-minute drive to the airport fielding Pieter's solicitous enquiries about her, I found myself praying that she was not in fact ill.

Apart from a crowd of holidaymakers at one end of the departures hall queuing to check in for the flight to the Canary Islands, the airport was more or less deserted. Less than a dozen people were at the gate for the London flight. None looking like they might be a Belarusian secret agent. With nearly an hour to kill, my thoughts turned to where to stay when I arrived. It was late, so it would have to be a hotel for the night. Then find an apartment tomorrow? Maybe Airbnb for a week or two? As soon as the Central Asia project was finished, I could head down to Lanzarote and stay with Bea and Humphrey. I'd be safe there. For a while, anyway. On a whim, I texted Sonia. Apart from anything else, I was feeling embarrassed at having ignored her messages for nearly a week.

Sonia was thrilled that I was coming to London ("I've got so much to tell you!"). Having turned down her entreaties to come and stay the night on her sofa ("it doesn't matter how late you get here. I don't mind waiting up") in favour of the airport Travelodge, I accepted a plan to meet the following afternoon at a bar in Canary Wharf, first insisting she promise me we wouldn't drink as much as the last time.

24 – Escape to Larnaca

Opening the door of the limo that had brought him and Laoban to the front of the private aviation terminal at Dubai, and looking up at the sleek white jet, steps lowered and awaiting them, Ronald remarked "Don't tell me you finally bought Rob a plane to fly us around in?"

"Absurd! Have you any idea how much these cost?" Ron shook his head. "I imagine he's rented it. Even that's going to be astronomic."

"Wrong," said Robert, coming down the steps to join them. "I've borrowed it. No charge. Well, apart from refuelling it for the return leg. Anyway, where are Beatrix and Humphrey?"

"They're on their way. Five minutes," replied Laoban.

"Are you flying us direct to Lanzarote, then?" asked Ron.

"Sorry, no. This baby doesn't have the range, and I only got to borrow it by agreeing to pick up the Sheikh's wife and daughters and bring them home. They probably won't be happy having their holiday cut short by a couple of days, but the big man is happy because he doesn't have to pay for contract pilots. He's got all the money in the world, but's as mean as they come," added Robert.

"How did you know this Sheikh, then?" enquired Ron.

"I used to fly through here a lot. Before Smith days. Needed friends in high places to get a plane in, refuelled and back out again with no questions asked. Did a bit of piloting for him as a favour in return."

"That sounds intriguing. I thought that refuelling stopovers were a routine thing."

"Oh, they are. If the flight plan and manifest are in order."

"So, what were you doing? Running drugs? Contraband?" Ron's eyes were glistening, thinking that this sounded very exotic.

"No, just government business."

"Surely that's all above board?"

"Not if your final destination is Guantanamo and your unwilling passenger has friends or family in this country."

"Oh. I see. I think." Ron didn't really see, but vaguely remembered reading something about rendition flights a few years earlier. "Anyway, where are you flying us to now, then?"

"Larnaca." Seeing the uncertainty on Ron's face, adding, "Cyprus. Lots of commercial flights from there, so you won't have to wait long. I've messaged Maria so she can get that sorted before we land. Board now, before anyone else sees you. I'll go and look for Humph and Bea. They may be stuck at security in the terminal. Don't fly off without me."

"Are we all going, then? Shouldn't at least one or two of us stay until the end of the conference?" asked Ron.

"The only one of you who's not compromised is Bea," said Rob, "and Humphrey won't leave her behind. I've got to bring the plane back, so I and the boss will be here again tomorrow."

Laoban was already in the cabin, reclining in the front-row seat and deep in conversation on her phone. Ron went to the back and had hardly had time to get seated before the others joined them. Rob pulled up the steps, closed the door, and motioned to Laoban to join him on the flight deck.

The team must have all dozed off, because the next they knew was being jolted awake as the plane touched down in Larnaca. As it taxied to the terminal, Laoban reappeared, at some stage having changed into a pilot's uniform. As soon as they had pulled to a halt, she opened the door and pushed out the steps. "Wait in the terminal! Transit area! Do NOT go through passport control!" she screamed at them. Ronald shook his head. Why she always had to act so aggressively and treat them as small children remained a mystery to him. But standard and wholly expected behaviour from her.

The private aviation terminal was small and had no transit lounge as such. Instead, just a couple of grey metal benches in front of the passport control desk. Beatrix, Humphrey, and Ronald sat side by side on one of them. The area was deserted, not even an officer behind the desk, but silence seemed the best policy. Accompanied by a lot of finger-tapping and fidgeting while they waited for Laoban and Robert, who were taking an extraordinarily long time.

The delay, Laoban told them when she materialised, was because she had been on the phone catching up with Maria. Toshio had been rather successful with his hacking of emails, and there were developments to discuss. Nothing related to Fullerton-Price, who, it seemed, was singularly focused on negotiating the sale to a customer in Iran of second-hand machinery to manufacture plastic bags. However, the others were interesting. Ryan had been sent copies of shipping documents for a container full of medical equipment that was due to be unloaded from a ship at Dubai the next day, destined for a clinic in Baku, and had forwarded them to Kulov instructing him to 'do the usual'. Meanwhile, Kulov himself had received an email from a clinic in Bokhara complaining that their order had still not arrived. He had replied telling them the ship had been delayed because of security issues in the Gulf, but the order was on its way and would be with them in another week or so.

Ronald, who had been taking notes on a pad, broke the silence as the team sat digesting this information. "Conclusions. Mallory is in cahoots with Kulov, but FP is not involved, so far as we know. The container arriving in Dubai today or tomorrow will be picked up from the port by Kulov's men against documents authorising them to take it to Baku. Somewhere along the way, the container will be diverted, presumably to Bokhara. Where is Bokhara, anyway?"

"Uzbekistan," replied Beatrix. "Which might link back to where this all started."

"Indeed," replied Humphrey. "But we don't know where or how the container will be diverted. Surely that's part of the client's brief, so we need to find that out?"

"Exactly," said Laoban. "Our contract with the underwriters is to establish the entire route of an insured shipment. It's no good to us if it just magically turns up in the wrong place. They'll simply refuse to pay us. Also, don't forget, it's not our business to stop the crime. That's down to the clients after we deliver our report. And after we have been paid."

"But now Kulov suspects we're after him, it's complicated. Not to mention being followed by the police in Kazakhstan," added Humphrey.

"The last thing we need is to be arrested in one of those countries. No one would ever know – and we'd never get home!"

"We still don't know who the man we met in Almaty is. Does he work for Kulov, or does Kulov work for him?" observed Ronald. "I've got some information to add. Things I discovered while I was working in the café in the Dubai mall. There was no time to tell you before. I think you'll find them rather interesting."

Everyone looked at Ronald, expectant.

"First one. You remember that all this started with an email that was sent to you, Humphrey, at hunterhealth.com?" Humphrey nodded. "Well, I mentioned then that there was also a hunterhealth.com.uz and maybe they made a mistake sending the email. I didn't think any more about it since then, but I thought now that I would look and see if there's a website." He paused for effect. "It's for a private hospital in Tashkent. They've got a second one in Samarkand. They're expanding and opening a new clinic in Bokhara. Which is where you say the email to Kulov came from, correct, Laoban?"

"Very interesting," she replied, tapping furiously into her phone. Realising she was being watched, adding, "I'm asking Toshio to see what email address that came from. Ronald, you said there was something else?"

"I found a blog post on a website for a shipping company." Seeing Humphrey shaking his head, continuing "No, not Kulov's one. It's in Singapore. Anyway, that's not relevant. The article was about what the author called the Bermuda Triangles for goods shipments, places where things often go missing in transit. One of those places is Turkmenistan. He says it's so secretive and bureaucratic that if something never arrives from there, there's no way of ever finding out what happened. The route from Dubai to Uzbekistan goes straight through."

"Lots of thinking to do," said Laoban. "There are no more flights to anywhere useful out of here tonight, so we'll check into an airport hotel and meet again over breakfast."

"A very early one, then," said Robert. "I need to get the plane back to Dubai. With the Sheikh's family. I've been given a take-off slot of 09:25."

25 – Getting a new look in London – Maria

Far too early, the roar of the first flight of the day taking off awoke me to the realisation that the room I had been given overlooked the end of the runway and had a window that didn't close properly. Together with the spartan mattress, cramped room, miniscule working space and a bathroom with a cistern that never stopped running, there was no question of spending a second night there. I showered and went out for a walk to think more clearly about what I needed to achieve before I met Sonia.

Most airports are miles from anywhere habitable, and surrounded by inaccessible security areas, warehouses and the like. This one is different. Although I'd flown in and out of London City many times, I'd never stopped to discover that there was ordinary housing and shopping just a short walk away. Emphasis on the ordinary. The buildings are fairly modern, I suppose, but what the estates lack in architectural merit they make up for with litter. A bit like suburban Rotterdam, but more brick and less concrete. It didn't feel like a place that anyone would choose to go unless they lived there. Close to the centre of town, but off the beaten track. Perfect for me.

I'd been walking for not much more than five minutes when my stroll took me around a corner onto a short street lined on one side with a three-storey block, even plainer than the ones I'd already walked past. Apartments above, but the ground floor level given over to a parade of shops. Maybe ten of them, but most boarded up with graffiti sprayed over the 'To Let' signs.

The convenience store windows were obscured and covered with metal grilles too, but the shop was at least open, light spilling out of the doorway. At the other end of the terrace, a middle-aged woman was raising the shutters on 'Daphne's Charming Cutz' hairdressing salon. Daphne herself. Presenting me with the ideal solution to the need to change my appearance. Wardrobe alone wasn't going to hack it.

Daphne's own hairdo didn't promise quality styling, and her salon was very basic. I don't often spend much on my hair, but when I do, I go to quite a select (and very expensive) hair stylists in Den Haag. But now I was in Docklands, possibly the poorest part of it too, and this would have to do. Once Daphne had overcome being distraught at my request to cut my long curls down to pageboy length, and had me confirm a dozen times I was serious (almost to the point I thought she might prepare a legal document and make me sign it), she did the necessary with efficiency and reasonable style. I toyed with having my remaining blond locks dyed pink or blue, but remembering Laoban's fury when I'd done that before, opted for dark chestnut. I looked in the mirror and didn't recognise myself. Box ticked. For a quarter of the price I'd pay at my normal salon.

Daphne being extremely chatty, I also engaged her in talking about whether she knew of any apartments in the area available for rent. The conversation was going nowhere until she realised I only wanted short term, a few weeks or a month at most. She stopped to call a couple of friends, chatting inconsequentially for so long that I thought I would be in the chair for ever. Although those calls yielded no results, Daphne suggested I ask Mr Gupta in the convenience store, who she thought had rooms he let out from time to time. "Mind you," she added conspiratorially, "I think they're for his type. Not fancy ladies like you."

Well, I was more concerned with discretion than style. Mr Rakesh Gupta, a small dumpy man in his mid-fifties, did indeed have rooms to let. Not just rooms, but a whole apartment in the next street, described to me in glowing terms as if it were the height of luxury. He insisted on taking me to see it immediately, calling out to an elderly woman behind the counter, his mother, as I later found out, to mind the shop.

Luxurious it wasn't. In fact, it was very basic, but clean enough, other than the lingering and indelible scent of curry, presumably the favoured cuisine of whoever had lived there before. There was a living room with a kitchenette off to one side, a bedroom just big enough for the two single beds in it, and a bathroom into which the architect had somehow squeezed a shower and a loo. I remarked on how small it was. "The estate agent calls it *bijou*," he told me with a proud grin on his face. "It means jewel!"

The only thing vaguely jewelled about it was the rent that Rakesh asked for. Five thousand a month! I knew London property prices were high, but wouldn't and couldn't pay that. But it met my essential needs. It was on the top floor (admittedly that was only the second floor) and on a corner, the windows affording views of both streets. It was a ten-minute walk to the airport if I needed to get away again in a hurry. There was working wifi ("cable television too!"). I offered two thousand cash up front, no questions asked. He came down to four. Just like bartering in an Arab market. Eventually we settled on two thousand five hundred cash, no tenancy agreement. Grudgingly, after my telling him it wasn't safe for a single girl like me, he agreed I could change the lock, as long as I gave him a key.

I went back to the hotel, collected my case, stopped by the airport to change five thousand euros from my emergency cash fund into pounds (no doubt at a terrible exchange rate), went back to the store to pay Rakesh, collect the keys and buy a few supplies, and back to my new apartment to get installed. Just in time to get a torrent of "where on earth have you been" messages from Laoban. She was in Cyprus, of all the unlikely places. Not that I ever knew where she would be from one day to the next. Or even one hour to the next. Luckily for me, she took no interest in my move to London. All she wanted me to do was to find out how to get one of the team into Turkmenistan and another into Uzbekistan. Urgently, of course. That would put paid to the afternoon. But first I called a locksmith.

I didn't have a British passport, but what I did have was a British social security number and a bank account in the name of Maria Landess. Even a birth certificate to prove that I was her, or at least allow me to pretend to be her. The real Maria Landess had, unfortunately, only survived to nine months old. Smith gave me the papers, soon after he'd furnished me with my fake Latvian passport in a different name. "Need to have you all legal, ha ha," he'd said. Feeling uncomfortable rather than legal at being given the identity of a dead girl, I had searched for her death certificate online and went out one Sunday afternoon to Loughton to visit her grave. Smith had chosen well, in that it was unlikely anyone would ever enquire about her; she was buried with her parents and brother, as they'd all died together in a car crash. I may have cried all the way back to town, but I've taken advantage of the identity whenever it was useful, and made regular little transactions on the bank account to keep it active. I never knew when it might come in useful. Like today.

Usually when I need to book tickets and hotels for the crew, I can simply go onto the internet, check a few options, pick what I think is best (or, if Laoban is watching, the cheapest) and book it all online in a matter of clicks. Easy. If they'd just wanted to go to Uzbekistan, that's exactly what I would have done. Not so Turkmenistan. Everything I read said whoever went would need a visa, and that they were very difficult to obtain, even for a tourist, which was always going to be the simplest option. Visitors needed to be sponsored by a recognised agent and go on a pre-planned organised itinerary accompanied by a Turkmen guide. Not the sort of arrangement a covert researcher would want. Even then, I read one had to apply four weeks in advance, and there were warnings and cautions that over half the visa applications were rejected.

Never give up. There was always a way, I thought. I searched for tour operators. Perhaps they had ways of getting visas faster. I could only find three that offered trips to Turkmenistan. Probably that was because of the visa difficulties. I called them all. The first didn't answer. Their office was in Bangkok, so nowhere near the country in question. I worked out it was ten o'clock at night there. Good reason not to answer the phone. Number two was in Istanbul. They had a tour going in three months' time. Would that suit? No, it wouldn't. Nothing sooner. But I elicited one useful piece of information. They wouldn't accept a solo traveller, as they said it was impossible to get a visa.

The third agency was in Tashkent. Eight in the evening there, so I doubted I'd get an answer, but tried anyway. After about ten rings, it was picked up. Thank goodness for an enthusiastic agent greedy for business at an inflated price. Their next group tour was months away, but, as long as they were happy to follow the same itinerary, they could arrange a private tour for Mr and Mrs Hunter, if that would suit? Rock, the man at the end of the phone, speaking perfect English, claimed that he had a contact at the Embassy who could get them visas in forty-eight hours, but they would have to go to Tashkent first to make the application.

Laoban wasn't enthusiastic about sending Humphrey and Beatrix together. "They'll think they're on another honeymoon," she complained. She told me she'd been trying to keep the middle-aged lovers apart, and they'd only ended up together in Dubai by a conspiracy of circumstances. I got the impression she was jealous. I pointed out that they could go to Bokhara and Samarkand on the same trip to check out the clinics, and the fact that wouldn't cost any more mollified her somewhat. Now all I had to do was get the happy couple from Larnaca to Tashkent. Surprisingly easy. Except that no sooner had I sent the itinerary, Humph replied, complaining. Not that the flight out was at six in the morning but that the connection in Istanbul was only just over an hour, and didn't I know how big the airport was? Tough, I thought, they'd just have to run.

26 – Back to Dubai – Robert

As I'd predicted, the Sheikh's wife wasn't too thrilled at having her holiday cut short by several days. Even less happy at having to get to the airport for a 09:25 departure. Laoban, who needed to accompany me as I had to have a qualified co-pilot, wasn't enthusiastic either, though for reasons of her own she wasn't sharing. On the other hand, the Sheikh's teenage daughters, all four of them, boarded the plane with alacrity, clearly happy to be going home. As for their luggage... well, suffice it to say that it weighed more than the combined weight of two pilots and five passengers.

With the early start, we landed back in Dubai at 14:00. Whilst the all-female family had to crowd into a minibus, the Sheikh had sent a stretch limo for me and Laoban. Proof of the pecking order in the Emirates, I suppose. We decided to go straight to the conference hotel, where it was afternoon break time, to check if all the men we were interested in were still there. I went into the exhibition, while Laoban, perhaps fearful of running into Kulov's heavies, dived into the mall. (At least, I assume she was not seeking retail therapy. That would be hard to imagine). The enthusiasm the delegates had displayed the day before had dissipated considerably, as their return to the conference hall was more of a shuffle than a stampede, and quite a few delegates took the opportunity to leave. I guess that 'Symbiotic Heterogeneity in Multi-Robot Infrastructure' just isn't that exciting a subject to delve into at four in the afternoon. Some of the exhibitors were packing up their stands, but Kulov was still there, now, much to my surprise, deep in conversation with EA. We'd been wondering what had happened to him. Not up to any good, I was sure, but there was no way of getting close to them without attracting attention. I couldn't see Kulov's men, but they had to be around somewhere. Maybe they'd learnt to be more discreet.

My phone, tucked away in a pocket, was vibrating nonstop, which meant new messages coming in. Since I couldn't achieve anything in the exhibition area, I walked out onto the kerb outside the hotel lobby to enjoy a bit of tropical warmth (Dubai doesn't really do fresh air) and see what they were all about. Maria telling us she was relocating to London for an indefinite period. I wondered why, and whether Laoban had approved it. After getting away from Smith a year ago, Laoban had forbidden Maria to base herself in London for unexplained 'professional reasons'. Maria and I always assumed that was because Laoban suspected we were an item and was jealous, and it was more important to have me in London than Maria. Anyway. More pertinent to the moment, another message advising that the ship carrying the container of medical stuff had docked at 1:30 that morning in Jebel Ali. It was scheduled to be unloaded before 23:00, as the ship was sailing out again after that to Mumbai. Which meant that the goods were probably already on the quayside. And, while I was reading that message, a new one came in. Toshio had intercepted an email from Kulov to a local truck company instructing them to pick up the container at 19:00, transport it to a trailer park near the Saudi border, confirm delivery and await further instructions.

I had no idea what level of security there'd be at a trailer park in the desert, but guessed it would be a lot less than at the port. I'd never had a reason to go there, but remembered being told that, apart from being immense, Jebel Ali was notoriously secure. Pictures of it on the web showed enormous areas populated with tens of thousands of containers. The intercepted emails meant we did now have the container number, but even if we could have got past the port gates, the chances of finding it without the right paperwork were vanishingly remote. Whereas locating it in a smaller trailer park, knowing roughly what time the container was arriving, was a different matter.

As it turned out, Laoban was thinking along the same lines. She messaged, summoning me to the second floor of the mall. The same place as where I had found Ron. Thinking about it as I rode the escalators, I could imagine her playing paintball, but not when there was a serious project underway. As for wedding dresses and baby trappings… Amusing but silly speculation. I found her in a mobile phone and electronic gadget shop, almost obscured by the two large stores on either side, each of which had huge displays of prams and baby strollers spilling out onto the mall.

Judging from the dust that had gathered on some of the items on display, the young Asian guy behind the counter didn't get much business and was proving very enthusiastic to have some late afternoon customers. I was more than surprised that Laoban would ask me to advise on which gadget to buy. I'm glad she did in this case, though, as I'm sure the cheapest one, which she would have bought had I not been around, wouldn't have done the job. She even agreed to buy two of them.

By the time we'd completed our purchase and returned to the hotel lobby, the conference was over and the only indication it had ever been there were the teams of men dismantling the exhibition. We sat in the lobby, ordered tea, and did a little research. Toshio told us that Kulov hadn't sent any more emails, so all we could do was guess his next steps. He probably communicated with his own team using secure messaging, which we didn't have access to, of course, only resorting to email to deal with outsiders like the haulage contractor. So, putting myself in his shoes, I reckoned that since he was in Dubai, he'd want to check on the goods for himself before they were taken onwards, and that he'd do that at the trailer park. Which was our own best chance of locating the container we needed to track. Unfortunately, said trailer park was close to the Saudi border, over three hundred kilometres and four hours' drive away. No nearby airport. I'd never realised such distances existed in the United Arab Emirates. The country looks so small on the map, and I'd only ever flown in and out, always either straight over the coast or due south over the Saudi border, never east to west.

Even though we weren't staying at the hotel, a five hundred dirham note judiciously palmed to the concierge rustled up a car to take us to the border and back again with a driver the man told me was guaranteed to ask no questions. I say car, but what arrived was a gargantuan gold metallic Cadillac

4x4. Not in the least discreet, but then, nothing much in the Emirates is. The windows were blacked out, and there was a matching black glass partition between the back cabin and the front seats. Much to my surprise, the driver was a young Arab, unlike all the taxi drivers who originate from the Indian subcontinent. He introduced himself as Ali, told us he was a university student and that the car belonged to his uncle, who he insisted was more than happy to have him borrow and drive hundreds of kilometres in it. I'd assumed that all the oil and gas around meant all the locals were rich, but he told me that his father only gave him a tiny allowance. He'd jumped at an all-night six-hundred-kilometre round trip drive, expecting to make enough to pay for his nightlife for a month. From our point of view, it was perfect; no traffic police or other authorities would question a local driving such an extravagant vehicle. I told him to keep the partition closed and, if he was stopped, try not to say that he was carrying passengers. For Ali, this all added to the excitement.

Laoban hadn't only been to the gadget shop, she'd also been shopping for clothes for both of us. That reminded me we were both still wearing our pilot uniforms. They'd been useful up to now, but weren't ideal for covert surveillance of a trailer park far distant from any airport and in the middle of the night.

As soon as Ali stopped hurtling around corners and was driving along a straight freeway, we got changed. We had left the city and there were no streetlights now, and with the tinted windows, both of us had all the discretion we might ever need. When I could see her again, Laoban was in another of those stretchy black jumpsuits. I'm beginning to believe she was a cat in a previous life. At least she'd bought me normal jeans and a sweatshirt. So, both of us dressed all in black, head to toe. Clinging. Fine in the air-conditioned car, but I hoped we didn't need to walk around outside too much. We'd die from the heat dressed like that. Her logic was good in all other ways. It was already getting dark, and we'd be much less conspicuous wandering around a trailer park in the desert at night.

Ali was having the time of his life, swaying to music and driving like a madman. Heaven knows what speed he was doing, but it was a wide, dead straight highway, and the only other traffic was slow-moving trucks in the nearside lane. Thank goodness for that partition sheltering us from him.

The sound of the Arab music he was playing was only faint on our side, but repetitious and irritating enough. The one time I opened it a crack to ask him something, I was knocked back by the sound. No way we would have heard each other, or he our conversation.

It had been dark almost all the way from Dubai, and after we had passed the bright lights of Abu Dhabi, the sky was a complete pitch black, and even if the windows hadn't been tinted, we'd have seen nothing. I assumed the landscape was desert. Occasional distant clusters of lights from a town or settlement. Flares from drilling rigs. Just shy of three hours out from Dubai, we pulled into an enormous filling station. Ali pulled the partition back and announced that we'd arrived. It had been a comfortable ride, but I was glad to get out. A huge canopy covered about ten islands with fuel pumps. Back to one side, an international chain burger restaurant. Beyond that, I could see gantry lights illuminating what we'd come for, a sizeable parking lot. Inside, there were dozens of trucks lined up, but also a long row of trailers with their containers but without a tractor, presumably delivered there by one carrier and awaiting another to collect. Nine o'clock. We'd made good time, so were destined for a long wait. If our container was being picked up from Jebel Ali at 7, I calculated it wouldn't reach here until midnight at the earliest. Three hours. Even ordering and eating the super monster half-pounder spicy lamb burger with extra-large fries and onion rings wouldn't keep us occupied for that long.

I was hungry, but our priority was a recce. Leaving Ali contentedly dozing in his uncle's car, Laoban and I walked towards the trailer park. Whilst there was no security on the fuel forecourt, and the few people standing around it paid us no attention, that changed once we had rounded the side of the restaurant. Not only was the trailer park floodlit as brightly as a sports stadium, it was ringed with a four metre high chain-link fence, bright yellow diamond signs every few metres warning it was electrified. A bonded customs facility then, one with a vague resemblance to a prison camp, with a watchtower at each corner, the one nearest us manned with a sentry in a reflective jacket, toting what appeared to be an AK47. Looking in our direction. I wasn't sure that he had seen us, as we'd been careful to stay in the shadows close to the back wall of the building, and the gantry lights were focused on the trailer park. But I couldn't be absolutely sure.

We stood still and watched as a truck arrived and drove up to the perimeter, flashing its lights. A guard appeared from a hut in front of the fence and checked the paperwork that the driver was holding out of his cab window. Satisfied, he talked into a handset and a gate slid open in the fence behind him. The truck drove through and the gates closed behind it. I could still see the taillights through the fence, and figured that the truck must have stopped at a second set of gates, in some sort of holding area.

"We need to get to our truck before it drives in there," said Laoban, stating what was now obvious to both of us. As long as we could be within touching distance of the container, we only needed a minute or two to complete this part of the mission. "Let's go back to the car. I have a plan."

I was glad she did, because I couldn't think of a way of intercepting a truck between the highway and the trailer park. Especially since we didn't know which truck it would be. One container looks just like another. Yes, they have ID numbers, but they're lots of digits, painted high on the back of the container and thus usually only visible as it's driven away, which is, of course, too late. All we could be reasonably sure of was that it would roll up within the next hour or two. Back in the car, we checked our phones. A new message from Maria, relaying information from Toshio that the local carrier had emailed Kulov, confirming their shipment had left the port at 19:37. Not quite three hours ago. We'd made it in that time, but that had been in a fast car with Ali, the crazy driver. At least another hour then, probably two. Helpfully, the agent had included the truck registration number. Except, as Laoban pointed out, all the number plates used Arabic numerals, which we didn't understand. In any case, her plan required Ali's help and cooperation, both eagerly given once he'd been woken up and fed a large burger and a giant strawberry milkshake.

Ali wasn't dressed as an official, but once he put his headdress back on – he'd taken it off when he was driving – he definitely looked smart and official enough. Laoban explained what we wanted him to do. He magicked up a clipboard from somewhere in the car and strode off to a position by the highway turnoff to the gas station and trailer park. Laoban and I sneaked away along the perimeter and on to the highway, avoiding all the bright lights. Around five minutes passed before the first truck arrived. Not the one we wanted, but Ali waved it down anyway, and engaged in conversation with the driver. Laoban had suggested he say he was a university student doing a thesis on road transport and was collecting statistics as part of the project. After a minute, the truck moved on towards the trailer park. Another truck arrived. Again, Ali waved it down. This time, a man walked over to him from the filling station office, obviously asking what he was doing. Ali's explanation must have convinced, as he wandered away, and Ali waved the truck on. Every few minutes, the scenario was repeated.

We didn't have to wait very much longer. The seventh truck was the one we were looking for, indicated by Ali waving it to stop with both his arms rather than just his right. I was confident Ali would spin out his questions as long as he could, but knew I still only had about a minute. Silently, I moved fast in a crouched run, skirting around the back of the truck and staying on the dark side, away from the gas station office and the burger restaurant. It proved easy enough to mount the two satellite trackers we'd bought in Dubai at the back of the lower crane holes, where they weren't visible and shouldn't be accidentally dislocated. What took the longest was opening the tube of superglue and squeezing out enough to be sure they'd hold permanently without sticking them to the gloves I'd picked up in the filling station, or, for that matter, to my fingers or anything else. Not so easy in the pitch dark. No way was I going to rely solely on the magnetic mounts the trackers came with. Deed done, I retreated into the night with just a second to spare. Well done, Ali.

While I'd gone, Laoban had photographed the container ID number and was checking the app on her phone to make sure the trackers were transmitting. All good.

Any doubts we may have had as to whether we'd got the right container were quickly dispelled when we walked back towards the gas station and saw Kulov and EA climbing out of a long silver Lexus saloon that had raced past us under the canopy and swerved in front of the truck, forcing it to stop just before it reached the perimeter fence of the trailer park. We held back, so we weren't spotted. Using the camera zoom on our phones, we could see Kulov talking animatedly to the truck driver and exchanging small sheaves of documents. EA hung back, but then strolled towards Ali, who had stopped another truck, maintaining the pretence. Our new temporary researcher was doing a sterling job, as EA was easily convinced too, and walked back to

Kulov. The two of them got back into the Lexus, drove over to the burger restaurant, parked and went inside, while the truck moved off towards the trailer park. I waved to Ali to come over, and we all got into the Caddy.

After congratulating Ali, I turned to Laoban. "Why do you think Kulov drove all this way out here to check the cargo?" I asked her. "It's his shipment. Surely he could check it out as it was leaving the port. Maybe even inside the port?"

"Obvious," she snapped. "You saw him switching the paperwork. I got a lot of pictures. He needed to do that before the cargo left the country, but after it had gone through the checkpoints along the highway." I said I hadn't seen any checkpoints. "There are turnoffs for trucks. The checkpoints are just canopies. Look like small filling stations. At the speed Ali was driving, I'm not surprised you didn't see them."

"So, what now? Back to Dubai?"

"I think not, we brought nothing with us, and there's no need to stay in the Emirates. Abu Dhabi's nearer. Let's get the first flight out from there."

"As long as Ali stops at the drive-through window so I can get another burger to keep me going," I replied, receiving a withering stare in response.

27 – Tashkent - Beatrix

As a little girl I'd loved reading stories set in the great Silk Road cities, and I was so excited to be following in the steps of Marco Polo. Samarkand, Bokhara… My head was full of mental images of colourful mosques and palaces, and warriors on horseback, galloping past traders in ethnic dress leading their camels and donkey carts taking their wares to market. Such thoughts weren't even dissipated by the modern ordinariness of the suburbs of Tashkent as we drove from the airport towards the city. I kept reminding myself I was in Uzbekistan to work, but I couldn't stop anticipating the exotic, and spent the entire journey squeezing Humph's hand. Now we were in the city proper, driving down wide avenues, a park on one side, a city square on the other. Suzana, the guide who had met us at the airport, turned towards us from her seat in the front.

"We're going to go to the office first," she said. "I know you must be tired from the journey, but we need to complete the formalities for the Turkmen visa this morning." I nodded. "We'll go straight to the hotel afterwards, I promise!"

Almost as an afterthought, she added, "I know you have another reason for coming here, not just for tourism, but my colleagues do not know. Your secretary Maria said we must keep it secret."

"Exactly," I replied.

"But it is important that you act like tourists. Even here in Uzbekistan, the police will become suspicious if you do not 'look the part', as you say, unless you have a special visa. And you came into the country as tourists, correct?" We both nodded. "So, look happy and take lots of pictures." Clearly a very serious instruction. I got the guidebook that I'd bought at the airport out of my handbag and showed her. "Very good," she said. "Carry it with you. Let them see it."

Suzana's office was a unit on a minor shopping street, between a pharmacy and a greengrocer. Just like a retail unit but without any signs, accessible only by keycard, the windows on the frontage obscured with vertical blinds. Four desks, three of them occupied, and a dozen or more filing cabinets. An awful lot of piles of unfiled papers. The antithesis of the paper-free office. Suzana sat us facing her at the fourth desk and cleared space simply by pushing everything in front of her onto the floor to her right.

When it came to Turkmenistan visas, 'formalities' proved a very inadequate word. Bureaucracy gone mad, in my opinion. All I'd expected they'd need would be a short application form and maybe a copy of our passports. Both of those. I'm used to scanning the picture page of my passport to get a visa. This lot wanted photocopies of every single page, including the outside cover. And the form? How many people even know the dates of birth and full names of both your grandfathers and grandmothers? Qualifications, education, with dates and grades, all the way back to high school? It would have been even more invasive if Suzana hadn't told us the rules, although Humph had already half-finished his form and had to start all over again when she said that he should put 'businessman' as occupation. He'd written 'surgeon'. "You'll have to explain so much more if you put that, or even doctor," she told him. "And then they'll probably refuse the visa. Write 'businessman'. They don't ask questions about that."

I asked Suzana if I should put 'business owner' and got a sharp look. "You are a housewife!" she said. Highly inaccurate. Not only sexist, but implied competence in hoovering and cooking. I have zero skills in either.

One of Suzana's colleagues led us into another room to take our pictures. A big gruff guy, wearing a khaki jerkin that gave him a military look, and out to prove his virility through the length of his camera lens. "Look more serious!" he told each of us, in a thick accent. Several times. Lined up there against the wall brought home to me how innocents, and not so innocents, must feel when arrested by the police and forced to have their mug shots taken.

It was more than an hour before we finished all the paperwork and could leave for the hotel and a desperately needed beer or two. Hours and hours of air conditioning had dried me out completely. "Tomorrow, we do all day city sightseeing!" said Suzana cheerfully. That sounded like fun to me, but Humphrey, the responsible one, interjected.

"I think we ought to make a move towards the border," he said. "I'm not sure how soon we need to go over, but best to be nearby and ready."

"Not possible," said Suzana. "Tomorrow morning Fydor, my colleague, will take the visa application to the Embassy. Perhaps there will be a problem. You need to be here in case we have to change the forms or need new pictures."

"You mean in case we didn't look serious enough," I replied, trusting she would catch the sarcasm. She didn't. Just nodded.

"So, tomorrow, you will be tourists here in Tashkent. You will take many photographs on your phones. Then on Thursday morning we will take the train to Samarkand, one night there. Then on to Bokhara. We can wait there for your news. Very pretty city. Lots of sightseeing. Good restaurants. You will like."

Our hotel in Tashkent was comfortable, fairly modern and on a small street in a residential area a couple of kilometres north of the city centre. We left our bags in the room and headed straight for the so-called Panorama Bar, sited on the rooftop. The panorama was of other rooftops and buildings. Perhaps when the hotel was built, it was the tallest around, at eight stories. Now it was dwarfed by its neighbours, a relative midget among giants.

I'd have more than happily gone straight to bed after slaking my thirst, but Humphrey had other ideas. Frustrated when he found out that the map on his phone was all in Cyrillic script, he'd texted Ronald to find the Hunter Health clinic and send the coordinates, so we could go and take a look. It was on the opposite side of the city to our hotel, but according to Google Maps, just a twenty-minute taxi ride. Well, twenty minutes after the point that Humph had convinced a reluctant taxi driver who didn't understand a word of English to follow the directions given by an online map. Or, should

I say, Humph's gesticulations, sitting next to the driver and waving his arms left and right as the phone barked out instructions to him. The cabbie spent the journey shaking his head and muttering unintelligibly. I assumed he was like his kind the world over and was telling us that there were much better routes, but no matter, we got there.

I'd imagined a 'clinic' to be relatively small, but this looked like a major hospital. With illuminated signs in English! An emergency department, three ambulances lined up outside it, double doors marked 'dental clinic' and another pair of doors signed 'admissions'. Plenty of people coming and going, and benches outside that had been commandeered by six elderly male patients sitting in their dressing gowns and slippers, all smoking as if their life depended on it. No time to stop and tell them that the opposite was true, as I followed Humph, already striding through the Admissions door and straight up to the reception desk. Manned by a smiling young man who admitted to speaking English.

"Do you have a list of the surgical procedures you carry out here? Perhaps a brochure?" asked Humphrey. Not what I was expecting him to say.

The receptionist looked quizzical. "We do a lot of surgery here. What is your condition?"

Humphrey laughed. "It's not for me. I'm the medical director of a practice in the UK. We have many patients interested in travelling abroad for treatment."

"But you have a state health service, surely?"

"Yes, but there are long delays, and private hospitals are very expensive."

The receptionist picked up his phone. "It's best you talk with our medical director," he said. "I'll check if he is available."

The medical director had gone home for the day, but his assistant, Svetlana Hematova, was not only available but thrilled to meet an important surgeon from the UK. She proved to be a highly enthusiastic saleswoman. How clever of Humph to think of this approach, I thought. Even if he was rather exaggerating his credentials. I'd been politely greeted as Humphrey's administration manager and thereafter totally ignored. Within a quarter of an hour, they'd discussed a variety of types of plastic surgery and dentistry. Finally, Humphrey asked about hip and knee replacements. "Of course," said Svetlana, reeling off a host of technical terms and abbreviations that meant nothing to me, but which Humph diligently nodded along to for a few minutes before asking the question we really wanted an answer to.

"Are you planning on using robotics?"

Svetlana was excited to tell him they were expecting to install and start using the latest equipment in the next two or three months. "It's a secret," she confided. "I wasn't supposed to say anything, so don't tell anyone, please. We're not making any announcement until the new equipment actually arrives and is installed. But it's really exciting, we will be able to do many more operations. And they will be cheaper!" Said triumphantly.

I think Humph would have gone on chatting, but I thought we ought to leave at that point. Enough research successfully completed for one evening! Svetlana quite understood that we'd left our business cards behind at the hotel and carefully wrote down the fake name and hospital that Humph gave her, insisting that we called her the next day to arrange a tour of the clinic. As we left, I took advantage of her talking to Humph and ignoring me to pick up the paper she'd made notes on.

Getting a taxi back to the hotel was easy. Fortunately, we didn't need Google's help this time, as I'd picked up a card with the name and address from the front desk before we left. Back in the bar, we celebrated our successful evening's covert research with a plate of delicious steamed dumplings, called *manti*, washed down with a bottle of Russian champagne. Then, while Humph went to the bathroom, I picked up the glossy brochure that Svetlana had given us. On the fourth page, I stopped. The smiling face that stared out at me was that of their medical director. I knew I'd seen him before. Talking with Fullerton-Price, thick as thieves, in the conference hall in Dubai.

I thought that our visit to the clinic had been a good initiative, but all that Laoban said when she replied was 'noted'. I didn't expect high praise, but surely she could have done better than a one-word reply? She really is a one. Probably still resenting that we were having a holiday, as she sees it, at the company's expense. Her reply also curtly informed us that the shipping container containing the robot was en route through Saudi and expected to reach Ashgabat in five or six days. Definitely long enough for us to enjoy some sightseeing along our way.

Our tour of Tashkent was a bit of a disappointment in that there weren't any historic buildings. Suzana explained that the old city had been flattened by an earthquake in 1966. So that's why everything was new. But it was still an attractive city with wide avenues, big squares and pretty parks, and I was enjoying myself. As instructed, I took hundreds of photos. I could have spent hours exploring the massive covered market. Humph, on the other hand, didn't get animated until Suzana took us down onto the metro system, travelling a few stops between stations that resembled cathedrals with marble pillars, lit by chandeliers. The station that Humph liked was one with walls covered with pictures commemorating space travel, Uzbek astronauts from Soviet days. He told us he'd been fascinated by space travel as a young boy and still hankered after being an astronaut. Something new to learn in a relationship every day.

Our tour concluded with a late lunch at a big open-air restaurant. There was only one thing on the menu. Plov. Or Osh, if you prefer. Two names for the same dish, a sort of rice pilaf made with meat and white carrots. A lot of carrots. I was fascinated to watch a team of chefs, more accurately described as muscled stirrers, cooking it in a row of enormous cauldrons, the heat from the steam eclipsed only by that from the fiery ovens on the other wall where other men were baking flatbreads, pushing the raw dough in and pulling out the cooked breads with long poles reminiscent of pitchforks.

Plov was tasty but rather greasy, and the lumps of meat in it were very chewy, if not exactly tough. "It might be horse," said Humphrey. Suzana laughed and said that she had ordered mutton for us, but they also had it with horse if we'd prefer? I was very surprised that Humph said yes, he'd have second helpings, but this time with horsemeat. He said he'd eaten it with Ron in Almaty. I don't think he actually preferred it. I'm sure he was just showing off.

28 – In the footsteps of Marco Polo – Humphrey

Tashkent, Uzbekistan

While we waited for the early morning train on the platform at Tashkent station I had to admit to Bea that the name Samarkand conjured up exotic thoughts for me too, ancient tales from the Arabian Nights vaguely remembered from my childhood. That was nothing compared to Bea's level of childish excitement as she paged back and forth through her guidebook. Suzana had told us we were travelling on the bullet train. It certainly looked and felt like the ones in Japan, though it moved too sedately for a bullet. But never mind, it was comfortable and only took two hours to reach Samarkand.

There, we were met by another guide, Bojan. A flamboyant character, to say the least, in his late twenties, with long black hair tied into a ponytail, and wearing a bright orange sweatshirt and royal blue long shorts. He was practically leaping up and down on the spot, telling us how excited he was to meet us. I was amazed by how fluent his English was, compared to Suzana and the few others we'd met in Uzbekistan, until he admitted to having grown up in the States. We spent the hot and sunny day making a whirlwind tour of mosques and palaces and museums and mausoleums, all covered in mosaics of colourful tiles, each more spectacular than the next, to a background of narration of Bojan's unceasing history lessons.

It turned out I'd got the Marco Polo bit right, as the intrepid explorer had indeed visited some thousand years before us, but I was wrong about Kubla Khan, who lived a century before Marco and never ventured far beyond his native Xanadu. However, his Mongolian countryman and successor, a nasty character called Timur, had invaded in the twelfth century and conquered an enormous swathe of territory, not just Samarkand and the rest of modern Uzbekistan but stretching up to Turkey and down to Pakistan, in the process killing or raping the humans and pillaging and destroying any buildings that lay in his path. I might exaggerate, but not much. Assuming Bojan's explanations were correct. It never became clear to me whether all the buildings we saw were spared by Timur or built after his demise. But they were very old.

I have to admit that Samarkand is a magnificent city, and that I was enjoying being a tourist so much that I forgot all about our mission. Until the evening, and the inevitable slew of messages and emails that greeted us then. Bea confessed she'd been sneaky and put both our phones into airplane mode early in the morning. True, our day would have been much less enjoyable, and possibly not enjoyable at all, if it had been interrupted as usual by new information and demands for updates. We agreed we'd blame bad mobile phone reception if, or rather when, Laoban or Maria commented on our prolonged unavailability.

The news was that our container had made it to Kuwait, and should reach Basra by the next evening. At this rate, it would take at least another three days after that to reach the Turkmenistan border with Iran. I briefly wondered how Laoban knew where it was, but she moves in mysterious ways and I'm quite prepared to believe she's psychic. The unstated good news deciphered from the messages was that we could go on being tourists for those few days. Left to our own devices, we secured an outside table at a brightly lit restaurant on the main drag where we could watch real tourists crowd towards the *son et lumiere* performance at the star attraction buildings, while savouring a variety of kebabs barbecued in front of us at the table and, at least as importantly, quaffing ice-cold beer. I was glad we didn't have to fight for a view of the light show, as our hotel had an almost perfect view from the roof.

When we got back to our room, we found a note from Suzana pushed under the door, telling us to be packed and ready to leave at 6am. An unpleasant surprise, since we'd been expecting to leave much later for the

10am train. Surely, she would not have us waiting at the station for four hours?

No, it turned out that we were booked on the 7am train. Suzana claimed there had been a misunderstanding, though frankly I didn't believe her, but apart from missing out on a proper night's sleep, it didn't matter. It would give us more time to be tourists in Bokhara.

I suppose I was half asleep sitting on a bench waiting for the train when Bea nudged me and pointed to a man standing near us on the platform. "Isn't that EA?" she whispered. It certainly looked like him, and dressed for business, not as a tourist, chatting with two other men. I had the feeling I'd seen one of them before, but it took a minute or two to come to me that he could very well be the man I'd met at the top of the mountain in Almaty. Of course, I hadn't seen his face there, but this man not only had the right build, but was wearing the same distinctive bright blue baseball cap.

Bea took a sharp intake of breath. "You see the third man, the one who has just turned towards us? He's the medical director of the clinic. Picture in their brochure. He was at the conference too. I saw him talking with Fullerton-Price."

Bea pulled out her phone and moved me into a position where she could take selfies of us with the group of men in the background. A few minutes later, after we'd boarded the train and found our seats, on the train, she edited the pictures, so that we weren't there, but the group of men was bigger and clearer, and WhatsApped them off to Maria.

I wondered what EA was doing there. Was he, like us, going to Turkmenistan? What was his business in Samarkand? Or Bokhara? And the black marketeer? Were they going to take delivery of the shipment, perhaps? Though officially it should be delivered to the clinic in Tashkent, of course. Lost in these thoughts, I'd hardly noticed when Bea had left her seat, presumably to go to the bathroom, but, being suddenly disturbed by a young man distributing bottles of water, I realised she had been gone for quite a time.

Fortunately, since she had the tickets in her handbag, she returned just as the guard was coming along the carriage. I remarked on how long she'd been away.

"Those men are in the carriage behind ours," she said. "There were empty seats behind them, so I sat and eavesdropped for a while. I couldn't stay any longer as the rightful owners came back. I think they'd been in the dining car."

What a good little spy she is. Makes me so proud. I wish I had her initiative. "What did you find out?" I asked.

"Thank goodness it's not one of those noisy British trains," she smiled. "It was still hard to hear much, though. Your man in the baseball cap didn't say anything. He was sitting in the row in front of the others. But EA was talking with the other man about a new clinic in Bokhara, so that must be where they're going. The medical director. Talking like he owns it, so I assume he does."

I reached into my bag, pulled out the brochure we'd picked up in Tashkent, and turned to page four. "This is him?" I asked Bea. She nodded.

We looked again at the pictures that Bea had snapped earlier. Although his face was partly obscured by the others, it was almost certainly the same man. Bea tapped out a quick update for Maria and Laoban and turned her phone off. I raised my eyebrows. "We're slowing down, so must be arriving. Let's not be disturbed on our sightseeing," she said, grinning.

Suzana, who'd been sitting elsewhere on the train, came to find us, and we alighted to find a rather dour-looking woman waiting on the platform holding a placard 'Suzana Tours'. That wasn't the name of the agency, but there was no doubt she was waiting for us. Not so much greeting us as acknowledging our arrival. Katerina was in her forties, and dressed like she'd acquired her wardrobe from a charity shop after everyone else had taken their pick. She didn't smile. All morning.

Suzana wasn't joining the tour. "I have business in the town," she told us. "I will come to your hotel when your visit finishes." We looked around, but there was no sign of the three men we were interested in. Something we'd have to worry about later.

So, we were left with Katerina. "You are too early for check-in at the hotel," she announced. "First, we will visit the Ark." I had visions of Noah and a parade of animals, but far from being a boat, the Ark proved to be a sort of castle. A fortified hill surrounded by a high wall. Whether they'd built the wall first and filled it in to make a hill, or started with the hill and covered it with granite blocks wasn't explained, though I worked out it was the latter. We climbed the steep ramp to the portcullis door and entered a set of courtyards of different sizes, none of them particularly interesting, stopping now and then for Katerina to reel off snippets of history lesson. Like prerecorded soundbites, delivered in a bored monotone. Her accent meant that much of what she said was incomprehensible, but given her attitude, neither of us was motivated to ask questions. The best part was the view over the city, all Islamic architecture with fine archways and blue-tiled onion dome roofs.

Afterwards, down in the city, we walked, mostly in silence, through the pedestrianised streets, visiting ancient buildings, former mosques and madrassars that had almost all been turned into souvenir arcades. Every few minutes Katerina would stop and recite some brief explanation that she had memorised and repeated countless times. Someone who could turn a fascinating historic city into a boring one. Bea tried to engage her in chit-chat. What was life like in Uzbekistan? Did she have children? Things like that. She told me that "it was like talking to a brick wall." I thought it rather unusual for a tourist guide. Normally they'll say anything to impress hoping to get a big tip. Even at the big tower, Minaret Kalon, she couldn't impress. A good guide would have made a meal out of the stories and myths over the centuries of people being deliberately or accidentally thrown to their deaths from the top, rather than a cursory "probably not true" and quick progression to the next sight. I was enjoying the history and architecture, but couldn't wait to get rid of our guide. Bea seemed to mind her less, being preoccupied with taking countless pictures.

Finally, at 2pm, we reached the hotel, another conversion of a historic madrassar, considerably more tasteful than the souvenir malls we'd seen earlier. I wondered if there were any left performing their original function of educating youths in the mysteries of the Koran. Katerina offered to wait while we unpacked and show us places to have lunch, but she was obviously more than happy when I said that I'd seen restaurants nearby and I was sure we would manage on our own. She hovered for a moment, hoping for a tip, and realising one would not be forthcoming, turned and left without so much as a goodbye.

The bedroom was beautiful, with a high arched window that had been fitted with stained glass, heavy carved wooden doors, prehistoric but clean and functional bathroom fittings and, unlike in Samarkand where the beds were like rocks, a comfy king size bed with a foam mattress. There was even a kettle to make tea. What there wasn't was wifi or a mobile phone signal, no doubt because of the heavy stone walls. We'd just have to go to the lobby to communicate with the boss.

Or, in the first instance, to a restaurant. With such an early start, and no breakfast other than a stale croissant bought from a place on the station, we were hungry. Our usual lunchtime choice of salad wouldn't hack it. We ordered osh, hoping it would be at least as good as we'd enjoyed the day before. It wasn't. Obviously cooked hours or days earlier and reheated in the microwave. Well, it filled a hole. Bea turned our phones back on. Just one message. Ah, the six-hour time difference. Still only nine in the morning back in Europe. Laoban must be somewhere else, or we'd have received more. The message was interesting, though. From Toshio, the internet guru we had neither met, nor knew where he was based. He had run the pictures Bea had sent from the train through some mysterious Artificial Intelligence software he had access to and got a lead on our baseball cap man. No name for him, but, if he was the right man, and he certainly looked the same, there he was, standing next to a known Russian mafia-style boss in another picture taken a few years earlier and stored on an Interpol database. Toshio's information was that the godfather character was now languishing in some gulag in Siberia. The sidekick, or whatever he was, was here in Bokhara.

After a well-earned siesta, we got directions from the very helpful receptionist to the nearest pharmacy and headed off in search of antacid tablets. Whilst delicious, osh is very greasy and indigestible. You have been warned. The short walk took us away from the historic centre, which is entirely pedestrianised, into the modern commercial area surrounding it. Leaving the chemists, I spotted our quarry, the three crooked men, getting out of a minibus a little further down the road. A lucky coincidence!

It was a wide and busy street, and it was easy to follow them until they took a turning onto a narrower side road. From the corner, we could see nondescript buildings for the first fifty metres, perhaps the backs of offices as there were no doorways, and after that what looked like a building site on one side of the road and a park on the other. The three men were walking slowly, talking to each other, and there was no-one else around, so we would have definitely attracted their attention had we followed. But we could linger on the corner discreetly enough, from where Bea could zoom in and take close-up pictures with her camera phone. Soon we got the answer we needed. The men paused for a while in front of the building site, then the medical director unlocked a padlock, opening a panel in the fence, and all three disappeared inside.

"I'm going to take a look," said Bea. "Stay here. They don't know me, but one of them might recognise you. If anyone asks, I'm a lost tourist." She pulled her guidebook out of her handbag, opened it at a map page for Bokhara, and wandered off down the road. She'd definitely have convinced me, making a show of looking at the building site, then at her map, then back again, then shaking her head and returning towards me.

"It's got a sign on it written in Uzbek or Russian or whatever language it is," she said. "I took photos. I'm texting them to Ronald to translate for us."

He didn't take long to respond. "All it says is 'Site of a new clinic, under construction, due to open early next year'."

29 – Using my initiative – Maria

London, England

With new locks fitted, I made my way back to the airport, taking a slightly longer route to avoid walking past Rakesh's shop. I didn't want to give him my spare key. Yet. I wasn't catching a plane today, but taking the little DLR train, well more like a tram than a train, to meet Sonia at Canary Wharf. The restaurant was at one end of a rather pretty aerial park that had been built on top of the new underground station. It was almost empty when I arrived at four-thirty. Still half an hour before the end of the office day, and probably longer than that before Sonia arrived. For the moment, it was big, dark and quiet, but looked set to become very noisy later, as a couple of 'roadies' were setting up the stage for some band that would be performing later. Given the size of the speakers they were hauling into place, we wouldn't be able to hear a thing. A passing waiter told me the show wouldn't start until eight, which gave us a few hours, but I chose a table as far away as possible anyway. I ordered a bottle of Pinot Grigio, a large bottle of sparking water, and a bag of nuts. When they were brought, I poured a thimbleful of wine into one glass for appearance's sake, diluted it and set about drinking the rest of the bottle of water and devouring the nuts. Lining my stomach for the alcohol to follow.

I wasn't left on my own for long. Sonia arrived earlier than I'd expected, well before five. Once she'd recognised me ("You look amazing! I'd never have recognised you! Your new hairdo really suits you!") she was super-enthusiastic and our inconsequential gossip consumed the time it took to see off the whole bottle of wine. We were so engrossed that it wasn't until I was trying to attract the attention of a server that I realised that the entire restaurant was now packed, with many people standing and drinking in the middle bar area beyond us.

Sonia was beyond excited I was planning on staying in London for a while and thrilled that I'd found a flat close to hers. If you call a twenty-minute bus ride or two stops on the DLR close. I suppose it is, in London terms. I briefly wondered what Laoban would think about me having a close girlfriend in London, but the wine helped ease any concern I had that cover would be risked. Well, never mind what she might think. I was happy. Sonia and I were getting on really well, and she'd just told me she was a member of a car club and she'd take me to Ikea on Saturday to get towels and a duvet and all the other stuff I needed to settle in to the flat. I hadn't even thought about any of that.

"Anyway, I've got something I've been waiting to tell you," she said. "I'm so glad you're here. I didn't want to call you about it because I know what you're doing is super confidential."

"That depends on what we're talking about," I replied.

"This is definitely a secret." Her voice had gone down to a loud stage whisper. I was beginning to wish we were in a quieter bar, but couldn't imagine anyone being able to hear what we were saying, even if they had a microphone hidden under the table. "One of the underwriters I work for, he's a lovely man, gets a lot of the business you're interested in from an insurance broker here in the City. You know how Lloyds works, don't you?"

"I've read up a bit, but please tell me in simple language."

"OK, well, ordinary people like you and me and ordinary businesses can't go straight to Lloyds to get insurance. Lloyds is like a huge club of individual underwriters. We call them 'names'. Some of them take on risks on their own, but for bigger things, they club together in what they call a syndicate. You and I, when we want to insure our apartments or our cars…"

"Or a shipping container full of medical robots?" interjected Maria

"Yes, exactly, so we go to insurance brokers. Basically, they are middlemen. We go to a broker, tell them what risk we want to insure. For ordinary stuff like cars and houses, there are big insurance companies. You don't need a broker. But if it's something special, like your shipping container, you go to a broker. Then they go and talk to some different Names or syndicates at Lloyds and, when they find one or more who will take on the risk, they negotiate the premium and write a policy. And add on their own fee, of course."

"Hmm. I think I get it. I'll have to read it up again in the morning when the effect of this wine wears off." They both laughed.

Sonia continued. "Anyway, my friendly underwriter's convinced that they're taking on dodgy business from one particular broker that they know will lead to claims, not to mention charging premiums that are way too low. Which means that he and the others in his syndicate lose money on every claim."

"Why did he tell you that?"

"Well, I think it's because one day I asked him if there were any unusual big claims for shipments to Central Asia." Sonia obviously saw the way I was looking, as she continued "really, don't worry, I was very discreet. I've worked for him for a few years and he's very friendly. I made sure to pick a time when there was nobody else in the office."

"So, you told him about us and what we are doing, I suppose."

"Well, I suppose I dropped a hint. I was very vague. Said I didn't really know anything about it. Well, I don't, do I?"

"You've been doing pretty well at putting two and two together," I replied. "I hope you told him to keep it to himself and not tell anyone."

"Oh yes, of course, of course." Sonia was blushing now. "Anyway, do you want to know the rest?" I nodded. "Well, he's not allowed to hire you direct. Your company, that is. Everything has to go through official channels. Except he says that he's told the right people and they've done nothing about it. So, he'd like your help. But unofficially. If you do find out what's happening, he says he will find a way of paying you. A success fee. Maybe you'll have to take out an insurance policy and claim on it!" Sonia found this idea hilarious. I thought Laoban would quite like it. And this was just another thread of a project we were already working on. We were hired by the American manufacturer, but if we could get two clients who didn't know each other to pay us for doing the same job, surely that was good business?

"This is definitely interesting," I said. "Does your man have a suspect? Any ideas on how we could get into this brokerage?"

"There are two partners in the brokerage. He doesn't know if it's just one of them or if they're both in on it." Then, after a pause. "It could all be quite legit, I suppose. They might just be incompetent, not follow the formulas on how to set premiums, things like that."

"Your man doesn't believe that, though, does he?" I asked.

"No. It's either one of them acting alone or both working together. I do have an idea how to get you in there, if you like?"

"Tell me."

"Well, now you're here for a few weeks, right?" I nodded. "And you can type and do filing and office stuff?" I smiled and nodded again. "Well, I know they're always looking for temp staff. I don't think they have any permanent positions except the two guys. The partners. The temps that they get always leave after a few days, so there's bound to be a vacancy any day now."

"How do you know this?" I asked.

"I'm friends with one of the girls at the agency they use," she replied. "It's the same one as we use sometimes. They're in the building next door, so we often run into each other in the coffee shop. Stop for a bit of a chat. You know how it is. If you come into the City tomorrow, I can introduce you?"

Goodness. Talk about friends with benefits. OK, maybe not in the usual sense. But Sonia was proving more than helpful. Not only bringing a business opportunity, but providing the means to achieve it. Had it been anyone else, I'd have been suspicious. Instead, I ordered a bucket of buffalo wings and a plate of loaded potato skins, resolved that in future when we were out together we would go somewhere with healthier and more diet-conscious bar snacks, and made a point of paying for everything to show my thanks. Not to mention ordering another bottle of wine. I was counting the glasses. Sonia was drinking two for every one of mine. Excellent, that was the plan.

The following morning, a Friday, I wore the smartest of the three outfits I'd brought with me from Rotterdam and, just before 11am, took up position at a corner table in the coffee shop next to Sonia's office building. I'd already clocked the employment agency a few doors down as I walked past. I'd been told that a decade or two before, there had been a dozen or more on every city street. Now, with most hiring done online, physical agencies were a rarity. This was obviously an upmarket one, as they had no job ads in the window, just an exhortation to phone for a 'personal' appointment. I bought a *ristretto,* with an extra shot of caffeine, in case I wasn't as sober as I felt.

I didn't have to wait more than a couple of minutes for Sonia, and only a few minutes more before Francesca from the agency joined us. Introductions and obligatory small talk done, Sonia came to the point.

"I was telling Maria about the temp job at that insurance company you told me about," she said. "Is it still available? Maria's not sure how long she will be in London and was asking me if I knew of any short-term jobs." Sounded very convincing to me.

Francesca looked doubtful. "Oh, the job's still going. There's always a vacancy there, even though the hourly pay is twenty per cent higher than our normal rate. I'm pretty sure Piers would like the look of you."

The subtext was pretty obvious. "So that's why no-one stays there?" She nodded. "That's OK," I said. "I've worked with more than a few of those sorts of men. I know how to handle myself. But thanks for the warning."

"Good. You can start on Monday if you want. Remember, you can walk out any time." Then, as if she had forgotten something, "You're not British, though, are you?"

"No, I'm Latvian. But I registered as a resident before Brexit kicked in, and I've got an NI number." Things I supposed I should be thanking Smith for. "And a UK bank account."

"You won't need them for this job. I'm afraid it's rather unofficial. Off the books. Unusual for these days. Cash in hand."

"Really? Why's it like that?" I asked.

"Plausible deniability. Nobody stays for more than a few days. If anybody ever asks Piers questions, he just says that he had this girl that he met, can't remember her name, helped him out for a day or two."

Well, I'd said I could look after myself. It seemed like this job would give me the opportunity to prove it. I nodded to signify that I understood and would go along with that.

Francesca smiled. "Perfect," she said. "What references can I give Piers?"

I grimaced. With my previous employer languishing in an Angolan jail, obtaining any written or phone reference would only be possible with the involvement of Laoban. Anyway, I doubted Piers would insist, given what Francesca had said. "How about 32 double D?" Francesca and Sonia collapsed in a fit of giggles.

The days were growing shorter and the weather was miserable in London, but the weekend proved to be fun, for me at least. Nothing significant seemed to be happening with the project. Humphrey and Beatrix were enjoying their sort-of-holiday in Uzbekistan. Ron was still in Cyprus, supposedly doing research, which probably meant checking out all the restaurants. Laoban and Robert the Bastard might still be in Dubai, but could be anywhere. They were messaging every day, but hadn't told me their location. Presumably, I didn't need to know. I'd written to Laoban explaining about the underwriter's concerns and my getting a job at the brokers, so, for once, rather than complaining that my moving to London was costing the company money and pestering me for an explanation, she actually congratulated me on my initiative. She should thank Sonia, really. Meanwhile, Sonia and I had the sort of girly weekend I'd heard so much talk about but never experienced for myself. Saturday shopping and sorting out the flat. Sunday joining Sonia's dance club. More than a few bottles of Pinot Grigio along the way, but staying sober enough to stop Sonia from posting pictures of us together on Instagram.

Come Monday morning, I donned the mini-skirted business suit and tight-fitting blouse I'd bought on the Saturday, spent ten minutes more than my usual two on makeup, and joined the commuters on the tube going to work. As I'd predicted, Piers was what the English call 'old school'. Late fifties, not fat but indisputably well-fed, too thick a thatch of hair to be entirely real, reminiscent of a certain American president but black instead of ginger, and a lascivious look in his eyes. He actually whistled when I walked through the door. Other girls would have screamed harassment and walked straight out again. I just saw it as testimony to my appearance – and my opportunity to manipulate. I was on a mission to unearth fraud, so had to get as close to the action as possible. I'd dressed for the part. Needs must.

30 – Mezethakia – Ronald

Larnaca, Cyprus

I've never really got into Greek food before. I don't think there were any Greek restaurants in Slough when I was living there, at least not any that did home delivery, or I'm sure I would have tried it. More recently, I remember being told it was much the same as Turkish food, and I have eaten in an awful lot of Turkish restaurants. However, within a day of arriving in Larnaca, I was disabused of any notion of similarity by the owner of a taverna where I went for lunch. I vaguely knew there were issues between the two nationalities, so, after the other diners had left, I decided I'd ask him what the differences were. I think the only reason he didn't hit me was because I was an old idiotic English teacher who couldn't be expected to know better. I didn't risk going back. Largely because his moussaka, which he told me was his 'signature dish', was swimming in oil and devoid of seasoning.

Of course, I hadn't been left in Larnaca to test out the restaurants, and Laoban's jibes about my weight still stung. Before she departed with Robert to take the plane back to Dubai, we'd agreed that it would be best for me to stay put for a few days, at least until the boss decided where I could best help the project, and she'd reminded me again to control my eating urges. Returning to Lanzarote would be a long journey, and in the opposite direction to where all the action was. Cyprus was another nice island with long warm sunny days. I found a guest house, sorry 'boutique hotel', at a room rate that I didn't think Laoban would complain about, in a street a few hundred metres from the beach and the city centre. Nice room, with an actual table and chair I could work at, very quiet and with good wifi. Milos, the owner-receptionist-general factotum, made me welcome, and was more than happy to map out all the best tavernas in town for me.

However, there was covert research that needed to be done. I had already started digging deeper into Kulov and his company. I wanted to see if I could find the names and details of any of his clients, where they were, what their business was, what goods he shipped for them. I found a Russian-language reviews website, something like Trustpilot, but with a lot more swearing. Either they had no moderator or liked the posts to be provocative. There were only four reviews for Silk Road Import Export, the company name under which Kulov was exhibiting in Dubai, but many more for his 'associate' companies in Kyrgystan and Kazakhstan, none awarding five stars, but none overtly negative either. Average rating 3.6. However, his Azerbaijani company not only had more than a hundred reviews, but most were negative, giving one or two stars. Most comments were brief, just a few words like 'will never use this company again' without explaining why. Two reviews went into detail, however. Each complaining that their shipments had been lost en route. Both had received something, but not what they had ordered. One was written by a private aircraft operator that had ordered a refurbished jet engine from a workshop in Spain. They'd received a container full of Chinese Christmas decorations instead. The other complainant was expecting parts for machinery for his food processing factory, but had a lifetime's worth of COVID test kits delivered instead. In both cases, Kulov, or his company, had denied responsibility, simply telling them that the paperwork was correctly processed and it must be the fault of the shipper. They couldn't be expected to look inside every container they transported.

Deciding this discovery represented a good day's work and thinking it would be a good idea to stretch my legs, I walked a couple of kilometres to the other side of town to Zak's taverna. My host at the hotel had called Zak to tell him I was coming, and must have impressed on him I was both a gourmet and an important customer, as I was greeted like a star restaurant critic. The establishment itself was quite humble. Not exactly a seafront shack, but not much more impressive, with just a few tables with colourful tablecloths. I was the only customer. Either nobody else had been told how good the food was here, or Milos had been lying to me.

He hadn't. The cold meze was remarkable, including freshly prepared tzatziki with a real zing of garlic and some secret herb, and taramosalata prepared with real smoked cod roe. I know, because Zak brought the ingredients to the table to show me. While I was demolishing a basket of pitta with the dips, a grizzled fisherman arrived carrying his basket of wares, from which I selected a beautiful dorada for Zak to grill. I wasn't sure I would ever really get to like retsina, but when no other wine is available and it's chilled close to freezing, it goes down very well. So well, in fact, that Zak thought it essential to drive me back to the hotel. Not because I was drunk, of course, really so he could remind me all the way to post reviews online. Being sure to mention his secret herbs and spices.

The following morning, I received an update from Humphrey and Beatrix, telling me about their visit to the clinic in Tashkent. More for me to research. Hunter Health claimed to be world leading, but possibly only in curing ingrown toenails or something else relatively minor, as their website, while heavy on superlatives, was scant on detail. 'Continuously expanding', 'wide range of treatment options', stuff like that. Nothing specific. Their medical director, Dr Ivan Zelkopf, was billed as being a graduate of Harvard Medical School with surgical skills 'recognised worldwide'. Harvard helpfully publishes a database of graduate names online, but despite trying a dozen different spellings, I couldn't find him. Unless he graduated before their records started in 1960. I worked out that would make him at least ninety years old. His picture suggested he was in his forties or fifties. I couldn't find any references to him on the web at all, other than for the clinic in Tashkent. Mystery man? Imposter? But his clinic was legitimate and well established, and the client site I'd found the day before was full of flattering five-star reviews. Fifty or more of them. If they were to be believed, that clinic worked miracles. Making the paralytic walk again. Healing the blind. Nobody claiming to have been raised from the dead, but it wouldn't have surprised me. My Russian is poor, but I spotted a lot of repeated phrase, as if all the reviews had been written by the same person. Probably anyone could post a review? I experimented. Yes, they could. Which only meant that

Kulov hadn't yet realised that he, too, could flood that site with fake five-star reviews for his businesses.

Real or fake, one new thing I learned from the reviews was that clinics sell their services to foreigners. Medical tourism. Faster service, cheaper prices. Especially plastic surgery and dental work, but once I dug deeper, I found some that even offered open heart surgery. I came across countless hospitals and clinics offering private medical services in Eastern Europe and Thailand, but none in Uzbekistan except Hunter Health. Again, they didn't specify what services they offered, just an open invitation to enquire for more details.

Personally, I felt hale and hearty, and my teeth were fine when I went for a checkup a month or two before. I called Josefina for a chat, to find out how things were in Lanzarote and for her advice. Everything was running smoothly, but she said she was missing me, which was nice. I asked her whether I should have plastic surgery. "Your head is too big, but I don't think any surgeon can do anything about that," was her riposte.

It was while I was contemplating lunch that it came to me. Of course! Humphrey had told the black marketeers he was interested in robotic surgery. I went back to the clinic website and filled in their enquiry form. Gave myself a false name, set up a new email address, and tapped out a message. "I need a knee replacement. Can you help?" Then, getting back to my previous thought process, left my room in pursuit of a light and healthy lunch. Souvlaki – just one skewer - and salad. No retsina, though. I needed to keep a clear head for more research in the afternoon.

By the time I was back in front of my computer, the clinic had replied, to say that of course, knee replacements were a speciality of theirs. Dr Michaela Romanovich was an acclaimed orthopaedic surgeon and would perform the operation herself. If my condition was not so acute that I could wait a few weeks, they were soon installing the latest state-of-the-art robotic tools that improved happy outcomes from 95% to 99%. All for eight thousand euros per knee. Claimed to be half the price of having it done in Western Europe. So much sales spiel, I was surprised they weren't offering a discount to do both knees at once.

All this reinforced the theory that Hunter Health was implicated in the scam. Unlike the medical director, Dr Romanovich's qualifications and experience were easy to find online. Even on LinkedIn. Nice photo. If I needed a knee operation, I'd like it to be done by someone so attractive. She had qualified in St. Petersburg in 2001, so along with other dates on her profile, I estimated her being in her mid-forties. Her work experience had her practicing in several hospitals across Uzbekistan and Kazakhstan. No mention of the Hunter Health clinic, though. Except that the address of her private consulting rooms in Tashkent happened to be the same as that of the clinic.

I wrote to Laoban to update her, and without waiting for her reply, wrote back to the clinic, expressing definite interest and stating my intent to visit Tashkent for an initial consultation. A near instant response to say that Dr Romanovich's next appointments were in two weeks' time. Would 3pm on the 14th suit, or would I prefer 4pm? The meeting could be by Zoom if it was inconvenient for me to travel to Tashkent. I booked the later time and said I would come in person, even though, then, I had no expectation of attending.

Not having anything else urgent to research, I decided to dedicate the rest of the afternoon to improving my Russian. No point in learning Uzbek or Kazakh, it seemed. As far as I could tell, the only people who used them for everyday communication were goat and camel herders on the steppes. Russian was the *lingua franca* across all Central Asia. Logical really, as all the countries were once part of the Soviet Union. I found a wonderful online language course employing artificial intelligence to critique a student's speech. All very clever. You listen to a phrase read by a native speaker, then repeat it aloud, then the computer speaks to you in English telling you what you got wrong, then you repeat the process until the computer voice says it understands you well. Wonderful thing, AI. A system with infinite patience, so better than any human language teacher. I should know. I was one for over thirty years. The system only works with students who actually want to learn, though. I can't imagine the brats in 4B using it. Unless it taught them indecent words.

Apart from speaking Russian to a computer, I also improved my education in Greek cuisine. I like the mezethakia concept very much, various small plates of whatever is going in the kitchen. Though some of the things I was served had probably been lying around for quite a few days. Keftedes, dolmades, you name it. My favourite was spanakopita, like spinach-stuffed samosas. Delicious, and a wonderful name that I wanted to go on repeating. Spanakopita.

The following afternoon brought an email from Beatrix telling me about the building site she and Humphrey had come across in Bokhara. I was embarrassed, thinking that I should have researched other clinics, particularly new ones, in Uzbekistan. I'd seen that Hunter Health claimed to be expanding, but had assumed that meant doing more things or making the building bigger, not that they were opening new branches. Google Earth showed the Bokhara site as a car park, but the date of the photo was two years previously, so presumably predated the construction. My internet search brought up ten other private clinics or hospitals in the country, though not one in Bokhara. Eventually, I struck lucky with the news pages of the city council's website. Just a short press release, dated four months previously, saying the mayor welcomed a 'massive private investment' to develop a new clinic in Bokhara that would offer all sorts of procedures currently only available in the capital, Tashkent. It didn't say who was putting up the money, nor did it mention Hunter Health, just said that it was expected to open in less than a year. I wondered how it fitted into the picture. However, one thing was certain. If EA was involved, something underhand must be going on.

31 – Bureaucracy bordering on the insane – Beatrix

Bokhara, Uzbekistan

There was no hurry to get out of bed. All we had planned was a lazy day in Bokhara. More sightseeing, stop and look at some of the souvenir stalls, maybe buy Humph one of those furry hats he likes the look of, even though I don't know when he'd wear it where we live now. Thus, knowing that the hotel served breakfast until eleven, we didn't leave our room until after ten-thirty. We hadn't expected Suzana to be waiting for us in the lobby.

"Where are your bags? We need to leave. Now," she said. Then, seeing incomprehension on our faces, "Did you not see the messages from your boss this morning?"

I looked at Humphrey, who looked sheepish. "No, sorry," he said. "We weren't expecting any news, so I turned off the phones to stop them beeping in the night. I forgot to turn them back on this morning." Heavens above. I love him dearly, but he needs to get over these romantic tendencies when we're working. Which reminds me to have words. I'd like it if he left it up to me when I turned my own phone on and off.

There were plenty of messages, one bringing important news. The container had been moving more quickly than previously expected, and was now expected to be brought across the border from Iran into Turkmenistan in two days. We needed to be in Ashgabat by then, and that meant leaving today. No furry hat then. We rushed back to our room to pack, Humphrey moaning about missing breakfast. Honestly, he's as bad as Ron sometimes.

By the time we got back to the lobby, Suzana was clutching a paper bag she'd filled with pastries from the buffet. I thought it was just that she was more sympathetic to Humph's breakfast demands than I was, but that wasn't it. "It is important you both eat something before you get to the frontier," she said. "There will be no time for lunch, and it is a long time until dinner. Also, it will help you with the stress." Stress? I wondered what she was signalling.

A car was waiting outside, and the drive to the frontier only took about half an hour, which flew by, filled with Suzana's instructions, repeated several times. "Don't think that Turkmenistan is like Uzbekistan or most other countries you've been to before. You can't just wave your passport at the officer and walk straight in," she said. I decided not to interrupt and say that it wasn't quite that simple anywhere. "You need visas. You have to pay cash dollars. I can't tell you how much, it changes all the time. Nobody knows how they work it out. Many officers will stop you many times. All will look at your passport and ask you questions. After you leave the Uzbek border post on this side, you cannot change your mind and come back. You must complete the tour itinerary. Understood?"

We nodded meekly. Humph whispered to me, "she sounds just like one of the sergeants in the air force I used to get briefings from."

She reached into her bag and presented each of us with a piece of paper. "Invitation letters!"

The documents looked like badly altered photocopies of a badly designed form. The only English words were 'Letter of Invitation'. Suzana insisted the 'letters' were all we needed. "They will exchange them for visas at the border post. Remember, each visa will only be valid for the itinerary of the tour and for five days. If you need to change anything for any reason, your guide will have to get permission from the ministry. Which will be difficult." And, after a pause, "or impossible."

Suzana was definitely doing her best to make our going to Turkmenistan sound as unappealing as possible.

"Your mobile phones will not work. You will find it almost impossible to buy a local SIM, but there is no point trying, as you would only be able to call local numbers. The hotels have wifi, but communication apps like WhatsApp and Telegram are forbidden, and you cannot access social media or any foreign news media. You should be able to send and receive emails, but they will be censored in both directions, so be very careful about what you write, and expect delays. Your colleague Maria tells me you have a code system, but messages mustn't look coded, so no odd words, strings of numbers or so on. But you won't know until you try. If the authorities do not believe you are tourists, they will say you are spies and put you in prison or deport you. Like Russia, but worse. So be very careful."

"It's really that restricted?" Humph asked. "It sounds completely closed off."

"They say North Korea is worse," said Suzana. "Oh, and remember also that your guide will be with you all the time. Twenty-four seven." Seeing my face, adding, "obviously not in your bedroom, but all the rest of the time. I don't know what he or she will be like, but be very careful what you say or how friendly you get. All the guides are state agents. Trust no one."

"Don't you know who our guide is?" I asked.

"No. The agency we work with doesn't tell us. Just that someone will be waiting in the customs area on the other side of the border, holding a card with your names. Don't look so worried. We send many tourists like this, and they all come back happy. You will be fine. Now, go," she said, opening the side door of the minibus and pointing towards the border post about two hundred metres further down the road. A metal gantry over the road, surmounted by a large crest on a roundel in the middle. High fences on both sides of the road. Soldiers standing to attention at twenty metre intervals. Grey clouds gathering on the horizon. Not exactly forbidding, but far from welcoming. Like something you'd see in films set during the Cold War. Not surprising, I supposed, since the border divided two former Soviet states. Humph and I strolled uncertainly along a two-metre-wide path, tugging our cases behind us. It was all eerily quiet; just the soldiers and us. Though, as we neared the border post, a truck slowly and noisily drove towards us along the road on our left, pulling a trailer with a huge and anonymous container into Uzbekistan. One day soon, I thought, another one like that will arrive, bringing our target cargo. Or not.

Suddenly, we had company. Two women in a hurry, running up from behind us and literally pushing us out of the way just as we reached the Uzbekistan exit counter. Both in their fifties or sixties, very short and dumpy, wearing what I suppose is ethnic dress, clutching voluminous bags with both hands.

"Turkmen grannies," the friendly officer behind the window told us in good English, after they had gone. "They travel back and forth every day, taking things they buy here to sell in their country. Very rude. Always pushing and shoving. You have visas?" We showed him the papers Suzana had given us and he nodded, gave me them back and stamped our passports. A three-minute walk to the Uzbek exit gate, where two more soldiers examined our passports. Every page scrutinised, every entry and exit stamp studied. Always the question "why are you going?" We still hadn't left Uzbekistan. A more-jovial-than-most soldier, perhaps some sort of commander since he looked slightly older than the others, pushed open the metal gate that barred our way. "Gate of No Return," he announced, chuckling.

I confess I hesitated. I turned to Humph. Checking first that the guards weren't listening, I said, "Tell me again why we have to go there."

"Because we're on holiday," he said. "It's all part of our grand Silk Road tour."

"Don't be so stupid," I hissed.

"Because the boss believes this is where the cargos or the paperwork or both get switched and she wants us to see what we can find out about that and take lots of photos. And, if we're really lucky, catch them red-handed." I didn't react, so he carried on. "Come on, you know this needs to be done. We get to see the sights as well. Very few tourists make it here, so think of it as a privilege. The boss is right. You and I are the only ones in the team who can carry off being a happily married couple on holiday."

He was correct, of course, but I still didn't move.

"What are you afraid of?" he asked. "The bureaucracy? It can't be that bad. Come on!"

He was wrong. The bureaucracy was even worse than Suzana had said or I could have imagined. Squeezed onto an ancient bus shared with what had now grown to a dozen or more Turkmen grannies and their bags, we were driven across no-man's-land to an isolated guard post where we were given a cursory medical exam, then by another bus to an immigration hall, not very large but bursting to the seams. A lot of grannies and a handful of bemused tourists like us, all fighting to get their turn at various official windows. As

Suzana had said, facing countless officials all dressed in military uniform, all asking us the same questions, all paging through our passports, stopping randomly at stamps they hadn't seen before. Many of them inventing some meaningless interrogation.

"Why does this stamp say Zimbabwe?"

"Because we went to Zimbabwe."

"Where is Zimbabwe?"

"It's a country in Africa."

"Why did you go there?"

"For a holiday." By now, frustrated, the temptation was to say that our real reason for going there was to cross into Botswana on a spying mission, but stopped myself. That would have been true, but not a good idea to mention it.

"Why are you here now?"

"For a holiday."

"Why here and not Zimbabwe?"

Seriously? Even without the stupid questions, the bureaucracy took ages and ages. Sometimes, when our passports disappeared behind a window for what seemed like hours, it felt like we were trapped in a purgatory we might never be allowed to leave. The whole story is so long and tedious that, when I told some of our residents in Lanzarote about it a few weeks later, I literally sent them all to sleep. Anyway, after what felt like a lifetime but was actually just over two hours, the last uniformed official returned our passports saying, "you are now in Turkmenistan, enjoy your vacation." Not exactly welcoming, but at least polite.

Sometime during our battle with the bureaucrats, and when we'd virtually given up hope of one ever appearing, our guide had turned up, claiming to have been waiting outside. "My name is Purli," he announced. Funny name, easy to remember, though. Definitely had white teeth. In his early thirties, slim and quite tall, wearing a brown and dark green checked suit, clearly showing its age as it was made in some sort of fabric that had stretched and faded in all the wrong places.

"You got here very quick today!" said Purli.

I looked at my watch. "It didn't feel quick to me. It's been at least two hours since we left Uzbekistan."

"Usually it is more. When it's busy, four or five hours." Easy to believe that. "We must walk this way," he said, "our car is the white one at the far end," pointing down the road. I suddenly wished I'd not been so worn down by the officialdom and stayed more alert, as, less than fifty metres ahead, a big, fierce-looking man was holding a car door open for a curly-haired man to get in. Just as we reached it, the car was driven away. I nudged Humphrey. "EA," I said. "He must have been in the immigration hall while we were there."

"Let's hope he didn't see us, then," said Humph, without much confidence. Against a background of a sea of Turkmen grannies, anyone else is conspicuous. Mind you, we hadn't noticed him.

32 – From the White City to the Flaming Pit – Purli

I'm going to be completely honest. Being a tour guide in Turkmenistan gets very boring. There aren't a huge number of sights here, nothing like as many as in other countries. At least that's what my guests tell me, and about half of the ones we do have are off limits to foreigners. Locals aren't very welcome either. So life is a lot of back and forth between two frontier posts to Uzbekistan, one leading to Khiva, the other to Bokhara, our capital, Ashgabat and the flaming gas pit in the desert – the only sight in our country most foreigners ever read about. I only manage to be with my family one or two nights a week, as I have to stay wherever my guests are staying. But I can't complain, even if I was allowed to. The job pays well enough; it gives me a little sideline in black market money exchange, and I get to meet foreigners who tell me stories of faraway places that maybe, just maybe, I will be able to go and visit one day. If the situation here changes. Which nobody thinks will ever happen.

For the tour I'm writing about, I had two guests, a charming couple in their forties. They told me they were British, but they had Irish passports. Since they were polite and I thought we might get on, I decided against reporting that straightaway. They looked very much in love. On Itinerary Number Four we are supposed to stop overnight at Mary, a city in-between the Bokhara frontier post and Ashgabat, and tour the ancient settlements of Merv, but Humphrey and Beatrix (difficult names for me to pronounce, so they said they were happy with Hump and Bee) were in a hurry to reach Ashgabat, so we missed out on those. Suspicious, I thought. I expect tourists who have come this distance and fought their way through our notorious immigration procedures to want to see and do everything. Talking of which, they also didn't seem to appreciate the new fast track visa processing our government recently introduced. Only two hours! It used to take all day.

Anyway, they were the customers, so we drove straight from the frontier to Mary International Airport, stopping only for twenty minutes at a hotel in Türkmenabat for a bathroom break and to buy some snacks for the drive. It's four hours to Mary, even with the driver the agency had wished on us. It's a good road, but there's nothing to see, just desert and scrub on both sides all the way. One of the problems we have as tour guides is how to entertain visitors on long drives like these. At least Hump and Bee asked a lot of questions, many of which I could answer truthfully. I got suspicious, though. It's true that there are a lot of container trucks that pass through the country on their way to Uzbekistan, Russia, Kazakhstan and Afghanistan, in fact there were hundreds of them on this stretch of road alone, but I've never before had tourists who were interested in them. Especially not ones who asked questions like "where do they park overnight?" I certainly couldn't answer that one. I assumed they just kept going, but I suppose they have to stop somewhere sometime. I wondered if I should put this in my daily report.

We reached the airport more than an hour before the flight to Ashgabat, which was just as well, as it took most of that time to check in and go through security. Mind you, if you arrive two hours before the flight, those things take two hours. Our officials are past masters at stretching procedures to fill the available time. Hump and Bee say it's quicker where they come from. The plane never leaves late, though. Every time I go, I wonder why it's called an 'international' airport, and why they built twelve departure gates when there are only two flights a day, one in the morning, one in the evening. Perhaps one day it will get busier.

It takes only 30 minutes to fly to Ashgabat, but it's the best way to travel, as both tourists and guide are sick of the monotony after four hours of driving, and the rest of the road to the capital is potholed and takes another six hours. The plane was full, but Hump and Bee were the only tourists. As usual, all the rest were business people, working in the gas drilling industry that goes on in the desert.

Every visitor is fascinated by their first sight of Ashgabat, and Hump and Bee were no exceptions. The White City. Everything is white. Well, not the asphalt on the road, of course. I also admit some buildings have gold and dark wood detailing, and the many statues of our beloved leader Berdimuhamedow and his predecessor are, of course, golden. But all the buildings are faced with white marble, all the cars are white, all the buses and trucks are white. Well, almost. Occasionally a silver or grey one slips through, but it's a brave driver who risks confrontation with our guardian police force. At night, coloured neon signs light up the city and there's an impressive enormous illuminated horse's head rearing over the Olympic stadium in the city centre, but by day when the lights go out, it's all white. I'm proud of my city.

Hump and Bee were impressed, just as I expected. I even anticipated their question about where all the trucks were. Driving round the outer ring road was the answer. I knew that answer. But why did they want to know? By then I was certain that they weren't tourists, or that if they were, that wasn't their only agenda. Arriving at the hotel, after marvelling at how huge and white it was and checking the wifi worked, which seemed to be their top priority, they asked me how they should change money to pay for dinner. That gave me the excuse I needed for a small black-market transaction. I whispered that the official rate at the hotel desk was six to the dollar, but I could offer them fifteen. Most tourists look scared at that point and won't do the deal, but Hump and Bee were completely calm with it, like they did it all their lives. Hump picked up a city map from the reception desk, spread it out on a table in the corner of the lobby, pushed sixty dollars under it and towards me, and I pushed nine hundred *mana* back. Very professionally handled. Good for me, as my neighbour gives me twenty to the dollar. Better still this time, as I discovered Hump had given me eighty dollars, not sixty. He winked and said, "keep the change." Very nice man. I was revising my opinion of them being difficult customers. I'd keep their interest in trucks to myself. At least for now.

I waited five minutes after they went to their room before I went to mine. Next door, as usual. I took out my microphone with its sucker pad from my backpack and attached it to the communicating door. Part of a guide's job is to listen in and write anything interesting they hear into their nightly reports. It's something I hate. Always extraordinarily tedious, often difficult to hear clearly, mostly mundane conversations when I can, sometimes acutely embarrassing. I often wonder if guests realise they're being listened to. Hump and Bee might have, as there were long stretches of silence interrupted by unnecessarily loud calls of "have you brushed your teeth, darling?" and things like that. I certainly didn't hear any conversation worth reporting, but had to write something to prove I'd been doing my job. 'Guests talked about what a beautiful city it is and complained to each other that there was no toothpaste in the bathroom.'

In the morning, I went to meet them in the breakfast room. They told me they were amazed that it was so vast, with a high ceiling and tables and chairs that they said looked like they came out of Versailles, wherever that is. In France, apparently. No guests ever commented on that to me before. All our hotels are much the same as each other. They were looking intently at the map Hump had picked up the night before.

"Ready for our city tour?" I asked.

"Yes, please," said Bee, more enthusiastically than I'd expected. "Please can we go to the Wedding Hotel?"

The so-called Wedding Hotel is an enormous building, on the edge of town at the top of a hill. It's all white, of course, and I think it looks like a monstrous spy camera atop a pile of triangular blocks. It's a favourite place for weddings, which is how it got its name. It's on the itinerary, but nobody had ever before asked to go there specially.

"Aren't you already married?" I asked.

They assured me they were, but that they had 'heard so much about it'. That made no sense. It was suspicious. I knew I ought to make a call to get a supervisor to take over from me, but they were much nicer customers than usual, I was enjoying their company and they had money. I made a snap decision to trust them. The nearby tables were all empty, and the ceiling was too high for microphones, but I kept my voice low, anyway. "What exactly do you want?" I asked. "I might be able to help. If I can."

Bee and Hump looked at each other and obviously decided to trust me in their turn. Bee said "We need to find out what happens when a certain container truck passes by here on its way to Uzbekistan. Sometime later today, we think. We were told there's a place where they check lorries that's just off the ring road, near the wedding hotel. We just want to have a look."

An unusual request to be sure, but as long as it was just taking a look from the outside, I couldn't see why that would be a problem. I thought I knew where they meant, but it wasn't a place I'd ever taken much notice of. A yard about the size of a football pitch, full of trucks. I've seen it from the top of the hill by that hotel, a place we always stop for photos. I wondered if that would be enough for them. Doubtful. I told them to meet me outside in ten minutes and went to see what driver I'd been assigned. The agency always has four or five cars lined up outside the hotel, and I'm supposed to take the first one in line. Some drivers are more friendly than others, though. Luckily, my friend Bayram was one of the ones waiting. We live in the same zone and we went to school together. I think of him as my brother. He was third in line, but knew the drivers in front, and they willingly shunted positions.

As it was about half an hour's drive to the wedding hotel, I told Hump and Bee that we'd stop at some other sights along the way. It seemed they were in no hurry. While we drove, speaking in our local dialect, I asked Bayram about the truck depot. It was indeed the one visible from the hill. He wasn't confident of getting closer, telling me it was a bonded customs facility at the end of a road that went nowhere else and was guarded by soldiers.

The view from the top of the hill was good, and it looked to me like Hump was taking dozens of pictures with his phone. I was relaxed, waiting for him to finish, when Bayram shouted "look out!" A police car, sirens blazing, racing towards us and screeching to a halt. An officer jumped out shouting "no photos!" Now I was going to be in trouble. He'd just confiscate the phone from Hump, but it would be all my fault. I should have told him it was forbidden to photograph government facilities.

Hump, however, was acting remarkably cool. "No problem, officer, I won't take any," he said. The officer looked at me to translate; obviously "no photos" was the limit of his English. Hump offered his phone to show that he had only taken pictures of the hotel itself, nothing below. Surprising. I'd seen him taking plenty, and he hadn't had time to delete them. Perhaps the police were having a 'be nice to tourists' campaign, as the officer nodded, saluted, got back in his car and drove off. Seeing my surprise, Bee smiled and said, "our secret."

After the police went, Bayram wouldn't even consider trying to go nearer to the truck park, but Hump and Bee didn't seem to mind. "It's too secure," Hump said. "We're looking for a place where cargos or papers can be switched."

"Where's the truck going after here?" I asked.

"It's supposed to be heading for Uzbekistan," Hump replied. "But not the frontier we came across, if our information is right. I can't remember the name."

"Dash something," said Bee.

"Dashoguz," I said. "In the north. It is on your itinerary, so we can go. I remember seeing a big field where trucks stop on the way, about a hundred kilometres from here. There's a fuel station and places for drivers to sleep. I've never been close, but I've seen it from the road. Perhaps that's the place you're looking for." Hump and Bee looked excited. "We'll go in the morning, early. Be ready at 7."

"But we might miss the truck," said Hump. "I don't suppose it will stop here for very long."

"It's a customs facility," I replied. "Turkmen bureaucracy. It won't leave until morning, even if it's already there. Trust me."

"Will we be coming back?" asked Bee.

"No, after that we're going to Darvaza. It's also on your itinerary. All tourists go there. You'll like it."

"What's there?"

"They didn't tell you about it? A crater in the middle of the desert. A big one. With flames coming out of the ground. The only one of its kind in the world. A sight to behold, indeed."

33 – The policy of dealing with an insurance broker – Maria

London, England

Piers was very 'old school' indeed. Like Arbuthnot-alias-Smith when I first went to work for him. His idea of hiring a temp was to have a young woman on call all day long to bring him cups of coffee and buy pastries from the deli up the road, all the while smiling sweetly. There was no paperwork to handle or letters to type, though at one point on the first morning I thought he was going to come out with the old chestnut "Take something down, Miss Maria." Not that I had an intention of letting him anywhere near my knickers until I'd completed my mission of discovering the truth of dodgy insurance deals. And not even then.

The office was on the ground floor, behind a shop front, a single large room with five small desks, one enormous one in pride of place for Piers, and a dozen filing cabinets. Three of the desks had nothing on them except dust. The fourth had a computer and nothing else. Mine, temporarily. The fifth was the domain of the one other man in the office, Mr Patel, an Indian gentleman in his sixties. When I introduced myself, he told me he was a partner and the accountant, giving me the impression that he thought he was wasting his time telling me even that. I suppose he had a point, if girls only lasted hours or days.

By late morning, I'd determined that not much insurance was being brokered in that office. Piers spent a lot of time on the phone, though from the little I could overhear mostly organising a golf weekend somewhere in

Portugal. Mr Patel had a desk in a corner of the office, with a stack of three filing trays to his left and three to his right. He kept himself to himself, occasionally removing a sheet or two of paper from a tray on one side, examining it, adding a note or two in the margin and finally transferring it to one of the trays on the other side. Both Mr Patel and Piers had computers on their desks, but neither was switched on. This was a paper-centric business. No electronic records. Strange.

At precisely eleven, Patel rose from his chair, went to the kitchenette, and made himself a cup of tea. I offered to make it, but he refused. At one point, Piers called across to him and he leapt from his chair in a surprising display of obsequiousness and deference. Was Piers perhaps a minor Royal? I didn't think so.

I'd brought in a salad for my lunch, partly as a defence against any possible invitation to eat with Piers and partly hoping he would go out and I would be left alone to poke about for a bit. Neither ploy worked. Piers simply sent me out to buy a sandwich, "not one of those prepacked ones", for which he gave precise instructions (rare roast beef, thinly sliced tomato sprinkled with salt, on a thickly buttered bap, definitely no margarine, one teaspoon of horseradish sauce, the whole to be cut in half). When I repeated that in the deli, the girl behind the counter instantly replied, "you're not working for that creep, are you?" His infamy goes before him.

Returning to the office, and with nothing better to do, I arranged his sandwich on a plate, poured him a glass of water from the cooler, and placed them by his side on his desk. First grope of the day. Well, a chunky hand run up my right thigh. Almost all the way up. Better grin and bear it, if that was as bad as it would get. I gave him the sweetest smile I could conjure up in the circumstances and moved a few centimetres away.

"I'm very happy just to be your waitress," I said, "but it's a waste of my talents. I was hoping I would be able to help with some of your office work. Insurance must be so interesting."

He raised his eyebrows. "Well, I was hoping to explore your talents. But insurance, seriously? What do you know about insurance?"

"Well, not a lot. Only what everyone knows. You pay a premium to a company just in case something horrible happens. Like you crash your car or your home gets robbed. I was hoping that you would teach me. I think you'll find I'm a fast learner."

"That's very good. Very good indeed. Yes, indeed, I can teach you a lot. We don't do that sort of insurance here, though. We are specialists. Insurance for international goods shipments."

"Fascinating. You mean like when someone moves house from one country to another and all their furniture has to be sent there?"

"In a way, but even more specialist. Companies that manufacture big, expensive machinery and sell it to customers in another country. Like this," picking up a folder of papers from his desk. "A Rolls-Royce car built here that's sold to a customer in Qatar. Or this one," picking up another folder, "a ten-million-pound yacht being delivered to a customer in Port Moresby."

"Where?" I asked, genuinely not knowing.

"Papua New Guinea," he replied. "The other side of the world."

"You must be ever so rich to insure something like that. You mean that if the yacht sinks or something, you have to pay the customer ten million?"

"Not me personally. We're brokers, not insurers." I did my best to look mystified, to encourage him to continue. "What I do is find an insurance company or underwriter that will take the risk. Negotiate the premium. Get the cover the customer needs at the best price. We just take a percentage."

"Amazing," I replied. "Is there a lot of business like that, then? It seems very quiet here." Then, acting as if I had said something wrong, "Oh, I hope you don't mind me saying that."

"No, no, not at all. Because we are so specialised, it comes and goes. Some days are quiet, some days we are very, very busy. You'll see."

"You must be incredibly clever to do this. Are there lots of brokers like you?"

"I'm the best," he announced, smiling and puffing himself up, and moving a hand to pat my bottom, which I artfully avoided. "Everyone knows Piers Pritchard. But now I have some calls I need to make. Perhaps we could continue this talk about insurance n over a drink later?"

"That would be wonderful, but today I can't. I'm sorry," I pouted. True, I'd promised Sonia and Francesca a post-mortem glass or two. "Perhaps tomorrow?" He smiled broadly and shifted position slightly towards me, a good prompt for me to move further away. "What can I be doing that's useful in the meantime?" I asked. "Apart from bringing you coffee, that is."

"Well, you could file these folders. Take a peep inside and you'll start to see the sort of things we do."

"I can do that. How does your filing system work?"

He laughed. "I have no idea. That's something the girls take care of. I'm sure you'll work it out." He reached out a hand absent-mindedly as if to stroke my thigh goodbye.

There was no filing system. At least, not for anything recent. Three of the cabinets had a semblance of an alphabetic ordering system, but all the files in those were years old. Thereafter, I guessed, girls before me had simply dropped folders into the first random drawer that they opened and just shut it again. I assumed that either there was never a need to retrieve a file once consigned to a cabinet or that my predecessor would simply have to plough through piles of papers until the required document was found. But now I had my excuse to be nosy. I had a brief upset with Mr Patel when I attempted to open a filing cabinet that he claimed as his, but once the demarcation was clarified, I set to work to rebuild the filing system. Giving me the justification to peek inside any file I wanted.

I told Piers what I was doing. Not only did he approve, he looked thrilled. Probably because it signalled that I was planning on coming back the next day. And the day after that, if he behaved himself when we went for that drink. Well, he tried it on a bit, but it wasn't too difficult to keep him under control once he realised that the fact I kept coming to work meant he'd get another try another day.

By Wednesday evening I had made great strides with the filing and, just a few minutes before five, had located the paperwork for the various shipments of medical equipment being consigned to Uzbekistan and Kazkhstan. I finally went for the drink I'd promised Piers, having put it off again from Tuesday mainly because I wanted to line up Sonia and Francesca to sit in the same bar and observe. I figured Piers was just an old lecher, but wouldn't have put it past him trying date rape drugs on me.

On Thursday morning, I arrived with a present for Piers. Expensive looking, but bought for five pounds in a drug store. A heavily discounted box set of out-of-date men's toiletries. He was more than grateful, insisting that he had to take me out to dinner. I just hoped he'd get the hint and spray the deodorant on first.

My plan for the day was to study the files I'd found the afternoon before. There were five in the last year relating to shipments that FutureHealth had sold and Kulov's companies had handled. I sat at one of the empty desks near the cabinets and pulled the folders towards me. Two were for similar equipment for delivery to Azerbaijan. Both had been delivered, no claims made. The other three, though, were for delivery to Uzbekistan. Two had got lost in transit and had given rise to claims. The third was still en route. Presumably the one that our team was following? The premiums also varied considerably. The shipments that had arrived had cost eighty thousand dollars each to insure, but the premiums for the other three were closer to twenty thousand each. Same insured value, similar route, at least on paper. On other forms, I found that the starting premium was about eighty thousand for all of them, but the three in question had a seventy-five per cent discount applied. Scribbled in the margin of the calculation sheets, 'agreed with,' followed by an unreadable scribbled name and Piers's initials.

I was so deep in concentration that I was completely startled when a hand reached over my shoulder, pointing at the files in front of me. Mr Patel. He moves silently, that one. "What exactly do you think you are doing, Miss?" he asked, sounding suspicious.

"Piers said I could learn about insurance from the files," I said, thinking quickly. "These ones were banded together. The risks look similar, and the underwriter is the same. I was just trying to understand the differences." I hoped that sounded innocent enough.

"Your job is to do the filing, not study the paperwork," said Mr Patel, very sternly, moving round the desk, closing the files and picking them up. The situation had registered with Piers, who, unusually, had got up from his chair and come to find out what was going on.

"This young lady was looking inside the Silk Road files, Mr Pritchard Sir."

Piers looked at me quizzically. "Why were you doing that, Maria?"

"You did say that I could learn about insurance by looking at what was in the files, Piers. I'm sorry if I've done something wrong." I screwed up my face, looked down at my lap, and tried to conjure up some tears.

"Where did you find these files?" Piers asked.

"In that filing cabinet," pointing at the one where the drawer was open and putting on my best choked-up voice.

"Patel, explain. Why were these files left there?" Piers sounded quite angry. I was no longer the one in trouble.

"One of the girls last week must have put them in there," he replied. "I'll lock them up right away, Mr Pritchard Sir." He did exactly that, clutching the files close to his body to stop any papers escaping from them, and slowly walking backwards towards his own fiefdom.

I wished that I'd thought about the files being sensitive and Patel not being as docile and wrapped up in his work as he always appeared. If I'd been more careful, I could have photographed the page showing the discount, maybe more. I doubted Piers would have noticed. While I could still visualise it in my mind, I attempted the best reproduction I could, using the stylus and notepad on my phone. Agreed with who? It looked like it started with a K. Or could be an F?

I was glad that the clock was ticking up to five and even more glad that Piers had an 'engagement I can't myself get out of' in the evening. Masonic, judging from the clues. I was looking forward to getting back to the flat, having a long hot shower, ordering a pizza and spending the evening doing my real job, sorting out what needed to be sorted for the team.

Those hopes were dashed by what, or rather who, was waiting for me on the pavement outside. My father.

No warm family greeting, of course. Just "I've been looking for you. Come with me."

34 – One container looks much like another – Humphrey

Ashgabat, Turkmenistan

Exactly as Suzana had warned us, the only working communications with the outside world from Ashgabat were the emails we could send and receive using the very slow wifi in the hotel. The code system we use is based on John Le Carré novels, currently The Russia House. Our problem was that we'd left our paperbacks somewhere, and only had the ebook, which has completely different page numbers. Fortunately Bea, who's a bit of a whiz with a computer, managed to reformat her copy to more or less match and, after a couple of hours of frustrated attempts, we succeeded in decoding the messages we received from Maria and Laoban. Some words were missing or unintelligible, but we had enough to learn that whatever method they'd been using to track where the container was located had stopped working soon after it had crossed the border into Turkmenistan at 07:05 that day. Thus, we could be sure that it was in the country, but not exactly where it was now. If it had been taken to that depot in Ashgabat, it might have arrived there around the time we were looking down on it from the hill above. On the other hand, it could have been driven somewhere else. Anywhere. Well, anywhere on the very limited network of roads in Turkmenistan. Nothing we could do now except trust that Purli was right – and that he was as trustworthy as we were risking him being. Recipe for a sleepless night for both of us.

Somewhat nourished, if not invigorated, by the hotel breakfast, that comprised one cup of watery coffee, a sickly-sweet yogurt and a stale bread roll, we were ready to leave at seven. Purli had managed to get Bayram to drive us again, this time in an impressive and monstrous Land Cruiser. A white one, of course, but with distinctive gold-plated door handles and lettering. Even though Bayram was his friend, Purli took us to one side before we got in to tell us to be careful. "When I start to talk about the camel farms, ask to stop for a toilet break. I will have to tell you we will stop at the next town. When I do that, please make a fuss and ask to stop sooner. I will then ask Bayram to go to the camel herders' village where the truck park is."

"I thought you trusted Bayram?" asked Bea.

"Of course I do. He is my brother," Purli replied. "But we have to report everything we do and everywhere we go to our management and they will tell the police. It is difficult when everyone is watching everyone else. We are not allowed to take tourists to the camel village, so it is important that Bayram has a good reason that he can explain if he is interrogated."

It was now even more clear that Purli was taking a big risk for us. The irony of us being on a mission to spy on people who are obliged to spy on each other wasn't lost on me. I definitely didn't want to get Purli and Bayram into trouble. We might face a lot of bureaucracy, but however much trouble we got into, at least the authorities would probably allow us out of the country. They had to stay and face the music.

Bea put on such a good show of changing feet and fidgeting that I was afraid Bayram was going to stop at the side of the road rather than continue to the village, but at least he realised there would be no discretion for a western woman in a desert landscape with no vegetation, and accelerated down an unsignposted dirt track off the road. There it was. A corral with hundreds of camels. We hadn't even seen one until then, and I'd been wondering if Purli had got the wrong translation. An impoverished place. Semi-derelict wooden shacks and circular drum-shaped canvas tents of different sizes stood around the perimeter of the compound. Purli pointed at the tents. "Yurts," he said. "Where the nomads live. They can be taken down, rolled up, and put on the back of a camel when they move to another pasture."

"There's no pasture here," I said. "Just desert."

"There's a well, so there is water. An oasis." I couldn't see the palm trees I associated in my mind with oases, but decided not to say any more. Officially, we needed the bathroom. Unofficially, we were looking for a truck. As we drove round the camel paddock, the trailer park came into view. A few trucks, not that many, and a couple of huts. Bayram pulled up by the side of a portable building, the only thing that looked fairly modern and functional. Presumably the site office. Purli went in to beg the use of their facilities. In the five or six minutes we were waiting (Bea whispered she wasn't pretending any more and was now desperate) two trucks, each towing two trailers loaded with containers, lumbered slowly towards us and passed straight into the compound. No barriers or obvious security here.

I suddenly realised I'd not been as observant as I should have been. I nudged Bea. "See the second container on the second truck? 395217. That's the one we're looking for, isn't it?"

"Talk about good fortune," she replied. "And here's even better luck. We're allowed to use the loo." We went to where Purli was pointing, behind the office.

"It's a bit basic," he told Bea. "They're all men here." Bea, not in a mood to care about sanitation, raced off. I scanned the compound, counted eleven trucks, some with a single trailer, others with two. Three of the truck locomotive units, parked some distance away, were undergoing repairs of some kind. The only one I could see properly had two men actually doing something and five standing watching, no doubt providing their expert advice. Just like anywhere else in the world. As nobody was standing nearby, I strolled towards the truck with our target container, taking out my phone to take pictures. Purli, very curious, followed. As we reached the cab, the driver was just climbing down, clutching paperwork. He looked surprised to see us. Well, me I suppose, as I certainly don't resemble a Turkmen.

"Can you ask him where he's going after here?" I asked Purli, assuming the driver wouldn't understand English. Purli looked like he'd rather not get involved, but nevertheless spoke to the driver. A more animated and longer discussion than I had expected, involving much pointing at the office, to where the driver walked off.

"He says that he only goes as far as the frontier at Dashoguz. An Uzbek driver will take the trailers onwards from there. He was in a hurry to go to the office because he was told to pick up new documents for the shipments here, and he needs to leave soon. He is worried he will be late."

So, what we'd heard was right. This must be the place. A hotbed of fraud in the middle of nowhere in a one of the most secretive countries on earth. Switch the paperwork in order that the container with the valuable goods gets classified as something else and gets delivered to the black marketeer's address. Then the other container, filled with something else, something cheap, is taken to the buyer of the valuable goods. And that wasn't the only deceit that might be happening there. Looking to my right, I could see a man up a ladder, smoothing out what looked like new self-adhesive numbering onto another container.

Bea had reappeared by then, and I left her with Purli while I headed for the latrine at the back of the office. As I finished, I turned to find myself facing two tall and heavy individuals who had materialised out of nowhere. Kulov's men, dressed all in black, and, at a quick glance, heavily armed,. Before I could react, one clamped a hand over my mouth while drawing a long, curved blade knife from his belt, while the other pinned my arms behind my back. A horrifying scream rang out from the other side of the building. Bea. My heart pounded. What were they going to do with us? I tried to shout, but the one in front barked, "Stop," pressing the cold tip of the knife to my throat.

The man behind shoved me towards a narrow alley between two rows of trailers. It was only a short distance, but with each slow step, my growing trepidation made the walk feel like it was taking a lifetime. I couldn't think of any escape. I could fight, but I had no weapon and wouldn't be able to overcome one, never mind both of them. All I could do was brace myself for whatever horror awaited at the end and stay alert for any opportunity of escape. In this remote place, with no one knowing where we were, nor expecting us to come here, Kulov's men could kill us, safe in the knowledge that nobody would come looking until they were long gone out of the country.

Suddenly, my saviour Bea materialised like an avenging angel, appearing to fly from the top of a trailer and, arms outstretched, landing on the knife-wielding thug in front of me, knocking him to the ground. Then, in one smooth movement she delivered powerful karate kicks to the man behind me. She's brilliant at martial arts. She's trying to teach me karate, but I just don't have the same flexibility in my body as she does. "Don't just stand there," she shouted at me, interrupting my contemplation of her skills.

We sprinted towards the Land Cruiser, where Purli, clearly enjoying the action, already had the doors open, waiting. As Bayram floored the accelerator, a cloud of desert sand engulfed us. Through it, I caught a brief glimpse of another Land Cruiser parked by the office — a silent reminder of how close we had come to catastrophe.

"What happened here?" I asked. "I heard you scream."

"Kulov pointed a gun at me," said Bea, "but Bayram crept up from behind and knocked him out. Strong and silent operator," she added, approvingly, reaching forward to pat him on the shoulder.

"Where's Kulov now?"

"Lying on the back seat of that car. Should be unconscious for a few more minutes yet."

"They'll be coming after us."

"Not in a hurry," said Purli. "Bayram took these," unclenching his fingers to reveal a handful of fuses. "Oh, and this," picking up a key fob from the well by the side of his seat. "They might have a spare key of course, but the truck won't move without the fuses."

So Kulov and his men had been following their truck. Finding us there must have come as a surprise to them. Would it make them change their plans, I wondered? Perhaps they wouldn't now go ahead with switching the paperwork. Though then they presumably wouldn't get paid. Something that Laoban would definitely have an opinion on and want to make decisions about, but we had no way to share any of the information with her. No way of getting in touch until either there was a wifi network we could log onto or we crossed the border.

"Is there a gas station or hotel or somewhere along the road where we can get wifi?" I asked Purli.

He shook his head. "Nothing until Dashoguz. Another four hundred kilometres from here."

It was frustrating that he and Bayram had mobile phones that worked, a convenience forbidden to us as foreigners. The eSIM in our own phones gave unlimited network coverage across 207 countries, according to the proudly worded emails I received almost every week. Almost the whole world. Except North Korea. And here. We couldn't risk asking our guides to send a message. In any case, they probably couldn't send anything out of the country. Only domestic coverage. Not beyond borders. It didn't matter, anyway. Even if we could have messaged Laoban, what could she or the rest of the team have done?

Purli might have been reading my mind. "We go to the gas craters now, and you will spend the night there. Then tomorrow morning we drive to Dashoguz and you cross the frontier back to Uzbekistan. I am calling the agency now while there is a signal to tell them of the small change to the itinerary, and they will send a message to your agency across the border, so they will be waiting for you. Do you want me to ask them to send any instructions?"

A perfect opportunity. Well, as perfect as it could be in the circumstances. "Please ask them to send this exact message. The chameleon should meet us. We have new papers."

35 – Not feeling the love – Maria

London, England

Father grasped me by the wrist, his hand a human handcuff, his grip impossible to shake off. I was forced to walk - he would have literally dragged me down Leadenhall Street had I not been anxious about breaking the heels on my shoes. What a ridiculous thing to worry over at a time like that. I know I looked terrified, but the commuters crowding towards us ignored me, their eyes focused only on the pavement and the tube station as they headed home. I was resigned to my fate. No point in fighting or screaming. Now he'd found me, there would be no escape.

We didn't go far, in fact just one block, entering the same building as Francesca's agency, but passing that office and going straight to the lift, where a security guard waited, holding the doors open for us. Sixth floor. A long, deserted corridor, plain, grey-painted wall on one side, frosted glass panels and doors on the other. Father opened one of the doors and pulled me inside. "My London office," he grinned at me, releasing my wrist and locking the door. "It is wonderful to see you, Mila. Even more beautiful than before! How is my little *rypka*?" He pointed to a chair for me, and sat himself on the desk, looking very pleased.

"It's not wonderful to see you, and I am not going back to Minsk!" I practically screamed at him.

"Don't cry, my darling. Smile, please! Of course you are not going to Minsk. Why would you want to go back there? Even I don't want to go back, but I have no choice." He laughed heartily. "But surely you miss your brother and your mother?"

"You know I don't." My mother had treated me horribly since I was a little girl, looking upon me as nothing better than an unwelcome servant, forcing me to spend my weekends cleaning, and telling me off for everything the rest of the time. She treated my brother like a prince, of course. Four years older than me, father had got him into the local KGB as soon as he was eighteen. I don't know what his job title was, but probably Chief Torturer. All he would talk about on the times he came home to dinner was of the revolting things he'd been doing to subversives. Mother lapped it all up, telling him what a good boy he was, how much he was helping the country and how proud she was, while regarding me simply as a waitress, making me serve him second and third helpings. Thank goodness my father had always treated me well, or my childhood would have been dreadful. I reviled the idea of going back.

"Where have you left your operatives?" I asked, noticing now that, apart from being on our own, the office we were in was completely bare other than a desk and two chairs.

"There's only me. Before there were sanctions, this was what we called our trade office. I've still got a key."

"If it's not to make me go back, why did you set spies on me in Rotterdam?"

"Ah, because I wanted to find you, to talk to you. You were very good at losing them. I taught you well!" He laughed again.

"They weren't very good spies. I spotted them straight away."

"Yes indeed. Not good at all. They are now being repurposed, as you say. But I think it is really that you are brilliant. I am so proud of you. You have done well. And you have a very good little business."

"What do you know about that?" I asked, thinking that he more than likely knew everything.

"I know you work with a small team of researchers who blend into their environment so well that nobody would suspect them, and that they are much more clever than they appear. I would be proud to have such a team working for me. I heard how you found the drug factory in the jungle. That was very well done. And I am very glad you managed to put away that Smith man. I did not like him. Very smarmy. Very corrupt. He treated you badly, and I cannot forgive that."

I'd calmed down now. He opened a drawer in the desk from which he extracted a bottle of vodka and two glasses. "To celebrate," he announced, pouring. I allowed myself to clink glasses and downed the shot in one. "I thought you would be in London," he added. "I had everyone looking for you here. It was very smart of you to move to Rotterdam, an excellent place to hide. My people only saw you there by accident."

"How did you find me here in London?"

"Coincidence!" he laughed. "I saw you here, in the lobby. You were coming out of the office downstairs with two girls. You were chatting, so you didn't see me." I cursed. OK, this meeting wasn't going badly, but I had feared the worst after Rotterdam, and getting friendly with Sonia and Francesca meant I had let down my guard. "I am so glad I found you again, and to meet today. I go home to Minsk tomorrow."

"I'm not coming with you," I said.

"No, no, of course not. I don't want you to. You are happy here. And more useful, I think. I think maybe we can help each other."

"My help?" I didn't like the way this was going. I didn't want to be his Belarus asset in London. Or Rotterdam. Or anywhere. Or being expected to become a double agent.

"Well, your team's help, actually. The project you are working on is of great interest to me."

I wondered what he knew. "What project?"

"The one in Uzbekistan. Black market medical equipment."

"What is your interest in that?" I asked, cautiously. No point in denying anything. He and his minions probably knew the lot.

"The two men who are organising stealing and selling the equipment are wanted by us. I will tell you frankly, it is embarrassing. They are Chechens. Mafia. Very dangerous men. They killed many soldiers. We and our friends in Moscow have been after them for years. We finally caught them two years ago when they passed through Minsk. Moscow was very pleased. Then they escaped when we were transporting them to a camp. So, of course, Moscow is now angry. We need to get them back."

227

"Why do you need our help? Uzbekistan used to be a Soviet country. They speak Russian like us. It's easier for your men to move there than ours."

"No, it's not. Uzbeks don't like Russians. Or Belarusians. And these Chechens are very careful, nobody ever sees them. I think you are setting them a trap. Your customers want them taken down, so if you hand them over to us, they will be happy, we will be happy. Everyone will be happy. Will you help?"

"I thought all the Chechens you were after were terrorists. These are just thieves. Black marketeers."

"No, they are terrorists, too. They need money, so they invented this plan to steal very expensive equipment and sell it. Not just medical equipment, other things too."

"You said we could help each other. What can you do for us?"

"Your team has not seen these men's faces. I can give you photographs so they will recognise them when they see them."

"And?" I waited.

"The woman you call Laoban has been giving you lessons in selling, I see. Yes, also I can give you money. It will be a little complicated, but it can be arranged."

"Hmmm. How much?"

"Shall we say a million euros?"

"I will ask. But what exactly do you want us to do? Make a citizens' arrest and then phone you?"

Father laughed so hard that it took a minute before he could speak again. "I think you will catch them in Tashkent, no? I have people there. Very good people. Vasily and Igor. Perhaps you remember Vasily? He came to our house sometimes." I nodded. Yes, I remembered him. Very tall. Ugly face. Five years older than me? Always trying to flirt, playing the strong man and showing off his abs, as if I cared. He'd won some championship, though, so he had to be good at fighting. "When your team is in place and the trap is set, you call them and they will come at once. Any time. If your team needs extra muscle, Vasily and Igor will help. But they are to make the arrests and take the men away."

"Not the Uzbek police? Surely they should be the ones to make any arrest?"

"No. The Uzbeks are too gentle. And they are useless. Their own FSB has been trying to catch the men for months. They asked their colleagues in Kazakhstan to arrest two of your own team in Almaty, thinking they were the criminals. Fortunately for your friends, the Kazakhs are even more useless. No, tell them nothing. If the Uzbek police ask your people about it, they should say that two men they had never seen before came and helped the criminals escape. Once we have them back in Minsk, we will make an announcement."

"I have to discuss with Laoban."

"Of course. Here is my Signal Messenger address. It is secure, but still, be discreet." He held out a scrap of paper and I snapped a photo of it. A string of characters that could mean anything.

"Always. So… Can I go?"

"Won't you have dinner with me, *rypka*? Your dear father? For old times' sake?"

"I'd rather not. You said you were here alone. Am I going to be followed?"

"No. This is just between you and me. It is better that my colleagues know nothing about this. Go. The fire exit is at the end of the corridor. A lot of stairs, but no alarm."

I got up and, almost involuntarily, gave him a hug. I was still free. But an unwelcome reminder that, in another sense, I would never be free again.

36 – Out of the frying pan – Beatrix

Somewhere in Turkmenistan

We'd left the truck stop several kilometres behind and were back on the main road, which was progressively deteriorating. The first section from Ashgabat to the turnoff for the trailer park had been a wide asphalted highway. From there on, we started to encounter more and more potholes and then completely broken sections of road, eventually narrowing to a single carriageway. Wherever he could, Bayram drove off the road and parallel to it across the desert. Faster and not as bumpy. Mostly, the landscape was unrelenting desert, with minimal scrub vegetation and no sign of civilisation. After fifty or sixty kilometres, we started seeing asphalted roads and dirt tracks leading off the highway, with signposts that clearly meant something to somebody, but not to us. Like 'A2Z3', 'C99J'. "Gas fields," explained Purli. "The codes for the drilling rigs. Gas is our country's main export."

We also saw camels, sometimes in herds, being driven by a shepherd (or should that be camelherd?), sometimes just a few ambling along on their own. I know nothing about camels, but they looked malnourished at best, skeletal at worst. Well, I couldn't see any vegetation for them to eat. Purli explained they were bred by nomads for transport, milk and meat, and without being asked promised to take us to a restaurant in Dashoguz if we had time to try camel kebabs, of which he was very fond. Not something I could get enthusiastic about. No doubt Ron would like them.

Despite the bumpy ride, both Humph and I dozed off, regaining consciousness when catapulted out of our seats and hitting our heads on the roof. Should have been wearing our seatbelts. The Land Cruiser had left the road, and we were now driving cross-country on a very bumpy track, bordered by hills on either side. Cresting one of them, we saw a huge crater below us and, a hundred metres to the right of it, twenty or thirty yurts. "Darwaza!" announced Purli. "The famous gas crater. The yurts are the hotel for you tourists."

He told us that to see the crater in all its explosive glory, we needed to wait until nightfall, another hour and a half. In the meantime, we would have dinner. Colleagues of his were preparing the meal in the so-called 'hotel'. Bayram dropped the three of us in front of the yurts and went to park the car. As soon as he left, Purli gave us some instructions, whispering as if the desert had ears. "This is your yurt," pointing to the one we were sitting outside. "Bayram and I will stay in the one next to you. But I am afraid that if we stay the night here, the truck you are interested in will arrive at the border before we do. I assume you want to get there first? Or at least around the same time?" We nodded assent. "So, after you have your dinner, go and look at the crater. It is very special. Then come back and call me. Tell me you cannot stay in the yurt overnight. Say it is too uncomfortable. Anything. Just make a lot of complaints until I call Bayram and tell him we will have to drive to Dashoguz tonight. Then I will arrange for you to stay in the hotel there, and that way you will be at the border first thing in the morning."

I stopped him. "I already looked inside the yurt. There's nothing there. It's just a tent. A big tent."

"You have sleeping bags on the floor there. I can find you more sleeping bags if you want," Purli continued, speaking at full volume now that Bayram had rejoined us.

"There's no toilet either," I said.

"It's the square hut up the hill. There is a shower there, too." It looked a long way off. "But let's eat now. Here is the food."

Quite a number of tourists were arriving for dinner. I couldn't decide if they'd been hiding in yurts or just arrived by bus. Not that it mattered. The new arrivals all looked Chinese. Purli told us that most people visiting Turkmenistan were Chinese, Russian or Mongolian.

Dinner comprised barbecued chicken and beef ("sorry no camel"), tomato and cucumber salad, and orange juice from a carton. Simple, but plenty to satisfy our ravenous and carnivorous cravings. I always try to be vegetarian, but gave up on the first day in Central Asia. I was certainly too hungry to be content with just a tomato and three slices of cucumber.

Purli was right about the crater. I'd seen the flames leaping from the rocks when we arrived, but that was in daylight. By night, it was spectacular. Huge. "The gates of hell," he called it. He told us it was formed when there was drilling for gas about forty years ago. The land simply collapsed, like a sinkhole. The gas seeping out of the rock had caught light and the flames had never gone out since. Purli was seriously upset that the government was saying they were planning to extinguish it. As far as he was concerned, it was the number one tourist attraction in the country, and if the flames went out, he'd be out of a job. We looked around just in case Kulov and his men had come, too. It would have been easy to get rid of them here. Or, I suppose, for them to get rid of us. Surprisingly, the rusted and broken metal fence meant there was nothing to stop someone falling (or being pushed) into the crater and then going up in flames. I wondered if anyone had met their fate like that here. Probably, I decided.

Back at the yurts, no play-acting was required to complain in the strongest and loudest terms about the accommodation offered. No way was I prepared to stay. It wasn't just the hard floor with no mattress. I wasn't in the girl guides any longer, thank you. Worse, I had now visited the facilities at the top of the hill and could declare them a hundred times more insanitary than the latrine in the truck yard. Which was saying something. And walking there in the dark would be a trial, even with a torch. All the light from the burning crater seemed to be focused within it. True, we had the moon and stars, a night sky more amazing than I ever remembered seeing before, but that wasn't the point. Poor Purli, he'd not anticipated such a rant. A simple "sorry we're not staying" would have been enough.

I felt more sorry for Bayram. Instead of the sleep he must have craved, he had to wake up and drive us nearly three hundred kilometres on a road in appalling condition. By night. Not that he seemed to mind. I expect he didn't want to sleep on a yurt floor, either.

We were far from the only ones on the road. Plenty of trucks, lumbering along and rocking at petrifying angles as they hit potholes. I was surprised more didn't fall on their sides, but Humph said it wasn't as bad as the road he'd been driven down in Kazakhstan. The appalling road surface didn't deter Bayram from driving at a hair-rising speed and overtaking everything else on the road, the Land Cruiser jumping in every direction. No napping this time. And seat belts very definitely on! I was glad the Land Cruiser was the luxury soft leather upholstery version and not the hard wooden seat variety that we'd had on our safari adventure in Africa a few months beforehand. Strange that two such different vehicles have the same branding. Humph said the engine or chassis or something like that must be the same. I kept watching the trucks we passed to see if we saw ours, but no. Hopefully, we were ahead of it. Though they could have changed the numbers on the container, as we had witnessed being done.

After two hours, the road surface suddenly improved, and Bayram could drive at even higher speeds. An hour more, and there was street lighting, and I could see blocks of flats, warehouses, buildings of all types. Civilisation. "Dashoguz," announced Purli. "I already called the hotel."

The town didn't look very prepossessing, in fact rather industrial, and it wasn't bleached like Ashgabat. The hotel stood out, though, the entrance and lobby being all white marble, very ostentatious. We would not have long to enjoy its comforts; it was already past one in the morning when we arrived, and Purli was expecting us to leave again at eight. "The border post doesn't open until nine, so there's no point going earlier," he told us. Our bedroom was big, the bed was comfy, there was a clean bathroom we could reach at night in a few steps without fear of losing our way or getting bitten by a cobra. It had everything we needed. Except wifi. A faded and peeling notice on the back of the door in several languages said this was for 'technical reasons'. We'd just have to hope that the message we'd sent via Purli had made it through.

The hotel had a take on breakfast that I'd never seen before. Individual sealed plastic bags appearing to contain an apple, a wafer biscuit, and a fruit bun. I say 'appearing' as we didn't actually get to open one of them. The rather fierce lady at the door and in charge of handing out the breakfast bags consulted her list and told us that since we had checked in after 10pm, none had been ordered for us and nothing was available. "Try the coffee shop," she instructed. Which opened at midday. With Humph still grumbling about his empty stomach, we left for the border, and reached it in less than ten minutes. Bayram drove slowly past a long line of trucks waiting to cross. None of them ours. Could it have gone through already? Purli insisted that no, that would be impossible. The border closed at ten the previous evening and, even if the driver had left from the truck park right behind us, he wouldn't have reached by then because he would be driving much more slowly than Bayram. That was certainly true. Humph and I discussed our options and agreed there was no point in waiting for it to roll up. Better to catch it on the other side. We said our farewells, but Purli wouldn't let us go without leaving him our names and address in England. "I hope that things here will change and my daughter can come and study in your country and you can help her," he said. Humph took the proffered notebook and duly wrote in it. False names and non-existent address, of course.

"You will be the first to cross. It will be very quick today," said Purli.

We were certainly the first foreigners, but there was a long line of Turkmen bag ladies ahead of us, jostling each other, off for their day's marketing in Uzbekistan. Once we reached the window (we only had to go to one of them!) the formalities took only five or ten minutes. After our previous experience, we weren't surprised that the two-minibus transfer across no-man's-land took the longest time. But we reached the Uzbek side in less than ninety minutes. Better than I'd been expecting.

Waiting for us, inexplicably dressed in matching dark blue zip suits with white piping and matching caps, stood Laoban and Robert. As we walked down the path from the Uzbek border post, the boss stepped forward. "Who's Camille?" she snarled. Now, did Purli change the name in the message, or is this Maria guessing how Laoban would react and being discreet? Well, one way or another, the message worked. Probably just as well not to say anything more about it.

"Nice to see you too," said Humph. Ignored. Why was Laoban in such a bad mood?

"And why do you want newspapers? Can you read Uzbek or Russian?" She thrust a rolled-up paper towards us.

Ah. The penny dropped. "We don't. The message should have said that the truck has new papers." We explained what we'd seen and that the truck was likely to cross the border soon. Needless to say, we got no sympathy for our encounter with Kulov and his merry men, nor for the mountain of bureaucracy and thousand kilometre drive we'd had to endure to find out what we had. Rather, it seemed that in Laoban's opinion we had failed in our mission by not actually seeing the new paperwork, determined what was in the container it had been switched with, and establishing where the 'good' container was now going to be taken. Nothing less than a miracle was going to be acceptable to the great Laoban this morning. She pointed to a red car parked fifty metres up the road. "You can go. The driver will take you to a hotel in Urgench. Await my instructions there."

"All right," I said. "But before we go, tell me why are you dressed like Formula One drivers?"

A withering stare. "Uzbek traffic police." Followed, muttering under her breath, by "Camille. Honestly," and shaking her head as she turned away.

"I told you she wouldn't be amused," I said to Humph as we walked towards the car. "And that, if I'm not mistaken," nudging him and looking at the passenger in the front seat of a silver minibus, "is EA. Again. No doubt waiting for Kulov and company."

37 – Planning the next steps

Near Urgench, Uzbekistan

Laoban and Robert stood by a lay-by turnoff a kilometre down the road from the Dashoguz border crossing, trusting that their disguise really did make them look like Uzbek traffic police.

"Dokumenty!" Maybe Laoban had been practicing her Russian pronunciation, or maybe it just was what the driver was expecting, but no sooner had Robert waved the truck to a halt and Laoban barked her command than the driver uncomplainingly pulled to a halt and pushed a folder out of the truck window at her. She took her time studying the forms, making sure the inbuilt camera in her spectacles had taken a few images of each page, before handing them back to the driver and waving him on.

They got back in the car they'd hired and drove slowly towards Urgench, the nearest town. Two kilometres later, they passed the truck stopped by the side of the road. Two cars behind it. Kulov's two men were putting out red triangles, presumably to discourage anyone else from stopping. Kulov himself was nowhere to be seen. EA and another man, who they decided must be Zelkopf, the medical director, were deep in conversation with the driver. They took no notice as the passing car lingered a few moments before driving on.

Half an hour later, and having changed out of their police uniforms, Laoban and Rob met the others in the Urgench hotel coffee shop.

"Humphrey, Beatrix, take a look at these pictures," said Laoban.

"They look nasty. Who are they?"

"We believe they are the ringleaders. One of them is the man you saw in Almaty, Humphrey."

"What about Kulov?"

"He's just their agent. Does what they tell him to do. Gets a cut as well as the delivery costs. Much more profitable for him."

"How did you get these pictures?" asked Beatrix.

"We have a new client who has provided them."

"Hang on," said Humphrey. "That means we now have three clients? All for the same job? The manufacturer, the insurance underwriters, and this new one? Who are this lot, then?"

"I'm not allowed to say."

"Why not? I thought we were partners in this enterprise."

"Yes, but. Really, I cannot tell you." Not like Laoban to look apologetic. They sat in silence for a moment, staring at her, eyes to eyes.

"Rob, you know, don't you?" said Humphrey.

"No, actually, she won't tell me either. I've asked a dozen times. It must be something top secret."

"Don't tell me we are now subcontracted state players?" said Beatrix. "Who are we agents for now?" It was obvious from Laoban's expression that she'd hit a nerve. More silence. This time for longer. Eventually broken by Humphrey.

"All right, these are the guys we are looking for. This could be the one that I met in Almaty, although the only bit I saw properly is his forehead. I assume they are dangerous?"

"Very. Utmost care. Remember, they know what you and Ronald look like, and they may know about the rest of us too."

"So, what's next?"

"The new shipping documents are for the same clinic, Hunter Health, but an address in Bokhara. That must be where you went, correct?"

Beatrix nodded. "But that's nothing more than a building site right now. Do you think they're just going to dump it there?"

"I suspect this is more complex than we thought. They're not stealing the equipment and selling it to someone else. They're selling it to the company that originally ordered it."

"What do you mean?"

"The crooks have switched the containers and are going to deliver the wrong one to Tashkent. Kulov will say it's not his fault, that the paperwork must have been switched somewhere. Hunter Health and the Americans, FutureHealth, will both claim on their insurance."

"OK, but what about the container they ordered?"

"The crooks sell it to them. For a fraction of the price that they paid FutureHealth. So they get what they wanted in the first place, but save hundreds of thousands of dollars."

"Sneaky. Why's the container being driven to Bokhara, do you think?"

"Perhaps they think it's a good place to hide it for now. Maybe they're going to build the new clinic around it. Or take it to Tashkent later. Robert, as we discussed in the car, I want you there in Bokhara to see what happens when it's delivered. And before you say anything, there are no planes. The only way to get there is road, and the driver's waiting. If you leave now, you'll hopefully overtake the truck on the road and watch it arrive." Robert nodded, wished "good luck" to the others, and left without a backward glance.

"What about us?" asked Beatrix. "I wouldn't mind a nap, but I'm guessing we're not going to get to stay here."

"Correct. You're flying to Tashkent at 17:00. Suzana will meet you at the airport when you arrive. Our Maria has booked you a different hotel to last time. One that's near the clinic."

"What's the point, if the container is going to Bokhara?" asked Humphrey.

"A different container will be delivered instead. Right paperwork, wrong container, you understand? We need to know when it arrives, who opens it, what's in it and where it was supposed to go before the papers were changed."

"That sounds like some very exciting sightseeing," laughed Beatrix.

Laoban was in no mood for levity. She never was. "The container could arrive as soon as tomorrow. It is possible they will open it while it is still on the back of the lorry, expecting to unload it. Or if they have ground space, perhaps the container will be offloaded. Keep us informed. A car will be at the door of this hotel to take you to the airport at 14:00. You can do that 'sightseeing' you enjoy so much until then. I don't think Urgench is very interesting for tourists, though. It's a shame you will not have time to visit Khiva. Now that really is a beautiful city."

38 – Watching and Waiting
– Robert

Well, either the truck driver was taking it *really* slow, or I'd left before he started driving, or he got lost, or he'd been sent to another address altogether. Whatever, despite my crazy Uzbek driver breaking every speed limit, and his assurances, supported by Google maps, that there was no other road from Urgench to Bokhara, at least none suitable for heavy trucks, we didn't pass the container. Nor any other truck loaded with a similar container. I wondered what had happened to the trackers I'd managed to attach to the one we were after in the Emirates. They'd kept transmitting all the way to the Turkmenistan frontier, then simply stopped. We knew satellite phones weren't permitted in Turkmenistan, or Laoban would have given them to our guys. Now Humph had told me about their bureaucracy, my guess was that the customs authorities had devices that identified satellite trackers and found them that way. Anyway, whatever the reason, I had no way now of knowing where the container was. Bugger. I'd just have to go to where we thought it would be taken, lie low and wait for it to arrive. If it ever did.

Markusz, my driver, eventually located the clinic site. As the guys had said, it was tucked away down a side street, a long cul-de-sac off a busy shopping street. A dead end, and dead in every other respect. Nobody. No activity. Perhaps that was because it was Sunday. Was Uzbekistan Muslim or Christian, I wondered? The shops we'd passed on the main road were open. The clinic site itself was fenced off and ran for about a hundred metres along the cul-de-sac. Opposite and beyond was open ground covered with scrub. A big billboard sign, all in Russian or Uzbek. Probably a 'For Sale' sign. But no houses or apartments, no offices, and no reason for anyone to come this way unless they were going to the site. Or to park their car. Or possibly to abandon it, since the few cars there, all parked right at the far end of the road, looked well past their drive-before date. Which hopefully meant that traffic wardens didn't venture down this way.

I had Markusz drive me back to the airport just outside town that we'd passed on the way, and from there sent him on his way back to his home in Urgench. Bokhara is not a busy airport, and my arrival on the scene didn't coincide with any of the three flights that day, so to say that the rental office guy was surprised to get a customer at four in the afternoon would be an understatement. I had to wake him up. There weren't many cars to choose from, and I picked a black Kia hatchback, the most common and nondescript of those on offer. The car being fairly new and freshly washed, my second stop (the first being to go to a supermarket to stock up for the night shift) was down a country lane where, with the help of a plastic cup conveniently thrown by the side of the road, I scraped soil from the adjacent field and sprinkled it liberally over the bonnet and boot. If I got lucky, there'd be a shower before the morning to turn it into mud. I drove it to the clinic lane, parked in front of the other cars, made sure the number plates were caked with soil too so they couldn't be read from a distance, and settled down to watch and wait.

I've spent a lot of nights sitting in cars, watching and waiting, snatching a catnap when it felt safe, snacking on chocolate, crisps and nuts when peckish, so I've come not to mind it so much. I'd rather be tucked up in a bed, of course, but there'd be another night for that. With company, if I was lucky.

I was really glad, though, that I wasn't having to do this stakeout in mid-winter or mid-summer. Markusz had told me how extreme the temperatures could be, over forty degrees in July, and often minus forty in January. I couldn't turn on the aircon or heating in the car, as that would also turn on the headlights, so surveillance today, in early October, the weather an equable twenty degrees, was as pleasant as it gets. I opened a window a crack.

As dusk encroached, I was glad to see that although there were streetlamps, they weren't working. At least, not in this street. I could see lights on the high road at the end. I doubted anything would happen overnight, but if anyone walked this way, it was unlikely they'd spot me.

Drinking two cans of high-sugar and far-too-high-caffeine drinks stopped me from dozing off, which was just as well, as the street was suddenly illuminated by the headlamps of a truck turning into it from the main road. Two in the morning. It stopped a hundred metres ahead of me, by the side of the site fence, and the headlights went out. I guessed it was bringing the container we were tracking, but it was impossible to see much, even with the mini binoculars I always carry in my bag. I must buy night vision goggles sometime. The streetlights in the main roads had gone off at midnight, and thick cloud meant there was no light from moon or stars. I spotted a brief flicker in the driver's cab. Then nothing. I figured he'd parked up for the night and would wait for the builders to unlock the site in the morning.

But no, after half an hour, two more vehicles turned onto the road. An SUV followed by a biggish van. Both pulled up on the opposite side of the road to the truck. Four shadows emerged from the SUV. Two normal size men, two hulks. Presumably EA, Kulov and his two men. The big guys went to talk to the truck driver while the others disappeared around the side. Probably unlocking the site doors. It was no good my staying in the car. I needed to get up there. Without being seen. That was a problem. Even though it was dark, the thugs would be bound to see movement as long as they stayed where they were, however quiet I could be. I weighed up my options. Apart from making a noise, opening the driver's door would turn on the interior lights. There was a switch to turn them off somewhere, but I couldn't find it without turning on my torch. Instead, I decided to take the risk of opening the hatchback. It was impossible to do that without making a bit of a racket. I just had to hope that the noise didn't carry down the street. Clambering into the back was the easy bit. Pulling the back seats forward proved a struggle, since the release mechanism turned out to be on the other side. But, once I'd finally wriggled into the boot space, I easily found the escape cord, yanked it and the door unlatched and lifted an inch or two. I was surprised how quietly it opened. Quality Korean engineering. I pushed the hatch open just enough to clamber out and pulled it back down again.

Now I was outside, behind the car, and could watch the activity. Nothing happened for a minute or two, but then Kulov's men walked away from the cab. There was a mechanical roar as the driver started the engine and slowly reversed the truck into the building site. Although the headlights were on, they didn't look very strong. The noise of the engine and the beep-beep-beep of the reversing warning siren would easily mask any sounds I made. The driver would be concentrating on his mirrors, and the big men would no doubt be shouting instructions to him, helpful or otherwise. Time to make a move.

Creeping along the edge of the road towards the site as stealthily as I could, I made it as far as the start of the fence without being detected. Because there were high stacks of building materials piled up by the side of the road, I hadn't noticed before that the fence continued back from the road at a right angle to fully enclose the site. Not only was there just enough space left for me to squeeze through and hide behind the bricks and blocks, but those gave me something to clamber up on, so, lying flat, I had a high view over the top of the fence.

The yard stretched out below me, illuminated by strong arc lights. A hut in one corner, probably the site office. A mechanical digger and two cement mixers parked next to it. A few piles of concrete blocks. No actual construction. The clinic still only existed on the drawing board. There was a lot of activity going on, though. The container was on one of those trailer beds that tip, and the truck, having already reversed to the right position, was now inching forwards, in the process slowly letting its cargo slide onto the ground. I hadn't seen that done before and was surprised at what a smooth and quick process it was. The container was on the ground in less than a minute, and as soon as it was clear, the driver levelled the trailer bed and drove out of the site. I could now see that both the SUV and the van had been moved and were now parked inside the yard. The man I'd assumed to be Kulov most definitely wasn't him. This looked like Ivan Zelkopf, the clinic director. He hurried to close and lock the gates behind the truck while the thugs set to work opening the container. They and the van driver then unloaded the container, struggling with the many big and clearly heavy packages cocooned in foam and bubble wrap that they then loaded into the van, while Zelkopf, now armed with a clipboard, shouted instructions and checked off each item against a list. EA was just standing around idly, his hands in his pockets, looking around him. There wasn't much to see in the site itself, and I was afraid he was going to look up towards me, but luckily he didn't.

It took barely fifteen minutes to transfer the cargo from container to van. EA got in the van by the side of the driver, Zelkopf opened the gates to let it out and the van drove away. While that was happening, Kulov's men had put ladders up the side of the container, one at each end. The one nearest me was attempting to scrape off the letters and numbers from the end door with some sort of chisel, while the other, now dressed in a protective suit like a spaceman, had started up a noisy industrial spray gun and was painting his end of the container. It brought back memories of being locked inside a shipping container with the rest of the team in Africa last year, somewhere in the jungle far removed from any road or port. I wondered how many containers were abandoned or purloined and started a new life, legal or illegal, in unlikely locations around the world.

Finally, Zelkopf and the men turned off the lights, locked up the yard and left in the SUV. I had to credit them for a very efficient operation; less than an hour to drop a container, transfer the contents to a van and anonymise the container, turning it from red to black. All in the middle of the night. Now, where were they driving to?

There was no point in staying around Bokhara anymore. I went back to the car, got in the elegant way, via the driver's door, tapped out an update report to Laoban, and set the satnav for Tashkent. Seemed to me that was the obvious destination. As I'd expected, I caught up with them quite soon. Zelkopf was following the van, and that wasn't breaking any speed limits. As I'd do myself. Take it easy, keep the contents safe and avoid getting stopped by traffic police. That reminded me to clean the number plates. I didn't want to be stopped either, and the road being largely deserted probably meant that any highway patrol that was out and about would likely stop anything and everything, if only just for their own entertainment. After a brief stop to clean up the car, I caught up with the Zelkopf convoy again, overtook and drove at the speed limit for about ten kilometres until I passed the next police patrol point. A few hundred metres further on, finding a side road, I pulled in, parked and waited for them to pass again.

Twenty minutes. Too long. They should have reached me long before then. There'd been no traffic at all passing in either direction, so I hadn't missed them. I put my binoculars in my pocket, got out, and walked back along the road, staying on the verge where I could drop low or lie down if any vehicles approached. Rounding a corner, at last I could see lights. The checkpoint. Two uniformed police with their backs to me, silhouetted by the lights of the van, stopped in the middle of the road. Facing the police, and dwarfing them, two other men.

39 – Room 616

Tashkent, Uzbekistan

"Be sure to insist on a room on the top floor at the back," Suzana had told them at least five times since leaving the airport. "Honestly, I don't know why, but Maria booked the hotel and insisted that I tell you." Now Humphrey and Beatrix were at the hotel, they were having difficulty convincing the front desk clerk to agree to their request.

"The lift is very slow," he told them. "If what you want is the view, it's much better from the front. You can see the park from there."

"Really, but no, a friend who stayed here told us we definitely had to insist on a room at the back," said Beatrix, trying an encouraging smile.

"But we arranged one of our best rooms on the second floor for you. I think you will be much more comfortable there."

The mantra drummed into Bea at an early age was that if you meet an obstructive bureaucrat, or a man who was not doing what you wanted him to do something for you, cry. Tears always worked. It had been her grandmother who taught her that, and over and again she'd proved how wise those words were. Faced now with a disconsolate woman apparently weeping into her husband's shoulder, the clerk relented. "OK, I will give you room 616. It is quite comfortable, but if you don't like it when you see it, come back and I will give you 213."

Room 616 was, to be frank, a bit basic, and no doubt 213 would have been nicer, but it had the essentials: bed, bathroom, television and power points. More importantly, it had a window that afforded a perfect bird's-eye view of the rusty grey roof of a warehouse, two empty parking lots and, beyond those, their focus of interest, the rear of the Hunter Health clinic. The clinic itself was quite large, four stories high and wide – Humphrey estimated that, as a hospital, it probably had a hundred beds – and there was a large walled yard behind it. The part of the yard next to the clinic was covered with a canopy. It was getting dark, so they couldn't be sure, but in one corner it looked like construction work was under way, an extension to the existing building. Two ambulances were parked, backed up under the canopy, but otherwise, the yard was empty. As might be expected on a Sunday evening.

"Does one of us have to stand here all night watching?" asked Bea.

"Not if this little trick works," said Humphrey. "You're not expecting any calls, are you?"

"No, I don't think so."

"Then give me your phone." Humphrey took it to the window, plugged it into a charger, and fiddled around with it. Satisfied, he turned back towards Bea, who had kicked off her shoes and was adjusting pillows to make herself comfortable on the bed. "Nice modern TV. Let's see if it's up to this." He turned on the flat panel television on the wall and adjusted the settings, then went back over to Bea's phone and opened the settings menu. "There!" The image of the back of the hospital appeared on the TV screen.

"How did you manage that?" asked Bea.

"It's because I'm brilliant. Screen mirroring. Your phone is filming the yard, and the image is being transferred to the television."

"And what would we have done if the TV didn't work, smarty pants?"

"I'd have mirrored the image to my phone, and we could have watched that. Either way, we can lie in bed and watch the back of the clinic. Much more comfortable on the television, don't you think?"

"It's possibly the most absorbing programme I've ever seen," said Bea, observing a scene where precisely nothing was moving. "Brings binge watching into a whole new dimension. But I'll be expecting you to provide some added stimulation." She grinned.

Despite, or perhaps because of, said stimulation, they failed in their plan to take turns at watching through the night and were awoken at 3am by a siren tone on Humphrey's phone. A high alert message from Robert, to warn them to watch for the van heading their way. Cue Beatrix and Humphrey leaping out of bed and anxiously peering down at the clinic.

"I don't know what that dark lump in the yard is," said Humphrey. "I'm pretty sure it wasn't there before."

"It can't be important, surely?" said Beatrix. "It's not moving, and it's not a vehicle. Is this video setup recording?" Humphrey nodded. "You can always rewind it, then."

They watched in slow motion as, at 1.21am, a man pushed the 'dark lump' out of a back door of the clinic and left it in the yard. "Linen for the laundry to pick up," said Beatrix, going back to the window. "Nothing for us to worry about. But this might be. Come and look." She opened the window to get a clearer view. They watched as a truck loaded with a container manoeuvred, reversing down the road adjoining the yard at the back of the clinic, where it juddered to a halt.

"That can't be the container we were tracking before," said Humphrey. "We now know that was dumped in Bokhara. So what's this one?"

"The switched container, I suppose. Going to be delivered with the right paperwork but the wrong contents. Either that, or it's not for the clinic."

"There's nowhere else on that road to deliver a container to. The driver's obviously going to wait until they open. It's only 4am now, so probably a few hours. Let's go back to watching on the TV."

Beatrix hesitated. "I think I'll stay by the window. Avoid temptation. Concentrate on the job. You get some shut-eye, and I'll wake you in an hour or two to take over. I'll send some pictures to the team now."

She didn't actually wake Humphrey until seven, not so much because she wanted a nap herself, but because she couldn't tolerate his snoring any longer. More aggravating than the constant drip from the cistern in the bathroom. In three tiresome hours, nothing had moved down in the yard. The truck was still there, and there had been no sign of activity from the clinic.

Humphrey had his usual priorities. "I wonder if this hotel does room service breakfast," he said, lifting the receiver of the phone by the bed and engaging in a conversation with the receptionist, who, it seemed, had never heard of such a luxury. "No," he said, putting the phone down, "but we can go and get a tray and bring it back to the room."

"Alright. I'm dressed, so I'll go down. Take over watching. Keep your eyes peeled."

Beatrix was back in five minutes, bearing a tray. "Juice, coffee, some sort of pancakes and curd cheese."

"No eggs and bacon?" asked Humphrey, feigning disappointment.

"This is what there was. Take it or leave it. Oh, and there are two very suspicious-looking men by the front desk. Plain clothes, but I think they're police."

"Presumably not anything to do with us." An assumption instantly disproven by heavy knocking on the bedroom door. Humphrey turned off the television, while Beatrix called "just a moment" and went to the window to retrieve her phone. The banging on the door continued. Humphrey opened the door to two men, both in their thirties, both with crewcut hair, both dressed in near-identical dark blue suits, white shirts and ties, both unmistakably police.

"What are you doing here?" asked one, in clear but slightly accented English.

"We're on holiday," said Beatrix. "Doing the Silk Route."

The policeman grunted. "Passports." Beatrix rummaged in her bag and handed them to him. He leafed through them. "You come here before, you go to Turkmenistan, then you come back here. Why?"

"We didn't see as much as we wanted of Tashkent when we came before."

"You were here for two days before. I think you can see everything worth seeing in one day. Why are you staying in this hotel? It is not for tourists."

"Our agency booked it. It's a very nice hotel."

The officer looked very dubious. "Why did you ask for this room?" Ah, so that's why they're here. The front desk clerk must have told the police they were suspicious. Or were they planning to watch us? Bugs and cameras in room 213?

"My wife hates it when the sun shines into the room first thing in the morning," said Humphrey, in a sudden flash of inspiration. "The agent who brought us here told me the front of the hotel faces east, so we asked for the back. And a high floor because we like being far away from the traffic noise." Invented on the spur of the moment, but it seemed to convince the policeman, who handed them back their passports.

"Enjoy your holiday." Then, turning back as he left, "Welcome to Uzbekistan." Yeah, right, thought Beatrix, breathing a sigh of relief, putting the 'do not disturb' sign outside and closing the door.

While they'd been dealing with the police, the gates of the clinic compound had been opened and the container truck was in the process of reversing in. A welcoming committee of a small group of people stood waiting.

"I think the man on the left is Kulov," said Humphrey, playing with the zoom on his camera phone. "Then there's two women and a man, all dressed in medical coats, and a young guy in jeans and tee shirt. He's a photographer, or at least that's what he's doing. Taking lots of pictures. I suppose that's to prove what's in the container."

They watched as the truck parked in the yard. The driver climbed down from his cab and, after talking to the group, opened the doors of the container. This resulted in visible commotion in the group, one of the women throwing her hands in the air, the man and Kulov climbing up and into the container and throwing boxes out of the back. Was their shock at what was inside contrived, or had this group seriously been expecting the container to be loaded with the equipment they had ordered? As this was going on, a woman police officer walked through the open gate from the road and approached the group. It didn't look like she was welcome. She was clearly demanding papers. The driver went back to his cab, pulled out a folder, and gave it to her. After that, she disappeared from view around the back of the truck for a few minutes – had she gone inside the container? – before reappearing and with hand signals indicating to the driver that he should take the truck away.

Beatrix and Humphrey didn't have to wait long to find out what was in the container. A message from Laoban. "It's medical equipment, but not what they ordered. Enough masks and bandages to get through the next pandemic. They've refused delivery, and Kulov told the driver to take the trailer to some lorry park."

"So she was the police officer we saw down there," said Humphrey. "Didn't even need to change her outfit from when we last saw her."

Another message pinged. "Suzana is coming to take you for a city tour. Go down to the front desk and tell her you don't feel well, then go back to the room and keep watching. The van Robert messaged about is expected in the afternoon, but text immediately if anything interesting happens."

40 – Not just a travel agent

London, England

Maria was relieved not to have to go back to Piers' office. Returning to her flat after her encounter with her father, the first thing she did was email the insurance underwriter telling him what she had discovered and attaching a screenshot of her attempt at remembering the scribble in the margin. Early the following morning, as she was getting ready to go to the office, he replied to say, much to her surprise, that he knew exactly who was said to have agreed that enormous discount, he was entirely satisfied with her work and no further investigation was required. She forwarded the email to Laoban and called Francesca to tell her she wasn't going back, and confirm that, while she was still joining her and Sonia for their Friday night drinks, please could they meet somewhere different and further away as she didn't want to risk Piers walking in on them. She suggested Francesca tell him she was leaving because she was scared of Mr Patel. Nothing at all to do with having her thigh stroked every time she took him a coffee, of course.

She could now spend a day catching up with the team and checking what she needed to do for them. Humphrey and Beatrix had just arrived in Ashgabat, Robert was on his way to Uzbekistan to wait for the container to arrive, Ronald was researching and eating his way through an expense account in Cyprus and Laoban was, well, where was she? Wherever it was, she wasn't saying, but she was sending and answering messages twenty-four hours a day, most of them urgent commands. Did the woman ever sleep? Didn't she at least allow others to get a little rest now and again?

Maria had been surprised that Laoban was enthusiastic about cooperating with Belarusian KGB. Working with or for a state security service seemed alien to their normal business, and Maria's first-hand experience in her teenage years had been that most of the operatives had been clumsy and heavy-handed. As likely to frustrate the mission as help. But Laoban was always attracted by money, and the prospect of another client for a project they were already undertaking and being paid for was just too tempting. She was probably in Minsk right that minute, negotiating with Maria's father. Unlikely for any ordinary individual, as getting a visa would take weeks, but Laoban always seemed to glide ephemerally through borders as though she were a genie.

On the Saturday, Laoban told Maria to arrange for Ron to go to Tashkent to follow up on his knee operation. "He'll know what it's about, but tell him he has to leave on the next flight," she told her. Maria was anticipating Ronald complaining and saying how happy he was in Larnaca, but he seemed genuinely excited. He didn't even object to a journey that would involve changing planes three times, in Amman, Dubai and Doha, and would take nineteen hours door to door. He even sounded proud that he was saving the company a princely fifty-five dollars.

That was the easy bit. What was problematic was what Ron would need to take with him to convince the specialist in the clinic there that he was serious about needing a knee replacement. He could fake pain and limping, but couldn't risk them insisting on doing x-rays on the spot. Maria turned to her friendly hacker, Toshio, who was quite excited at the prospect of infiltrating something more interesting than the email systems she usually needed help with. Two hours later, he sent her a link to a file sharing site with a dozen image files he'd filched from the server of a private orthopaedic hospital in Germany. MRI scans and x-rays of an arthritic knee, that he assured her were from a sixty-five-year-old man who had been operated on the previous week. She messaged Ron to find an internet café or shop in Larnaca to download the images onto a CD that he could take with him. He proudly replied that the hotel owner's son had done it for him for free. Another five-dollar saving to make Laoban happy, then.

It proved to be a busy Saturday. At midnight, after an enjoyable evening of salsa class and an obligatory follow-up glass of wine with Sonia, she returned to the flat to be greeted by a long string of increasingly urgent missives from the boss. More flights to book. First to get Humph and Bea onto a Sunday afternoon flight from Urgench to Tashkent. Then, much more thrilling, she, Maria, was being asked to go to Tashkent as well! At last. She'd been thinking for months that Laoban was overlooking her skills as a front-line facilitator, just treating her as a glorified travel agent and switchboard operator, and on this project had increasingly resented being left back in Rotterdam or London when surely, in those Central Asian countries, her fluency in Russian would prove useful. Not only that, but Rob would be there, too. She wondered if he'd still be ignoring her. She hoped not. The ice was thawing. She booked herself on the direct flight the next afternoon. Surprisingly, it was the cheapest option.

Thus, by midday on Monday, the whole team was in Tashkent. Suzana had them all staying in different hotels, but said she would come round them all with a coach at 6pm to take them for a collective 'Tashkent by Night' tour. In reality, an information exchange and briefing while being driven around the city in a bus with blacked-out windows. Essential preparation for the big day. Tuesday.

41 – Knee surgery

Tashkent, Uzbekistan

With Humphrey on one side and Beatrix on the other to support him, Ronald walked unsteadily towards the front desk, putting his weight on his left leg and dragging his right behind him, as he'd been practicing. "I'm hoping to see Dr Romanovich," he said.

"Do you have an appointment?" asked the receptionist. Or was it a nurse? Dressed like one, anyway. Middle-aged, blond permed hair. Glasses with heavy black frames. Somewhat forbidding for someone whose job it is to make patients welcome and at ease, Ronald thought.

"Well, yes, I have, but it's for next Tuesday at 4. I wasn't expecting to be in Tashkent today, but I had to bring my travel forward, and so I was hoping she would be here."

"She is here, but she has a full list today. She is a very busy surgeon. You will need to come back next week when you have your appointment." The receptionist went back to looking down at a magazine on her desk.

Humphrey butted in. "I and my assistant were here the other week. I met with Svetlana Hematova. Perhaps we can see her?"

"She is not in the clinic today."

"I don't mind waiting for Dr Romanovich," said Ronald. "If you could please ask if she could make a moment to see me?"

He thought at first that she was ignoring him, but it seemed she was just finishing reading a paragraph, as at last she looked up. "I will call her secretary. Wait over there." Ronald hobbled over to a bench by the wall and watched the comings and goings. It was certainly a busy clinic, but almost everyone who passed him knew where they were going and didn't trouble the receptionist. He tried dropping his folder and kicking the legs of the bench to get her attention, without success. After what felt like an hour but was really ten minutes, he went back to her desk.

"Did you speak to the secretary?"

"No. Her line was busy."

"Please, can you try again?"

"Her line is busy." Realising that Ronald didn't believe her, she moved her magazine to reveal a panel on her desk with a lot of buttons. She pointed to one lit up in red.

"Perhaps I can see someone else? Perhaps Dr Zelkopf?"

"He is not here in the clinic today." Trotted out automatically. A standard line.

"Oh. I thought that was him. Look. The man walking down the corridor." He pointed to his right, where Zelkopf was fast approaching. The receptionist looked at him accusingly, but Ronald smiled. "Dr Zelkopf!" he called out.

Zelkopf looked at him and then addressed the receptionist. "I told you already. No appointments today." He turned to Ronald. "I'm sorry. Who are you? I don't think we've met?"

"Your picture is in the brochure," said Ronald, waving it. "My name is Jones, Ronald Jones. I was hoping to see Dr Romanovich. I have come all the way from England. For a knee replacement."

"And you are?" Zelkopf asked Humphrey, ignoring Beatrix.

"My name is Doctor Humphrey. I came and spoke to your colleague Dr Hematova recently about introducing clients for elective surgery in your clinic. Mr Jones here is a patient of mine."

Health tourism was a business he was desperate to develop. Zelkopf's attitude changed in an instant from accusatory to placatory obsequiousness. Though they were still getting nowhere. "Dr Romanovich is very busy. I'm sorry, but you will have to make an appointment."

Ronald explained he had one for the following week. "Even if I can't see the doctor, perhaps I can see your facilities? My consultant here, Dr Humphrey, has warned me to be very careful going abroad for treatment."

"Yes, of course. I know there are many clinics in other countries that are not good at all. But our facilities are first class. You will have excellent care here, at least as good as you would get back home in England. In fact, better, I think. Here there is no waiting list!"

"Except for appointments with Dr Romanovich," said Ronald, smiling.

"Ah. Yes. Let me see what I can arrange," said Zelkopf. "Come with me."

As they walked away, a young woman with short dark hair and dressed in a grey tracksuit approached the desk, said "laundry" in Russian and, without question, the receptionist directed her down another corridor.

Opening one door after another as they went along, and in something of a whirlwind, Zelkopf enthusiastically showed Ronald, Humphrey and Beatrix consulting rooms, a private ward and an x-ray suite, introducing members of his clinical team at each station. Eventually they reached a waiting room. It reminded Ronald of the one he had once sat in for ages in Slough General Hospital, the key difference being that the latter was full to bursting while this one was completely empty. Zelkopf led them through it, and without knocking, opened another door. "Allow me to introduce you to Dr Romanovich," he said. Not overwhelmed with patients, then. The doctor looked much older than in her picture in the brochure. In that one, no doubt photoshopped, she appeared quite glamourous. The reality was different, her face almost haggard, though redeemed by an enormous smile and rapturous welcome. Ronald thought for a moment she was going to hug and kiss him. More like greeting a long-lost relative than a new patient needing a knee prosthesis. Ron suddenly remembered that he'd forgotten he was supposed to be limping and in pain, and sat down with an exaggerated groan of agony. "It only hurts like this sometimes," he said. "But I can always feel some pain." He explained about his appointment and coming to Tashkent earlier than he planned.

"But it's perfect," said Doctor Romanovich. "My three o'clock has cancelled, so I can see you right now, Mr Jones." Humphrey and Beatrix remained standing, while Zelkopf seated himself in a chair by the side of the doctor, obviously planning on joining the consultation.

"Call me Ronald."

Her smile grew even broader. "And you can call me Michaela. Do you have your x-rays to show me?"

"MRI scans too," said Ronald, extracting the envelope with his fake medical papers and the CD from his folder. Michaela opened it carefully, holding the disc gingerly by the edges and inserting it into the computer in front of her. While she was looking at the images, Zelkopf said, "we are soon going to have our very own MRI scanner here in the clinic. We are expanding! Adding new equipment all the time!"

Dr Romanovich joined in the enthusiasm. "It is very exciting! We have just had delivery of the latest robotic surgery tools for prosthetics. I plan to use that for your knee replacement operation. In America, they have shown that it improves patient satisfaction from ninety-five to ninety-nine per cent!"

Zelkopf stopped her from carrying on. "We are not announcing this yet, and Dr Romanovich should not really have mentioned it. Please do not tell anyone else. We have to wait for the equipment to be installed and tested first, which might not be for another three months."

"I don't want to wait that long," said Ronald. "Can't you test it on me, or is it too much of an ethical risk, or too dangerous being the first patient before full operational standards?"

"No, not dangerous at all," said Dr Romanovich. "But it is true, you will have to wait a little. I will discuss with Dr Zelkopf to see if I can operate on you sooner. At the first opportunity."

"This all sounds very exciting, though," said Humphrey. "Could we perhaps see the equipment? I'd be very interested. I've read so much about robotics."

"I'm sorry," said Zelkopf. "The equipment has only just arrived and we have not yet unpacked it."

"That's disappointing," said Beatrix. "Dr Humphrey is such an enthusiast for medical advances and robotics." Humphrey nodded vigorously. "We have other patients waiting for surgery that he was hoping to transfer here," she continued.

"I'm sorry. Who are you?" asked Zelkopf, finally acknowledging Bea's presence, and as if noticing her presence in the room for the very first time.

"I'm Doctor Humphrey's personal assistant. I organise all the patients and schedule their treatments. I was hoping you would introduce me to the person here I would have to liaise with in the future. But perhaps in the circumstances…" she left the sentence hanging.

"My dear young woman, that will be Svetlana," he said. "I will introduce you to her later." Bea didn't bother to tell him she had already met her. So much for her not being in the clinic today, either.

"I think we had better leave," said Ronald.

"No, please," said Doctor Romanovich. "I can see how bad your knee is from the scans here. I can operate on your knee tomorrow if that's convenient?"

"Without robotics?"

The doctor nodded. "The conventional way is very successful."

"I'm sorry. I don't want to risk being one of the ten per cent dissatisfied if I can halve that risk by having the surgery done robotically. I think you said that you had another clinic that could do robotics more immediately, didn't you, Doctor Humphrey?"

It was plain that Zelkopf didn't like the idea of ten thousand dollars hobbling out of the door. "I'm going to make an exception this time," he said. "I will show you the equipment. But you must understand that it is not fully unpacked, not installed in theatre and not tested. You must not take any photographs or tell anyone at all about it until we make our official announcements. Is that understood?"

Everyone nodded agreement.

"This is most exciting," said Dr Romanovich. "I haven't seen it myself yet!" They filed all together out of the consulting room, led by Zelkopf, back down the long corridor, past the reception desk and then into the rather shorter corridor opposite. Zelkopf pulled keys out of his pocket and unlocked a set of double doors. Another corridor, this one clearly backstage, stained grey paintwork on the walls, a battered rubber dado rail skirting them, peeling vinyl flooring beneath their feet, flickering fluorescent lights above their heads. "Everything you see here will be refurbished next month," said Zelkopf, guessing their thoughts, and pushing open the bar that secured the doors at the end, which were marked as an emergency exit. They walked out of the building and stood under the canopy.

The ambulances Humphrey and Beatrix had seen earlier had gone, the space now occupied by a big van, back doors open, with two men unloading boxes and what was clearly medical equipment, white objects wrapped in copious layers of bubble wrap. Registering the faces of the two men, Bea nudged Humphrey. He nodded. The black marketeers, or master criminals, or terrorists. Dangerous men, whatever their description. Definitely them.

Zelkopf started talking animatedly about the equipment, pointing to various items. None of them took any notice of the girl pushing the laundry trolley across the yard until she whistled. Within seconds, two more men dressed all in black leapt down from the wall surrounding the yard, pointing guns at the black marketeers and forcing them onto the ground. One of the men in black rapidly incapacitated both of the criminals, cuffing hands and ankles. A second whistle from the laundry girl was quickly followed by a deafening crash as a black Hummer cannoned through the closed and locked gates and screeched to a halt in front of them. Laoban, once again dressed in her police outfit, bounded out of the passenger door, while the driver, also dressed as a police officer, started taking photos with an SLR camera. The mystery men in black lifted their two captives into the back of the Hummer, got into the cab and drove it out of the yard, tyres screeching and leaving a cloud of exhaust fumes behind it.

It all happened so quickly that even Zelkopf hadn't realised what was taking place around him, but now he raced towards the open gates, pursued by Beatrix, who grabbed his arm and somersaulted him over her shoulder, leaving him lying unconscious on the ground. "Was that display really necessary?" asked Humphrey, rolling his eyes skyward.

"I suppose not," said Bea. "But I enjoyed it." She pulled some cable ties from a pocket and trussed up Zelkopf's arms and legs.

"Where did you get those?" asked Humphrey.

"I always carry them. Never know when they may come in useful."

Humphrey shook his head. "I'm learning new things about you every day."

They'd been joined by Ronald and Maria, who was no longer pretending to be a laundry maid and was now busy on her phone calling the local police. A distant crescendo of sirens suggested they were already aware and on their way.

"Where's Laoban gone?" asked Ronald.

"My guess would be to change," said Maria. "The police wouldn't approve of an imposter."

"Also, if I'm not mistaken, to send the news to our clients. Claim our fees. She never hangs around when there's money to be had."

"The other policeman, the one driving the Hummer and taking the pictures, has disappeared too," said Humphrey.

"Didn't you recognise him?" asked Maria. Humphrey shook his head. "Robert," she explained.

"I do like Robert. Always there when you need him to get you out of a scrape," said Ronald.

"How I wish that were true," sighed Maria.

"Who were the guys in black and balaclavas, Maria, if they weren't police?" asked Beatrix.

"Ah," she replied with mischief in her eyes, "Our new clients. Taking delivery of what they had ordered. The real police will be here any moment, I think. Better we get out before they arrive."

42 – Basking in the lap of luxury – Maria

Tashkent, Uzbekistan

From the pitch of the sirens it was obvious the police would be driving into the back yard any second, so I hurried the team back into the clinic and along a service corridor that ran straight from the rear of the building to the front courtyard. I'd discovered this route while spending most of the morning there pushing linen trolleys. Luckily, the commotion at the back didn't appear to be noticed by people at the front entrance, where everything seemed to be normal. Ron, no longer the doddery old man that I first met in Panama two years ago, went straight to the first taxi in line. Bea and Humphrey, always the more uncertain ones, needed some quick reassurance that it was all right for them to go back to the hotel and wait in their room for further instructions. "It might not be until the morning, but keep checking," I told Bea, realising that it would be down to me to get them all out of Tashkent and it was too late to fly anywhere that evening, even if there were any flights going anywhere useful. "Get the next taxi. Go now!" I told them, pushing Humphrey in the small of his back in the right direction.

I got as far as putting my hand on the door handle of the third taxi when a smartly dressed and rather dishy young man appeared next to me. "Miss Maria?" he inquired, speaking Russian. "I am Piotr. Your car is waiting over there. Please follow me." OMG. We wrap up the project, get the criminals arrested, and just as I relax a little, I get kidnapped? My nerves went into overdrive. I tried to picture in my mind the street layout around the clinic so

I could make a run for it. All dead ends or wide roads. Nowhere I couldn't be followed. On the other hand, the man didn't seem threatening, and he certainly didn't look athletic or have the physique for thuggery. He must have known what I was thinking. "Please, trust me, it's all OK," he said. "We are just here to take you to your hotel. Our car is more comfortable than a taxi."

That was true, at least. Accepting my fate, I climbed into the back of the long black limousine and sank into the pillow-like comfort of the seat. "I hope you are comfortable?" said my abductor. "We will go to your hotel now. I have a message to give you." He handed me an envelope, closed the door and got in the front seat next to the driver, who I now saw was a real chauffeur, wearing a peaked cap with a crest on the front. I no longer needed to guess who had arranged this transport. I only knew one person with diplomatic connections.

Unsealing the envelope, I pulled out the card inside. "To my *rypka*, to thank you for a job well done. Please accept the little hospitality I have arranged. You deserve happiness and a reconciliation. Remember, you are free, you can walk away at any time." The thought of reconciling once more with my father made me shiver just a little, but that aside, I had to admit the message was quite sweet. I found myself trying to imagine Laoban writing thank you cards to the team!

I was still giggling about that when the car pulled to a halt and the door was opened. I looked around. "But this isn't my hotel," I told Piotr. The one I'd booked into was a modest two-star place, out of town and near the airport. The huge tower in front of me, all mirror glass and marble, proudly announced itself as the InterContinental. Way outside Laoban's price range.

"You've been upgraded," said Piotr, handing me a small black folder with an electronic key inside. "You are already checked in. Room 1101. Your baggage has been transferred. The bill will be paid by the Embassy. Please enjoy your stay." He held up his hand in a small gesture of farewell and got back in the limousine, which immediately moved away, gliding noiselessly back onto the road and merging with the traffic.

Well, trusting Father's comment that I was free to be true, and a genuine demonstration of his good faith, I decided, as they say in England, not to look this gift horse in the mouth. Anyway, I was here, I had work to do booking tickets to get all the team out of Tashkent, and I knew this hotel would have first-class wifi. A rather ridiculously uniformed bellhop opened the door for me, another called the lift, and I ascended to discover what room 1101 held in store for me.

A suite. Filled with flowers. And, jumping up from an armchair and wrapping his arms around me, Rob! It was such a joyful surprise that we'd been kissing for minutes before I remembered he was a bastard and pushed him away.

"So, what happened? You got bored already with your new lover in London?"

Rob looked mystified.

"I don't have a new lover. You're my one and only."

"Don't lie to me. How long was it, three weeks, four? Secret mission, not calling, not answering messages?"

"Ah. I get it. I was chaperoning Inessa, the wealthy Estonian lady. You didn't seriously think I was with another woman, Maria? Well, in truth I was, but she's over eighty and all I did was drive her around London and make sure she didn't get kidnapped." I was sceptical and presumably looked it. Sure, it was the sort of business we did, but we always talked about what we were doing. And surely I would have been involved in organising a close protection mission like that?

"Laoban wouldn't let me tell you or anyone else," said Rob. "That woman is one of the richest people in the world, and was seriously at risk. Laoban had to commit to total secrecy in order to get the job. She made all the background arrangements herself." Rob told me the whole story. It took very little to melt my heart back to the way I'd felt about him before.

Changing the subject, "this is a wonderful surprise," I said. "When did you get time to organise all this?" I waved my hand around, pointing at all the flower displays and the rose petals arranged in the shape of a heart on the bed.

"Um, well, I wish it was all my idea," he said, "but it wasn't. I thought it was you. I was picked up by a young guy in a black limo who said you would be waiting for me. When we got here, he just gave me a room key and drove away. Obviously it's not Laoban. So who did all this?"

"I suspect it's someone I know, who's very rich and wants us to be together again." Surely the reconciliation Father put in his note was this one. Rob was clearly on the verge of asking more questions, so I held up my hand to stop him. "It's a long story. Complicated. Someone from my past. No, not a lover, nothing like that. I'll explain one day, I promise. But now, can we just get on with our reconciliation?" Rob smiled and nodded. "Well, there's a bottle of champagne on ice over there if you'd like a glass? Or we could just ruffle up those rose petals?"

43 – Epilogue – Ronald

Lanzarote, Canary Islands

One of the roles I've taken on board since joining Laoban's team, and perhaps the one I enjoy most, is that of chronicler. The boss believes it's necessary to provide each of our customers with a detailed report setting out everything we did for them, what we discovered along the way, outstanding items that still need resolution and so on. Extensive text, all accompanied by a copious number of photographs taken by the team, Laoban's logic being that the more words and pictures there are in the report, the more work the client will think we have done. I suspect all she cares about is justifying our rather immodest fees, but I know that clients really appreciate the reports, even if they do have to restrict them to a very small audience in their organisations and lock them away in a vault for ever after. Few clients would want the fact they bought our services, never mind the detail, to become known.

As soon as a project ends and I'm back in my new home of Lanzarote, therefore, I interrogate the team, make extensive notes, download all their photographs and then sit at my computer and do my best to write it up. As an author, I aim for the thrills of Mission Impossible and the word count of War and Peace. Obviously, I don't include every tiny detail, as many are of no interest to the client or have no financial implications, and some are just downright embarrassing.

Usually there's only one report to prepare, as we'll only have the one client for the project. This time, however, we had three customers, each with their own reasons for hiring us.

The report for the insurance underwriter was relatively short. He only needed a high-level summary of the black marketeers' criminal activities, the report going into detail on Maria's experiences, forensics and discoveries in her few days working for Piers in the brokerage. Everything the underwriter needed to sue Piers to recover his syndicate's losses and, in the process, put his brokerage out of business. Maria hoped the client would also take the report to the police and have Piers prosecuted for both fraud and sexual harassment, but I was sure that would not happen. It was only ever about the money.

Laoban told me that the mystery client who simply wanted to arrest the black marketeers for themselves had paid our fees even before she sent them the bill, so I was a little surprised that she wanted me to prepare them a report. Since the boss wouldn't say who the client was, we all suspected it was a state intelligence service, though opinions divided on which Central Asian state that might be. Not that it mattered. She seemed to think that sending them (whoever they were) a comprehensive report of how we tracked down the black marketeers would help her negotiate more business from them in the future. "Make the report as exciting as you can," she said. "Like a spy novel. Lots of action. Lots of hair-raising exploits." Well, the team had a few, but I wasn't confident I could make them sound all that thrilling.

I began by writing the report for the first client, the medical robotics manufacturer in America, because it would be the longest and most detailed, and so I could then simply edit out the dross and expand and embellish the "good bits" for the version for the state intelligence service, or whatever they were.

Read the three reports and you'd think that the mission had been totally successful. The black marketeers were out of action, arrested and taken away by a mystery organisation. Zelkopf was in the hands of the Ukrainian police and the stolen robots recovered. As far as our American clients were concerned, the risk of future shipments of medical equipment going astray down the Silk Road had been neutralised, at least for the time being. The brokerage that issued insurance policies that should never have been sold, and certainly not at a huge discount, would now go out of business, the principals made bankrupt and disqualified, and the underwriters would recover some of their losses. We had therefore met the objectives of all three clients, and they had all paid their bills in full.

The 'one that got away' was Kulov. A slippery customer if ever I came across one. Well, not a 'customer', of course. He not only had offices in at least five countries, but it seems had passports for all of them, and we suspected some others too. The American client really wanted to get him prosecuted, but for what? We had photographs of him exchanging paperwork with truck drivers in Dubai, but (were he ever caught) he could argue that, as the shipping agent, he was just giving the driver additional documentation that he needed. We had photographs of him doing the same in Turkmenistan, but the authorities there were only interested in how our team had managed to get into a restricted area, and for that matter, how they had entered the country in the first place.

A concern for both the Americans and the insurers was the risk of copycat crimes. On Laoban's instructions, in writing the reports I downplayed the risk, emphasising that Kulov was just a shipping agent, admittedly a crooked one, who didn't have the network or skills in finding customers that the black marketeers did. Since we had gathered no compelling evidence Kulov had committed any crime in a jurisdiction that was prepared to arrest him, the narrative that he was just a cog in a wheel suited us.

And, up to a point, that was true. But we'd omitted any reference to two other players. EA had definitely been involved. He'd cropped up several times, but we couldn't determine his role in this conspiracy. We didn't even know his real name, an omission that our team needed to resolve as soon as possible. For those reasons, I simply airbrushed him out of the narrative in my reports. Convenient for us, but perhaps not so much for our clients, as he clearly knew enough about the techniques and methodology of the crime to replicate it with other operators, should he so choose. EA also kept popping up unexpectedly on other projects too, something I could tell made Laoban nervous. We had been fishing in the same pool of Smith/Arbuthnot's former client list. It was now definitely a business priority to find out all about him.

Fullerton-Price, also omitted from my reports, clearly had nothing to do with the black-market medical equipment thefts that we'd been contracted to work on. However, the team had seen him spend significant time talking with EA and Kulov. What were they plotting, or what comes next, we cannot know at this juncture.

We weren't sure either about Ryan Mallory. There was nothing we could fix on him with certainty, but his appearance at the conference in Dubai, where he met Kulov, Fullerton-Price and EA several times made us suspicious. Perhaps he provided the black marketeers with the precise inside information they needed to know about shipments of medical equipment? Regardless of proof, our American client had no qualms about inventing some reason to "let him go" within hours of receiving our report.

It's always satisfying when I finish a client report that draws a clear line under the mission our team has completed. This time, what they achieved has made three clients happy, but for us, it's not the end of the story. For centuries, long before Marco Polo ventured down it, the Silk Road has been a corridor for trade, a not insignificant amount of it black market. With Kulov, EA and F-P at large, I suspect that will not change any time soon. And we are very much open for more business in that geographical region.

Anyway, in the meantime, our next important international mission beckons. Bea told me today that Laoban hinted to her she was negotiating something new and big. Bea is hoping it might be in the Far East, not a part of the world either of us have ever been to. Exciting as that all sounds, I wouldn't mind a few weeks' rest first. And, after kebabs for almost every meal for a week or two, the time and opportunity to explore the culinary variety closer to my home.

Thank You

I hope you have enjoyed reading this book. If so, please consider leaving a review, however brief, on Amazon or Goodreads. Reviews are critical to the success of any author, especially those without a big publishing house behind them.

Spies on the Silk Road is the third in a series. The award-winning first book, The Repurposed Spy, and its sequel, Spies on Safari, are both available from all booksellers.

For a free e-book copy of the prequel, The Apprentice Spy, subscribe to my newsletter at https://oliverdowson.com. Only free books, occasional newsletters and No Spam! – you can unsubscribe at any time.

Oliver Dowson
October 2024

About the Author

Oliver Dowson was born in Lowestoft, England. After studying mathematics, statistics and computer science at university, he spent a long career building a multi-national business from scratch, exploiting his love of foreign travel, cultures, languages and food. He has visited – so far - 149 countries for business and pleasure – and tries to add at least another new one every year!

Oliver is no stranger to writing, having been editor of both Imperial College and University of London Union newspapers in his youth, and writing many articles throughout his business career. Trapped by the pandemic, he wrote his first book, a travelogue "There's No Business Like International Business", published in 2022. Now, Oliver has now turned to fiction, publishing "The Repurposed Spy" to critical acclaim. It won The Wishing Shelf Bronze Award for Adult Fiction and the BookFest 2023 Gold Award in the Thriller-Espionage category. The sequel and second in this series, Spies on Safari, was published in late 2023.

When he's not travelling to more distant locations, adding new experiences and widening his knowledge of international cuisines, he lives less adventurously in North London and Oviedo Spain.

For more details and to stay in touch, see his website https://oliverdowson.com

Also by the Author

The Repurposed Spies series
The Repurposed Spy – book 1 in the series
Spies on Safari – book 2
Spies on the Silk Road – book 3

Other books
There's No Business Like International Business – a travelogue

Praise for The Repurposed Spy

'A smartly constructed mystery thriller with a strong, charasmatic protagonist. A BRONZE MEDAL WINNER and highly recommended!' **The Wishing Shelf Book Awards**

The Repurposed Spy is a testament to Dowson's storytelling prowess, plunging readers into a realm of subterfuge, disguise, and unexpected turns. For those with an affinity for espionage or simply a love for gripping narratives, this book is an unmissable treat.'

Literary Titan Gold Award winner

'There is something Orwellian about this story - the central character, Ronald Jones, kept reminding me of Winston Smith in 1984, always looking over his shoulder. The author keeps you on the edge of your seat throughout, wondering what will next befall this hapless and apparently reluctant spy. It is an intriguing tale, narrated in a light, slightly whimsical style that constantly keeps you off guard. I rattled through Oliver Dowson's debut novel at breakneck speed, anxious to get to the denouement. I wasn't disappointed, and neither, I venture, will you.'

Douglas Jackson, Author

"This is a spy thriller with a difference- I'm a big fan of this genre but I've never read anything quite like this. It's a great story which held my attention from the very first page and kept me guessing right to the very last! Definitely a fun read! I highly recommend."

NetGalley reviewer

"Somehow the author takes an incredible scenario and makes it credible. The story is written in such a way as to make me believe it was absolutely possible and I anxiously travelled along with the protagonist as he dealt with the unlikely hand dealt him."

NetGalley Reviewer

Praise for Spies on Safari

"The intricacy of the high-stakes game of cat-and-mouse that plays out across the pages is edge-of-your-chair excitement. Even though Spies on Safari is the second book in Mr. Dowson's series, it has brilliant qualities and rich adventure to make this novel worthy of standing on its own merit. Well done Mr. Dowson! I am a fan."

Feathered Quill review

"Spies on Safari is a novel that skillfully intertwines everyday drama with adventurous escapades. Dowson has crafted an entertaining and intellectually stimulating story, offering a fresh perspective within its genre."

Literary Titan 5 star review

"Dowson's narrative remains mature and insightful, allowing us to truly understand our protagonists and their choices. Fiction and reality, action, adventure, and a dash of mystery are intertwined seamlessly, keeping your head spinning with every turn of the page. A truly mind-boggling mystery at its core."

Authors Reading review

"The author has delivered again with a terrific follow up to the first book in this series, "The Repurposed Spy." The language and descriptions are evocative and quirky, bringing a sense of fun to a book which is also packed with thrills and risk taking. It's great to come back to the core characters again, each of which have their appeal, and the author breathes such life into the physical contexts in which the story takes place. It's not a cosy mystery, but the sense of coming back to something treasured is definitely there."

Amazon Australia reviewer (4 stars)

"The inimitable, almost mischievous humour that intersperses the often darker narrative gives the story a depth and readability which has led me to do very little else for a week other than finish the book. Great week though!"

Amazon UK reviewer (5 stars)

Oliver Dowson

Printed in Great Britain
by Amazon

48723082R00159